DIAMONDS
for the
DEAD

FORTHCOMING BY ALAN ORLOFF

Killer Routine

DIAMONDS
for the
DEAD

ALAN ORLOFF

MIDNIGHT INK
WOODBURY, MINNESOTA

First Edition
First Printing, 2010

Book design and format by Donna Burch
Cover design by Ellen Dahl
Cover photo © Ellen Dahl, cover background texture © PhotoAlto
Editing by Connie Hill

Midnight Ink, an imprint of Llewellyn Publications

Library of Congress Cataloging-in-Publication Data

Orloff, Alan, 1960–
  Diamonds for the dead / Alan Orloff. —1st ed.
      p.   cm.
   ISBN 978-0-7387-1948-1
   1. Virginia, Northern—Fiction. 2. Russian Americans—Virginia, Northern—
Fiction. 3. Jews—Virginia, Northern—Fiction. I. Title.
   PS3615.R557D53 2010
   813'.6—dc22   2009049626

Midnight Ink
Llewellyn Publications
2143 Wooddale Drive
Woodbury, MN 55125-2989 USA
www.midnightinkbooks.com

Printed in the United States of America

To Janet, the exquisite jewel in my life,
and
To Mark and Stuart, our two priceless gems.

ONE

No one had bothered to move the cane.

I stepped into the foyer and dropped my two large suitcases on the gray slate-tiled floor, eyes focused on my father's cane. It had come to rest at the base of the wall opposite the flight of stairs he'd tumbled down. No one had bothered to move it. Overlooked or ignored, didn't matter. Dead men had no use for canes.

Erik clattered in behind me. "Where do you want these, Josh?" Before I could answer, he dumped two duffel bags next to the suitcases. "How about there?" he asked, with a hint of a smile.

"Thanks. I'll take care of them later. And thanks for picking me up at the airport." The words came out lifeless. I'd taken the red-eye to Dulles from San Francisco after waiting standby all afternoon, too much on my mind to get any restful sleep.

"No problem. What are friends for, anyway?"

I nodded, keeping a snappy retort to myself. Didn't have the energy for verbal jousting.

Erik looked around, eyes never settling. "This place brings back memories. We had some good times here."

I nodded again. Erik Nolan had been my closest friend in high school and the best man at my wedding. We'd had *tons* of good times, here and throughout the Northern Virginia suburbs.

"Your father was a good man. He'll be missed by a lot of people," Erik said. "Katy sends her condolences. And her love, of course."

"Thanks. Give her a kiss for me," I said, stomach punctuating my request with a plaintive growl. A Snickers bar and four bags of stale airplane pretzels hadn't done the job. "Hungry?"

He glanced at his watch. "Sorry. Gotta run. Deposition."

"On a Saturday?"

"Justice never takes a day off," he said, then pursed his lips. "Listen, when you feel up to it, there's something we need to discuss. And sooner's better than later."

"What?"

"About the estate." In addition to being my best friend, Erik had been my father's attorney for years.

"What about it?"

"Oh, now you feel like talking?" Erik asked. I hadn't spoken much on the short ride over. Every time he tried to start a conversation, I'd cut him off. He tapped his watch with a knuckle. "Josh, I'm sorry. I need to get rolling. Got to stop home and change. Besides, it's business. We should do it at my office. I'm free between two and five this afternoon, if you get a chance."

"I'll try to squeeze it in."

Erik rolled his eyes, cocked his head. "You going to be all right?"

"Sure."

"How come I don't believe you?" he asked.

"I'll be fine. Really."

"Okay. I know better than to argue." As was his tradition, Erik engulfed me in a bear hug, one slightly less crippling than the hug he'd crushed me with at the airport. When he broke it off he said, "Anything you need, just holler." With a final pat on the shoulder, he pushed through the front door, jogged down the walkway, hopped into his car, and zoomed away. I guess justice didn't like to be kept waiting, either.

I closed the door and shrugged off my jacket. Flopped it on top of the bags. Worked the kinks out of my aching muscles, long trip finally finished.

My attention drifted back to the cane. I walked over and picked it up. Hefted it a couple times. Solid and smooth, save for a few chips gouged out of the curved handle. The beige rubber tip on the bottom contrasted with the dark wood. No ergonomic grip, no ornately carved ivory handle. No space-age lightweight alloy. No racing stripes.

Although my father had used a cane for years, I'd never thought of him as frail. Had others? I hooked the handle around the newel of the banister. The tip bounced against the post with a dull thump, sending a faint echo through the house where I'd been raised.

First food, then a nap. I still had a few hours before I needed to be at Lansky's Funeral Home to finalize the arrangements I'd started yesterday on the phone.

I wandered into the kitchen, trailing my fingers along the top of the old oak table we'd gathered around for family meals. I'd done my homework on it, played games on it, constructed papier-mâché volcanoes on it. Had countless conversations around it.

Back when Mom was still alive, and I was in grade school, and we resembled a regular family, dealing with all the mundane problems a family faces. Before my father got on my case for my lack of ambition and I tuned him out every chance I could.

At the fridge I paused, eyeing the lone piece of paper stuck to the door with the promotional magnets my father used to advertise his real estate business. A washed-out family portrait on frayed yellow paper, the artist's signature—JOSH, all caps—barely legible. Three generic smiling faces. A mommy, a daddy, and a boy, standing in front of a generic house, complete with smoke curling up from the box-like chimney. An authentic *Josh Handleman*, circa 1978, when I was about six years old. My Magic Marker period. My father never threw anything away, but I didn't remember seeing this masterpiece posted in such a high-traffic spot.

A low moaning noise startled me. I froze. Twenty seconds later, I heard it again, coming from the in-law suite downstairs. I tiptoed through the kitchen into the foyer. Stopped. Concentrated. Another moan. Or maybe it was a groan.

Had Erik returned to yank my chain? Unlikely, even taking into account his fondness for pranks. I considered calling the cops. Was I being skittish? What would they say if they came barging in, SWAT-style, and found a rabid squirrel running amok in the basement? I could do without the embarrassment—and the commotion. I slipped my father's cane off the banister and crept downstairs.

When I reached the bottom, I stopped. Five feet away, the bedroom door was ajar, but I couldn't see anything from my viewpoint. "Hello?" I called out, softly at first, then louder. "Hello?" I inched toward the door.

Rustling, followed by a muffled cough. Definitely not an animal. "Hello? Anybody there?"

No answer.

Stepping forward, I used the rubber tip of the cane to slowly push the door open. It creaked on its hinges.

A white-haired man in a gray cardigan sweater sprawled on top of the bedcovers, dirty black dress shoes still laced to his feet. One arm dangled off the bed, fingers six inches from an empty liquor bottle upended on the floor. The stink of sweat and alcohol and urine washed over me as I stood there, cane in hand, mouth agape.

The man opened his eyes, red-rimmed and glassy, tilting his head toward me. He cleared his throat, an underwater phlegm-filled sound, and blinked twice. Swallowed hard. Then his cracked lips parted, revealing a mouth half full of stained, crooked teeth.

In a scratchy voice he said, "Hello, Joshua."

TWO

"Who the hell are you?" I asked, pointing the crook of the cane at him. When he didn't answer, I lowered it, trying to appear less confrontational.

The man mumbled something and his eyelids drooped.

"Who are you? What are you doing here?" I wanted to poke him with the cane to get a response but mustered some restraint.

The man's eyes widened. "Your father was very proud of you. Very proud." He cleared some more gunk from his throat and ran a hand across his face. "He was a fine man, your father." I detected an Eastern European accent. Russian probably, knowing my father's proclivity for anything Soviet.

I leaned the cane against the nightstand. "What's your name?"

The man shifted and strained, grunting as he struggled to attain a sitting position. I caught hold under his arm and helped him perch on the edge of the bed, trying not to inhale too deeply. He was lighter than he looked and smaller than I first thought. His watery eyes focused on my nose. "Name's Kassian."

"Kassian? Is that your first name or your last name?"

"Just … Kassian. What people have been calling me all my life."

"What are you doing here?"

Kassian swept one arm theatrically. "I live here."

"Here? In this house? You live here?"

"Yes. Abe said I could live here as long …" Kassian's gaze flitted around the small room. "As long as I wanted." He belched, expelling a blast of fetid 100-proof air into my face.

I backed up two steps. "You pay rent?"

"No. Abe was a generous man. Very generous."

"How long have you been living here?" Aside from the empty bottle on the floor, the room was neat and tidy. A single framed photograph rested on the bureau, and the nightstand appeared freshly dusted.

"Moved in during the summer. July. Beginning of August. Maybe it was June." His eyes blinked slowly. "It was hot, I know. Very hot."

And probably as hazy as Kassian's recollection. I walked over to the bureau and opened the top drawer. Folded underwear on one side, folded socks on the other. I closed the drawer and turned back to Kassian. "Where were you before that?"

Kassian bowed his head and mumbled something. Could have been in Russian, could have been in Martian. His entire body trembled.

I sat on the bed next to him and waited a moment, then spoke in a hushed tone. "Kassian. Where were you before you came here?"

He lifted his head, eyes glossier if that were possible. "Don't send me back. Please don't send me back. They lock you in at night. Please."

"Where?"

"The shelter at the Hebrew Home. Please don't send me away." His lower lip quivered.

I didn't respond, trying to get a handle on things. The Reston Hebrew Home had an excellent reputation. Mom had spent her last three months in the hospice unit and we couldn't have asked for better care.

Kassian's face grew red. "Your father saved me. We had a deal. If he was here now, he wouldn't throw me out. No sir. He was a man of his word. His word." Kassian gritted his teeth, but he couldn't pull off the defiant look. Pitiful came to mind. "I don't have any other family. Abe was all I had."

I measured Kassian. A diminutive old man whom my father had taken in. Generous, kind "Honest Abe" Handleman, champion of the downtrodden. Who was I to break my father's promises? Besides, I was too spent from the last eighteen hours of misery to argue. I exhaled. "Relax, relax. You can stay. At least for a while, okay?"

Kassian's whole body unwound. His face brightened as he licked his parched lips. "I am very thirsty. May I have a drink?"

I picked up the bottle from the floor and examined it. Ruskova Vodka. Never heard of it, but judging from Kassian's condition, it did the trick. "Sure, but I think you need some coffee." I helped him to his feet. "Come on, let's go. Get you sobered up." Together, we made it upstairs to the kitchen. I got some coffee brewing while Kassian rested his head—facedown—on the kitchen table.

The foul odor in Kassian's room had quashed my appetite, just as the events of the last two months had beaten down my spirit. I'd caught my wife screwing my business partner. My father had tripped down the stairs to his death. And now I'd found a drunk Russian living in the basement.

I needed a nap. And a drink myself, something a lot stiffer than coffee.

———

When I awoke, I felt worse than ever. Exhausted and disoriented and physically ill. But I didn't have time to wallow in self-pity; I needed to get over to Lansky's to tie things up.

Down in the kitchen, I crossed my fingers and opened the junk drawer under the microwave, hoping my father's routines hadn't changed in the twelve years I'd been gone. I smiled to myself as I found his car keys, right where he'd been keeping them since I'd been old enough to drive and he'd had to share. I was planning to use his car to get around. He drove a Taurus, but I guess it was better than nothing. Maybe.

Next to the keys, his wallet rested on a pile of paper clips, twisty-ties, old batteries, and a bunch of other crap that had been accumulating since 1975. Stuffed into the wallet's fold was a bank envelope. I removed it and slid the pack of bills out an inch. Riffed through it. About six or seven hundred dollars, all in fifties. Mad money for a rainy day.

I started to close the drawer but hesitated. My father's old wallet. Smooth brown leather, worn shiny—twenty years old at least—with about thirty bucks inside. I put everything back the way I'd found it and shut the drawer, feeling a little like a Peeping Tom. Maybe I'd take a closer look in a few days when the shock of his death had worn off. Time *would* dull the pain, wouldn't it?

The wind fluttered a piece of flimsy corrugated cardboard someone had slapped over the broken windowpane next to the kitchen door. Where the rescue squad had to break in. According to the EMTs, my father died instantaneously from a broken neck sustained in the fall. No suffering. I wondered if that was true, or if it was just something they said to try to make the grieving relatives feel better. How could they know how much he'd suffered?

I leaned against the counter girding myself for an onslaught of childhood memories, but the rush didn't come. It was almost as if I'd never left—the surroundings felt so familiar. My parents bought this split-level house more than thirty-five years ago, back when Reston was still out in the Virginia boondocks and the notion of a "planned community" was novel. But while the town around us grew and evolved over the years, the carpet and furniture and wall hangings never changed. Even the less permanent things—the knickknacks and tchotchkes that had a way of infiltrating any home—were exactly as I'd remembered from my visit two and a half years ago, when Mom was fighting cancer. Her funeral had been the last time I'd been back. Now I had to plan my father's.

Before I left the house, I peeked in on Kassian in his basement room. He slumbered peacefully, so I let him be and drove down to the funeral home, preparing for the worst.

Mort Lansky, the funeral director, met me at the door, and he was exactly how I'd pictured him over the phone, which wasn't a good thing for Lansky. With his wrinkled parchment skin, chalk-white complexion, and beak nose, he looked as if he'd escaped from an old Charles Addams cartoon. Only his extra-firm hand-shake convinced me he was from my side of the grave.

I'd never had to do the dirty work before. When Mom died, I'd been assigned to other tasks while my father dealt with the funeral home. I didn't know what to expect, how it would affect me. In short order, though, Lansky's calm demeanor settled my nerves and an overall numbness enveloped me. An hour and a half after we'd started, everything had been selected and determined and chosen with the utmost of regard for the deceased's eternal rest. Tasteful timelessness. No expense spared. When we were finished, I felt relieved, even though I knew I'd just been handled and up-sold by a professional con artist dressed in a conservative dark suit with a deeply modulated voice meant to soothe.

———

After the fleecing at the funeral home, I stopped by to see Erik. It was after two o'clock, so I figured it was safe. I checked in at his firm's reception desk and ninety seconds later Erik came barreling through the door. This time he tempered his embrace, but I still felt the rock-hard muscles underneath. Erik prayed daily to the gods Cybex and Nautilus, and I often thought he chose his designer suits based on which ones showed off his chiseled physique the best. Today he wore a charcoal pinstripe with a muted purple shirt and matching patterned tie. A gold Rolex peeked out from under one cuff.

Erik ushered me back to his office, past those of a dozen other attorneys, many occupied. For the Saturday before Christmas, the office seemed busy.

We sat side-by-side on a black leather-and-chrome sofa, across the office from a modern metal-topped desk the size of a small aircraft carrier. On one side of the desk, a few file folders lined up like planes about to roar off into the wild blue yonder.

"Get some rest? You seemed pretty out of it this morning," Erik asked, leaning over and squeezing my shoulder.

"Some. Still a little tired."

"I'll bet," he said.

I gestured at his suit. "Nice threads. But isn't it the weekend?"

Erik clicked his tongue twice. "Need to look sharp. Big client this morning and Katy and I have a Christmas party to go to this evening."

"Right." Erik needed to look sharp all the time, whatever-sized client, whatever type party.

He touched my shoulder again, brow furrowed. "What's going on with you and Dani?"

My soon-to-be ex-wife. I hoped the surprise on my face wasn't evident—I hadn't told anyone about our breakup. A few lame, evasive responses entered my mind, but I could tell Erik was on to me so I kept mum and shrugged.

"I called your house yesterday afternoon before I got you on your cell. Dani told me you'd moved out weeks ago," he said.

"You didn't tell me you'd spoken to Dani."

Erik rearranged himself on the couch. "Sorry. Thought it might be better to talk about it in person. I tried this morning in the car, but you wouldn't have any of it."

I stifled a sigh. "Yeah. I guess things weren't working out too well. Hadn't been for some time now."

"I'm sorry man. If I can do anything…"

"Sure. Thanks."

Erik's tone brightened. "Hey, how's the liquidation business?"

I stared at him an extra beat. "I've moved on there too." No need to burden him with my soap-opera life now. There'd be plenty of time for that later, over plenty of beer.

"Okay." Erik patted his knee. Smoothed out the fine, Italian wool. In a few seconds, the uncomfortable moment had passed, and it was just two old buddies again.

"So, what about the estate?" I asked.

Erik took a deep breath. "Well, I wanted to tell you … But, well, let's just get right to it."

"Okay. Shoot."

"When your father came to me about doing his will, he made me promise I wouldn't breach my fiduciary responsibility to him. A client's wishes in this regard are sacrosanct, you know, and even if you are my best friend…" He paused and fixed me with a laser stare. "I would never violate the confidence of a client. Never. No matter what. So I'm sorry I couldn't tell you any of this before." Erik's glib patter sounded practiced, simply a different permutation of the words he used with his other clients.

"Right. Let the record reflect you're a true pillar of jurisprudence. Just spit it out, will you?"

Erik's face colored. "Okay. Sorry. It's just … this whole thing has me a little freaked." He got up, plucked one of the file folders from his desk, and returned. As he spoke, he glanced at the top sheet. "I'll spare you all the details for now, but bottom line, you get the house."

I'd already assumed that when Erik had given me the key this morning. Who else would my father leave it to? I was an only child.

"And all of its contents," Erik added.

Kassian's face—and breath—sprang to mind. I was sure Erik wasn't referring to the old drunk, but I saw no reason to bring him up. He was simply another guest star in Josh Handleman's secret soap opera.

Erik leafed through the folder and unclipped a small red envelope from one of the pages. "There's this, too. Safe deposit key. Virginia Central at Reston Town Center." He flipped it around in his hand, then read the number on it. "Box 112." He held the key-sized envelope out to me.

I took it and nicked at one corner with my fingernail. "What's in the box?"

Erik shook his head. "Don't know, but it's all yours. Probably family photos or birth certificates or baby teeth. Something with sentimental value."

"Not a million bucks in cash?" A grin spread on my face.

Erik swallowed. "No, don't think so. I checked the itemized list of assets your father compiled, and it didn't look like there was anything valuable that could fit into a box that size. Sorry." His Roman features tightened.

"Hey, not your fault my father wasn't loaded." I stuck the key in my pocket. I didn't care as much about money as most people, although having it was better than not having it. Of course, I didn't care much about old photos either.

Erik squirmed and consulted the folder again. "He left some jewelry—your mother's, I believe—to his sister Shelley."

"Good. She wouldn't want to be left out." Aunt Shel already owned a house, but she'd appreciate a few baubles. She was a lot more sentimental than I was.

A strange look descended over Erik. He seemed at a loss for words.

"What?" I asked.

"Listen, Josh. As soon as the paperwork for your father's estate gets filed, it becomes public record. So ..."

I shrugged. "So what do I care if people find out I inherited the house? Who gives a crap?" Sometimes he worried about the strangest things.

"No, it's not that," Erik said, as he closed the folder on his lap and took a deep breath. "It's the seven million dollars he left to the Reston Hebrew Home that people might give a crap about."

Holy crap, indeed.

THREE

Jews waste no time burying their dead.

My father died two days ago, on Friday, and if yesterday hadn't been *Shabbat*, we would have found a way to bury him then. So we had to settle for today, even though it was Christmas Eve.

The funeral service at Lansky's was mercifully short, as was the graveside ceremony at King David Memorial Gardens. The limo rides back and forth were uneventful. I shifted into detachment gear and rode the morning out, doing my best to support Aunt Shel while keeping my emotions locked down. I'd mourn by myself, later, in my own way.

Now we were in the City of Fairfax, sitting *shiva* at Aunt Shel's house. Shiva was similar to an Irish wake, if you took away the body, the copious amounts of booze, the merriment, and stretched it to an excruciating seven days.

All afternoon, a steady stream of people laden with food stopped by to offer their condolences. Aunt Shel and I had set up camp in the living room and—thankfully—our "guests" had finally given us a few moments of peace so we could decompress. Next to me, Aunt Shel balanced a Chinette plate on her knees, heaped past capacity with a hodgepodge of homemade food. A turkey drumstick, some potato salad with pimentos, a scoop of some indistinguishable casserole. Her fifth or sixth hard-boiled egg of the day—I'd lost count.

She picked up the drumstick and the plate listed to her left. After rebalancing it, she pointed the oversized hunk of fowl at me. "Why don't you get yourself a *polke?* It's getting close to dinnertime." A few dark crumbs of pumpernickel escaped her mouth. "And try some chocolate *babka* for dessert. It looked pretty good."

I glanced at my watch: 4:30. "Thanks, Shel. I'll get something in a few minutes." I'd tried to eat something right after we returned from the cemetery, but couldn't force much down. My body was still on West Coast time.

My pocket chirped. Out of the corner of my eye, I saw Aunt Shel frown, her entire face scrunching up in displeasure. I pulled out my phone, shielding it from her as best I could, and checked the number—Dani. I'd talk to her later. If I had my way, I'd never talk to her, but it wouldn't be up to me, it rarely was. She'd left me a handful of messages since Friday, and I knew she wouldn't stop until I called her back. Fidelity might not be Dani's forte, but she was persistent. When it suited her, anyway. I stuffed the phone back into my pocket, not wanting to further upset Aunt Shel.

A neighbor of Aunt Shel's took a seat next to us and started sobbing, a few tears leaving dark dots on the lapels of her navy suit. Aunt Shel rolled her eyes in my direction, set down her plate, and attended to her friend's grief. I tuned them out, more than content to take a break from talking and escape into my own thoughts.

17

Aunt Shel had insisted we sit shiva at her house, which was good by me. She'd also wanted to sit for only three days instead of the traditional week—also good by me. If she'd proposed a single night, I would have gone for that too. Luckily, my family considered the rules and traditions of Judaism merely suggestions, adhered to, altered, or ignored however we saw fit. Which again, was good with me. I wasn't much for carrying on antiquated customs, especially those I didn't even understand.

I got the part about wearing a torn black ribbon pinned to my shirt. There had to be some way for strangers to know I was in mourning. But no one had given me a good reason why we had to cover the mirrors, or why visitors had to drench the front porch with water as they washed their hands before entering. And no one explained—to my satisfaction—why Aunt Shel and I had to sit on uncomfortable metal folding chairs with short legs that Lansky's had sent over. *We do it because that's how it's done*, Aunt Shel had said, more than once. I chose not to point out any inconsistencies in her selective adoption of the shiva rules.

Another neighbor sidled up to join Aunt Shel's conversation, and the tone of their voices lightened the more they talked. Earlier in the day, I'd caught a few snatches of other conversations, and they seemed to be divided fifty-fifty: half centered around mundane topics like mah jongg and books and pot roast, the other half concerned my father.

They talked about how much of a *mensch* he was. Told amusing stories, most of which I had a hard time believing. The tales of his kindness and generosity and benevolence seemed to grow as the day wore on.

With only one or two exceptions, each mention of my father's largesse included a lengthy discourse on the new Handleman Library at the Hebrew Home. Everyone seemed to know about it but me. They all assured each other the upcoming dedication would take place on schedule. *Abe would have wanted it that way.* Every time they looked to me for answers, I kept my mouth shut and shrugged. Mr. Noncommittal, at your service.

I didn't know the majority of the well-wishers beyond their names and faces. Assorted family friends and relatives—very distant relatives—paid their respects and left, some staying just a few minutes, others as long as they thought proper. The last time I'd seen most of them was two and a half years ago, when we sat shiva for Mom.

Erik and Katy had come directly from the cemetery and stayed for about an hour before they needed to get on the road to her mother's for Christmas Eve supper. A couple of old high school poker buddies made an appearance, but seemed uncomfortable with the somber atmosphere and bolted quickly. Couldn't really blame them. Listening to old Jews *kvetch* wasn't very uplifting, and I certainly wasn't good company.

I never thought sitting around listening to people say good things about my family could be so grueling.

Aunt Shel's neighbors got up and said their goodbyes amidst a final burst of tears. Aunt Shel returned to her plate of food and spoke to me as if we'd been right in the middle of a conversation. "I've been telling him for years to move into a condo. Especially after Judy passed. Who needs the *farkakte* stairs?" She picked up her drumstick and waved it in the air like a conductor. "He should have listened to his older sister." She jabbed the polke in my direction, and a little flap of turkey skin flopped back and forth.

"Yes, he should have." I'd tried to persuade him to move, too, with the same amount of success. I nodded at the twenty or so people gathered in small groups in the living room and adjacent dining room. "Looks like he had a lot of friends."

Aunt Shel set her turkey leg down and frowned at the choices on her plate. "This is nothing. If it wasn't Christmas Eve, this place would be packed with *goyim* for three straight days. Wall-to-wall." She took a bite out of an unnaturally green pickle spear. "Tuesday's gonna be something all right."

I could see where the birth of Jesus outranked the death of my father in most people's eyes. "Well, we can sit for longer, if you want." I didn't, but I knew it was important for her to grieve properly. My father had been her closest confidante for the past fifteen years, ever since Uncle Don had his third—and final—heart attack.

She tsk-tsked me. "No. This is better for me. Don't need all those people traipsing through here making a mess anyway. They can send us a card." She busied herself with the food in her lap, done with me for the moment.

Throughout the day—at the funeral, in the procession, at the cemetery—I found my mind wandering back to the same questions. How had my father amassed such a fortune? And why hadn't I known about it? Erik had said he'd done well in real estate, and not just on the selling end. He'd invested wisely and as the Northern Virginia suburbs had exploded, so had the value of his holdings. But you sure couldn't tell it by how he dressed or what he drove or where he lived.

Erik had gone on to explain—in general terms—that my father had already set into motion some of his charity projects. I wished Erik had given me a few particulars, especially about the Handleman Library. Probably afraid of how I'd take it, my father a multi-millionaire, spreading cash around like grass seed, leaving his son out of the loop. Not for the first time in the past twenty-four hours, I pictured my father, martini glass in hand, lounging in a hot tub crammed to the gills with fifty-dollar bills. Utterly preposterous, but if you'd told me my father was worth multi-millions, I'd have said that was preposterous, too.

Across the room, the memorial candle on the fireplace mantel flickered as the front door opened. The sounds of a few more people trickling in floated through the air. I heard Lev Yurishenko before I saw him, his gruff, accented voice greeting people in the entryway. He'd been my father's best friend for as long as I could remember. When I was a kid, the old immigrant always greeted me with the same words—"It's your Uncle Lev, From Russia With Love"—right before he'd tousle my hair. Never liked it much. I think he got the message when I was about twelve and had grown taller than he was.

Lev had been the one to find my father when he came over for his weekly chess match; he'd been the one to call me Friday with the terrible news. Even though he was usually as stoic as a statue, the old goat must have been shocked when he looked through the front window and saw my father lying dead on the floor.

A moment later, he came striding toward us, heavy black overcoat still cinched at the neck, Lenin-style cap in place. In his left hand, he grasped a pair of worn leather gloves. As if he'd just stepped off the train from Minsk in pre-revolution Russia. He grabbed a nearby chair, dragged it in front of us, and eased himself down. Removed his cap. Hewing to the orthodox tradition in a shiva house, he waited for Shel or me to speak first.

Aunt Shel barely glanced up from her plate as she offered a slight nod in greeting.

"Hello, Lev," I said, rising.

He motioned me back down. "Sit, sit."

I had no desire to argue with Lev, so I sat. Even though I had six inches on him, I had to look up into his face, thanks to the shorty chairs. "I appreciate you coming back. But it wasn't necessary." He'd been at the funeral, of course, but he and his son Peter stayed in the background, not wanting to crowd us. After the cemetery, they'd stopped by for a little while, then excused themselves. I hadn't expected to see Lev again until tomorrow.

"No thanks are needed. Abe was like my brother. I will miss him greatly."

I nodded. "Is Peter here?"

Lev scowled. "No. He...he could not make it. He sends his best."

"Okay." I'd seen Peter two hours ago. He was entitled to a little break. What was it with fathers and their expectations?

Shel swallowed a mouthful of food. "Lev, did you get some rest this afternoon? Are you hungry?" I knew she'd miss mothering now that my father was gone.

"I am fine." He shook his head, slowly, sadly. "Abe had beaten me in chess three straight weeks. I had a new gambit I wished to try on him." He frowned. "I will have a difficult time finding another man who plays chess with so much passion as he did."

After a few more minutes of chitchat, I got up to stretch my legs. Lev followed me into the kitchen. "Come," he said, pulling me by my shirt into the corner, keeping my back to the other visitors buzzing around the congealing food spread out on the table. I looked down on him. Only about five-five or so, Lev maintained the bearing of a much taller, much tougher man. Maybe it was because he was always serious. I don't remember him smiling since right before the last time he tousled my hair.

"What?"

He peered around me and spoke in a hoarse whisper. "I am sorry. I do not wish to discuss this now, but I must. Please forgive me."

"What is it?"

"Joshua, this is not a matter that should be discussed in a shiva house, but it cannot wait. It is too important. The weight has been crushing on my heart." His accent thickened with every word. Two fingers still gripped my shirt.

"It's okay, Lev. This," I said, waving my hand in the air, "is mostly for Shel. She needs it. I'm not so *frum*. Say whatever's on your mind."

Lev took a deep breath and pulled me down closer so he could whisper in my ear. "Joshua, your father's death was not accident. He was murdered."

FOUR

I STEPPED BACK AND Lev's fingers slipped from my shirt. "What are you talking about? Who would kill my father? Why?"

Lev grabbed my shirt again and glanced around the kitchen. "Is he here?" Everyone had drifted away leaving just the casseroles and us.

"Who? What are you talking about?" I wasn't in the mood for morbid games. My head throbbed.

"Kassian. The weasel. He lives in your father's house, you know."

I stared at Lev.

"Do not play coy with me, Joshua. I saw you speaking with him this morning at the funeral."

"What?" I moved back, creating space between us. "I'm not trying to be coy. I just don't know what you're talking about. Why would Kassian murder my father?"

"He is an ugly man with despair in his soul. A leech. Where is he now?"

I'd arranged for a cousin of Aunt Shel's to take Kassian to the funeral. When he complained of feeling ill after the service, her cousin took him back to the house. "At home. Sick."

"Yes, vodka can make you sick." Lev sneered. "He killed your father. I know it."

"Kassian wasn't even there. He said he cleared out every Friday, when you came over to play chess. Went to one of the activity programs at the Hebrew Home, some music thing. Stayed for lunch, then watched a movie," I said. "I don't think he likes you." Actually, when Kassian told me he left every single Friday, he'd sounded more afraid of Lev than anything else.

Lev shrugged it off. "I do not care about who or what Kassian likes. He needs to be dealt with."

"Why would Kassian do it? My father gave him free room and board. My father was the only friend the poor guy had."

He pursed his lips. "I do not know why. But I am sure his reason makes sense only to him." Lev nodded, like he'd solved a riddle. "It was money. He knew your father had money and he killed him for it."

"What? He killed my father, ran away to the Hebrew Home to sing some songs, then returned to the house? That doesn't make any sense at all." I glared at Lev. If he was right about Kassian wanting money, the cash I'd found lying untouched in the kitchen drawer didn't make any sense either.

"I do not have all the answers yet. But I know he was murdered. I can feel it here," he said, touching his fist to his chest. "I know it. Abe would not just trip down a flight of stairs."

My fatigue had slowed my thinking, but things were starting to come into focus. "Lev," I said, putting my arm around his shoulder. "I know you loved my father. And it's only natural to be angry with him for leaving so … abruptly. But to accuse someone of killing him …"

"That is not it. You are—"

"Anger is natural, Lev. It means you are coming to terms with your grief."

"Yes, you are right. I am angry. I am angry at Kassian for what he has done." Lev brushed my arm away. "You do not have to believe me."

"What kind of proof do you have? In this country, we need evidence before accusing someone."

Lev stiffened. "I have lived in your country longer than you have been alive. Do not make the mistake so many of your fellow countrymen make. Do not be condescending to people born elsewhere. To do so accentuates your own ignorance."

I let the insult slide. "Did you tell the cops your suspicion?"

"No. I have not." His eyes narrowed to slits. "Not yet."

I sighed and softened my tone. "Lev, he fell down the stairs and broke his neck. It was a terrible accident. But that's what it was. An accident. That's what the police said, right?"

"Yes, they checked the doors. All locked," Lev said, meeting my eyes.

I stared back.

"And the dead bolts were secure," he added.

It took a few seconds for my foggy brain to noodle it through. "So there it is. You just proved my point. No one could exit the house without leaving a dead bolt unlocked. It had to be an accident." I exhaled, hoping I'd burst Lev's lurid fantasy.

Lev glared at me as if I were the village idiot. "Kassian has a key."

———

At first, waking up in my old bedroom was disorienting. But after a few days, it became oddly comforting. When I'd left for college, my parents converted it into a guest bedroom. Why they needed a second extra bedroom was beyond me; I was pretty sure they didn't entertain a parade of visitors. They'd taken down the posters of Theismann and Riggo and packed up my collection of Hot Wheels cars that I'd refused to surrender after elementary school. Given the walls a fresh coat of paint. Superficial changes only—it was still my room and always would be.

I rolled over and pulled up the covers, noting the familiar shadows caused by the sun sneaking in through the slats in the blinds. Amazing what came back to you. I'd been home for six days, and my body had finally adjusted to the time difference, so it wasn't fatigue keeping me in bed. I just wanted to take my time getting up. Let my head clear a bit. There was no place I needed to be today.

Christmas at Aunt Shel's had been quiet. A shuttle bus full of visitors from the Hebrew Home had stopped by on their way to dinner at a Chinese restaurant, but that was the only time the house held more than a few people paying their respects. She had been right about Tuesday, though. Non-stop action, all day long. Seemed half of Northern Virginia knew my father. His real estate colleagues. Neighbors. Old family friends. More folks from the Hebrew Home. And they all had good things to say about him. For me, a natural introvert, it was hard being "on" around all these strangers. I didn't know how people sat shiva for a week straight without going out of their skulls.

Fortunately, my days of sitting shiva were behind me. Yesterday, I'd recharged my batteries by sitting around watching hour upon hour of TV, inane talk shows mostly. In the afternoon, I'd taken a drive west on Interstate 66 to get some air, stopping at a little diner in Front Royal for dinner. Sat by myself and didn't speak to anyone, except the waitress. Even then, I managed to say little beyond "cheeseburger and fries, please."

Since Lev's accusation, I'd spoken to Kassian a few times, but wasn't able to carry on any kind of sustained conversation. My father's death had demolished him. He moped around, mumbling to himself, and spent most of his time sitting in the corner of his basement room, staring into space, uncommunicative. When I tried to comfort him, he just waved me off. But there were two things I noticed: Clear eyes and an absence of empty liquor bottles on the floor.

The conclusion I came to matched my initial reaction. There was no way Kassian had anything to do with my father's death. No way. Lev was wrong, dead wrong.

At around eight, I rose, got dressed, retrieved the *Post* from the end of the driveway, and drove to Starbucks at Reston Town Center. Sipped my venti and read the paper until Virginia Central Bank opened.

Just inside the entrance to the bank, an attractive young blond woman stood behind a podium, like a hostess at a fancy restaurant. She wore a headset, the thin, curved microphone stalk resting on her cheek an inch from the corner of her mouth. "Hello, how may I help you today?" She smiled, brilliant white teeth set off by a dark tanning-booth tan.

I started to answer, but she put up her forefinger and kept talking. "Yes, that's right, until five tonight and until eight tomorrow night. Thanks for calling." She pressed a button on her phone and nodded to me. "Good morning, welcome to Virginia Central. How may I help you today?" Her nametag read Cyndi Simpson.

"Good morning, Cyndi. I'd like to access a safe deposit box."

"Certainly, right this way." She gestured for me to follow and we zigzagged around a few other patrons waiting in line for the tellers. When we reached the vault in the back, Cyndi spoke to an older man. "Earl, would you greet our visitors while I serve this customer?" Her sweetly spoken request garnered instant action. Earl dropped what he was doing and hustled to the front.

She turned back to me. "Let's enter the vault, shall we?" She removed a lanyard—gray with little pink hearts imprinted on it—from her neck, and used the key to open the imposing door. "After you, sir."

Safe deposit boxes of assorted sizes lined each of the side walls. Cyndi went to a desk wedged into the back corner of the vault and picked up a red, leather-bound logbook. She flashed another blinding smile at me. "What number box?"

I pulled the key envelope from my pocket and handed it to her. "112."

She flipped a few pages and her green eyes lit up, matching her teeth in intensity. "You must be Josh Handleman!"

Her smile was contagious; I felt one of my own forming. "Yes, that's right. How did you know?"

"There are only two authorized parties on this account," she said, slipping into bankspeak. Then she switched back to Miss Congeniality. "How is the elder Mr. Handleman? I haven't seen him in a while. Such a dear man."

"He's … he died last week." The words came out brittle and without inflection, as if someone else were saying them. Someone in a faraway room.

Cyndi's hand covered her mouth and her face sagged. "Oh my. Oh, that's so …" She tried to get it together, wasn't completely successful. "I'm so sorry. That's just terrible." She gnawed on the inside of her cheek. "He was always so friendly. And he never failed to have a funny joke for us, too."

"Yes. It was unexpected." I swallowed and stuffed my hands into my jacket pockets.

She gazed off, eyes not focusing on anything in particular. I gave her a moment before clearing my throat.

"Oh. Sorry, I was just …"

"Would it be better if I dealt with the manager? You seem a little …" I didn't know how to finish.

Cyndi regained her composure. "I *am* the branch manager. I'm okay." With a final sigh, she opened the logbook again and ran her finger down the page. "Box 112. Here it is. You'll have to sign in." She placed the logbook on the desk. "May I see some ID please?" Then she shrugged. "Sorry. Regulations."

I showed her my license.

"Mother's maiden name?" she asked, with another shrug.

"Shapiro," I said. Satisfied, she handed me a pen and I signed in. Looking at the previous entry, I noticed my father had been in last Thursday. The day before he died. Prior to that, it had been a couple months since he'd accessed the box.

Box 112 was about two-thirds of the way up the wall, in the middle. Cyndi stood on her tiptoes—displaying nicely shaped calves—and stuck a key into each of the two slots. She opened the door and slid the long drawer out of its cubbyhole.

She held the drawer out to me. "Would you like a private room?" she asked, some of the perkiness drained from her voice.

"Sure. That would be great."

Cyndi showed me to a room and told me to take as much time as I needed. I thanked her and entered the closet-sized room, barely able to squeeze in between the door and the single chair. I set the drawer on the carrel-like piece of furniture that took up most of the space and pushed aside the chair—I wasn't planning to stay very long.

I flipped up the catch that secured the top of the metal drawer, but didn't open it. Took a deep breath. Was I prepared for what I might find, the last thing my father would give me? What if there were love letters from his mistress? What if there were bearer bonds worth millions? Maybe I should walk away and never return. Leave whatever was in the box to Cyndi. She seemed to care about my father.

I was being foolish. Erik was probably right. There'd be a stack of old family photos and Aunt Shel and I would spend an hour or two sifting through them, trying to identify all the people sporting odd hairdos and wearing dated clothes. Then I'd stash the pictures away in the attic, leaving them for someone else to go through when *I* died.

On the other hand, there might be some personal item of my father's that I could keep and treasure.

I opened the box and looked inside.

Empty.

FIVE

I wasn't angry or disappointed or perplexed. Well, maybe I was a little of all three. Did my father leave the empty box for me on purpose? Was this a hidden message from beyond the grave? Some kind of perverse motivational scheme he'd engineered to get me to see the value of amassing a nest egg? None of those explanations seemed likely. When he emptied the box last week, I doubted he knew he was going to die the next day. The photos or keepsakes he'd removed were probably in his dresser drawer at home buried under a pile of boxer shorts. Or not. I'd never know.

I found Cyndi and returned the drawer. She was back in perky mode, all smiles and good cheer. "Nice meeting you, although I'm sorry about the circumstances," she said, as she slid the drawer back into place and locked it up. She handed me my key. "Are you local?"

How to answer that one? "I've been living in San Francisco, but..."

Cyndi beamed at me.

"But I think I might stick around here for a while."

Her smile widened a hair. "Well, I guess I'll see you around then. If there's anything I can do for you, please let me know."

"Okay. Thanks." She closed the vault as I walked away.

I'd entered the bank with a safe deposit key and the excited anticipation of a child about to open a gift-wrapped birthday present. I left with a pocketful of nothing.

On the way home, I pulled into an elementary school parking lot and drove to the far end, where the spaces overlooked a playground. I killed the engine and sat there, watching a man play football with his son, probably about five years old. On every pass attempt, the boy would snap the ball to his father and run about twenty yards down the field before turning around. Then his father would wave him back, closer and closer, until the boy was three yards away. In a gentle arc, the father would toss the ball and the boy would make a valiant effort to haul it in, but he never quite managed the feat. After each miss, he'd fetch it and start over, resolve undiminished. While I watched, the ball hit the ground every single time.

After about a dozen tries, the father put the ball down and chased after his son in circles, laughing and waving his arms. Finally, he snatched his kid up and tucked him under his arm like a football, taking off down the field dodging imaginary tacklers, giving them the ol' Heisman stiff arm. The boy howled with delight.

I put my head down on the steering wheel, and for only the second time since I was a kid, I wept.

———

That night, I let myself into Erik's house and followed the noise of laughter into the den. I was the last to arrive for the poker game. A hand was already in progress, so I just nodded to the players and threw three twenties and a ten down on the table. Erik, who was dealing, paused for a split second and shoved a rack of chips in my direction. While they played on, I counted out three small stacks: seventy bucks worth of whites, reds, and blues.

When I was in eighth grade, Erik and I began playing poker. Lots of it. We'd play for nickels and dimes, inviting a revolving group of friends over to give them a few "lessons." Profitable for us, but its bigger purpose was to give us something to do besides homework and sports, something uniquely ours we could bond over. A core group of us played throughout high school, the nickels and dimes turning into dollar bills and fives. Somehow we squeezed in the weekly games between parties and dates and plain old screwing around. After I moved, though, real life got in the way and my friends became fewer and Dani wasn't too thrilled about me rolling in at three in the morning, wallet lighter by a couple hundred bucks.

Erik finished dealing the hand and his three eights held up. Only after he raked in the chips did he acknowledge me. "Hey, Josh, how's it going?"

I said my hellos. "Man, it's been a long time." On my right were the Spoletti twins, Matt and Goose. I'd known them since ninth grade gym class, when the three of us teamed up against hotshot Billy O'Rourke and a couple of his buddies in basketball and kicked their pompous asses. We'd played plenty of poker together, too.

Next to Erik was a guy I'd never met.

Erik introduced him. "Josh, this is Brandon Flannery. Buddy of mine. We work out together."

Brandon nodded in my direction.

"Good to meet you," I said.

He picked up his bottle of beer and tipped it at me, then busied himself restacking his chips. He wore a black Under Armour T-shirt that clung to his body like a second skin, but he was softer and dumpier than Erik, causing the T-shirt to bulge in the wrong places. Together with black sweatpants and a black Nike cap worn backwards, he looked like an out-of-shape poker Ninja. His dark sunglasses only made it more comical.

"C'mon ladies, let's cut the chitchat and kick this tea party into high gear," Erik said.

"Deal 'em," I said, as I rubbed the nappy green felt of the card table. I was comforted by that familiar feeling I got in my stomach right before the chips started flying. "This brings back memories."

Across the table, Erik cut the deck for Brandon. "Yes it does, my friend. We've played some," he said, as he gestured at the other players with his head, "but it's been way too long since we've had a sucker, er, you at the table."

We played for a couple of hours or so, and my stack gradually grew, mostly at the expense of the Spoletti twins. Some things never changed. I started to unwind, the first time in a long time. At the poker table, you could leave your problems behind, at least for a little while, losing yourself in the moment, absorbing the game's rhythms, watching the cards fall while you probed your opponents for weakness. Looking for the slightest advantage, searching for anything you could use to get inside their heads. If you got them to lose their composure—to go on tilt—your job was done. They'd get reckless and then they were toast.

Next to me, Goose crammed a handful of Cheetos into his mouth. More scrawny than skinny, more gangly than tall, Goose stood six feet plus a fraction, a good deal of it neck. "Hey, Matt. Tell everyone about the date you had last week." Some orange Cheetos dust drifted down from his mouth onto the table.

Matt nodded eagerly. "Okay, okay. So we're on her couch and we start making out, right? This girl's pretty hot, and we're really getting into it. So she starts playing with the buttons on her blouse and says, 'Would you like to see my puppies?' And I'm thinking, damn straight, those are some mighty nice puppies. I'll pet 'em too, if you want. So she screams out, 'Milton, Dante,' at the top of her lungs, practically deafened me. And five seconds later these two mangy mutts come bounding into the room, jumping all over us. It went downhill from there."

Amid the laughter, Goose said, "You didn't get anything, did you?"

"Oh, I got something," Matt said. "I got fleas."

I wondered how long they'd been rehearsing their vaudeville routine. Not long enough. When the groaning subsided, I asked, "What's this I hear about a fiancée, Goose?" He'd paid a shiva call, but we hadn't talked about his love life.

Before he could answer, Matt chimed in. "Goose is getting ready to mate for life. Aren't you, big bro?" Matt was eighteen minutes younger than Goose.

Goose chucked a white chip at Matt. "Shut the fuck up, will ya? Carla and I are not getting married. Not anytime soon, that is."

Good for him. Mating for life was overrated. Matt turned to me. "Don't ever believe what he tells you. He's a professional liar. He'd wear a skirt and heels to work if his precious Carla told him to."

"Fuck you," Goose said, as he stuffed more Cheetos into his mouth.

"How's Dani?" Matt asked.

I shot Erik a glance before answering. "Rough patch. You know how it is." I could feel everyone's eyes on me, waiting for more. "We're separated."

"Shit. I didn't know." Matt touched my forearm. "How you holding up?" he asked.

"Okay." Had someone turned the heat up in the room? For a minute, the only sounds were chips being rustled and Goose chomping on Cheetos.

Matt cleared his throat. "Sorry about your dad. He was a real good guy. He meant a lot to me." When he was a senior in high school, Matt's parents kicked him out of the house for smoking pot. My father took him in for a few days until things cooled down and his parents let him return.

"Yeah, he had a lot of admirers," I said.

"So generous, too," Goose added. "Really came through in the clutch."

"I guess," I said. As long as your last name wasn't Handleman. I'd had enough talk about my father during the past week—time to change the subject. "How's the world of software?" Matt and Goose had just secured some additional funding for a video game company they'd started a couple years ago.

"Great. We're going to launch a new product in a few months," Goose said, eyeing his brother. "Should be a winner."

Just what the world needed. More stylized video violence for adolescent boys.

"How's your business? Enough companies going under to support you?" Matt asked me.

Across the table, I noticed Erik flinch. "I'm going to try something new. Not sure exactly what, though," I said.

"How about we try playing some poker?" Brandon's loud, New York–accented voice interrupted our chat session. "Texas Hold 'Em. No limit." The table quieted as he dealt two cards facedown to everyone.

I glanced at my cards. Pair of jacks, a very good starting hand. When the betting got to me, I raised. Erik folded and Brandon called quickly. Matt also folded.

"How come all I ever get is garbage?" Goose said, as he mucked his cards into the middle, leaving Brandon and me head-to-head.

"Here's the flop," Brandon said. In Hold 'Em, you cobbled together your hand from the two cards dealt to you and the cards dealt face-up on the table. After the flop, there would be two more cards turned over in the middle, for a total of five common cards.

He turned three cards face-up. Jack, ten, deuce. I'd flopped a strong hand: three jacks. "Twenty bucks," I said, as I tossed two blue chips into the pot.

Brandon stared at me, although it was hard to know for sure with his shades on. After a moment, he tossed in two of his own blues. "I call."

He flipped over the next card. Two of clubs.

I'd lucked into a full house, jacks over twos, and struggled to maintain my poker face. I knew I had him beat—it was just a matter of how much I'd take him for. I figured he had a pair in the hole, which would give him two pair. Good, but a loser to my full house. As long as he didn't get extraordinarily lucky on the "river"—the last card—I'd take down the pot. My bet. I made a show of counting my chips and then pushed them in. "Fifty."

Brandon smiled. "You're full of shit. I can smell a bluff a mile away." He counted out his chips and splashed the pot with them. "I'll see your fifty."

Next to me, Matt and Goose stopped talking. Across the table, a strange expression came over Erik. This had turned into the biggest pot of the night, by a lot.

"Ready?" Brandon asked.

"Yeah, flip it over," I said, hoping for a small card, a rag. Anything but an overcard to my jack. If he had a pair of queens, kings, or aces, I didn't want him to suck out on me by getting a higher full house.

Brandon turned over the river card—a four. My full house stood up. I began counting my chips slowly, a ploy I used when I wanted my opponent to squirm.

Brandon banged his bottle of beer on the table to get my attention. "Erik's told me all about you, and he's right. Your life's fucked up," he said, as he pulled the last beer from a six-pack sitting on a small side table. "Job. Wife. Down the dumper." He stared in my direction. "That's rough. Maybe you ought to go on a little vacation or something. Cleanse yourself."

Erik spoke to Brandon in a low voice. "Don't be an ass."

Brandon kept staring at me.

"Thanks for the advice," I said, shrugging it off, trying to concentrate on extracting the most money out of Brandon. If I went over the top, he might fold. I needed to guess what size bet he would actually pay off.

"Losing your father. Really rough," Brandon said, slight smirk on his face. "Glad to see you could put it behind you and come play tonight. You're a strong man, Josh."

I gave him a fake smile, but didn't pursue it, trying to stay focused. I had ninety dollars in front of me. I figured forty would be safe and threw four blues into the pot.

Brandon didn't look down at his chips. He raised his sunglasses and set them up on his head. His eyes were dull, black marbles. "Were you guys close?" he asked. "See him often?"

I'd taken my share of needling at the poker table over the years, realizing it was just a strategy to put me on tilt. I clenched my teeth, determined not to give him the satisfaction, and willed my voice to stay steady. "We can talk about my father later."

"Come on, Brandon. Get back to the game," Erik said, always the peacemaker.

Getting back to the game sounded good to me. "It's up to you, Brandon," I said, but the words came out thin and tentative. A vision of my father in the hot tub flashed through my mind.

"In a minute, in a minute," he said. "I've got one more question." A diamond stud in his ear glinted.

Erik jumped in. "Brandon. Either call or fold. Come on, man. Be cool."

Brandon's eyes met mine. "How does it feel to have your father stiff you out of seven million dollars? I mean, he must have really hated your guts to do that, don't you think?"

I swallowed hard, my mind searching for some scathing retort, but nothing came to me.

In one swift move, Brandon pushed all of his chips into the middle. "I'm all in."

"Jesus," I heard Goose say. The surge of electricity in the room could have illuminated half the Las Vegas Strip.

All in? Was he crazy? "I call," I said, pushing my chips in as fast as I could. My pulse raced as I whipped down my cards. "Full boat. Jacks over twos." I extended both arms to rake in the mountain of white, red, and blue chips.

Brandon raised his voice. "Well, all I've got is two pair," he said. "Deuces and …" He snapped the two cards in his hand down on the table. "Deuces."

I froze, trying to take it all in. Then a wicked smile bloomed on Brandon's face and the black eyes smoldered. "So I guess that gives me four deuces. Read 'em and weep, Josh."

Tilt.

SIX

THE RESTON HEBREW HOME wasn't in Reston. Too many zoning restrictions, I guess. Or maybe the town council didn't like old people. Or Jews. Or maybe it was only old Jews they despised. For whatever reason, the sprawling campus occupied a dozen acres three blocks east of the town limits.

The Hebrew Home wasn't a single entity. A mélange of separate buildings housed an assisted living center, a hospice, a nursing home, a senior citizen recreation center, a homeless shelter, a geriatric-focused medical building, and various other units. Connected by a maze of walkways, tunnels, and skyways, you could get all of your business and visiting done without having to brave the elements.

The architecture represented an eclectic mish-mash of styles. Modern, traditional, glass, brick, what-have-you, all represented without a single unifying design. Whenever I drove up, I always imagined a bunch of preschool kids using different materials—Tinkertoys, Lincoln Logs, wooden blocks, Legos—to piece together their creations, only to dump them down on the playmat in haphazard fashion when they had to break for snacktime.

Named the Arthur Budzinger Building after one of the Home's founders, the main building contained the management offices and many of the common facilities. In a few hours, the Arthur Budzinger Building also would be the official home of the Handleman Library.

When I entered the lobby, bittersweet memories swarmed back from my visits with Mom. I'd spent more than a few afternoons sitting with her in the large, airy space, pleasant periods when she had the strength and desire to venture from her room. The constant buzz of visitors and residents milling about seemed to provide something—comfort, companionship, meaning—she had craved.

I took a deep breath, knowing the distinctive odor would trigger more memories, all the way back to grandmother visits at an old folks home in Jersey. No matter what name you used—retirement homes, nursing homes, assisted living centers—they all smelled the same to me, a mixture of Listerine and baby powder, with the faint scent of impending death layered beneath. I tried to shake off the past, but it clung to me like a tenacious burr in my sock.

I'd lobbied hard for Aunt Shel to join me at today's dedication, but she complained she was still recovering from the shock of my father's death. That, and she wanted to have enough energy to cook for the Shabbat dinner she'd invited me to tonight. I harbored hopes Lev might show up, too, although I had the sinking feeling he was avoiding me, not wanting to get into another argument. The couple of the calls I'd made to his house yesterday had gone unreturned. All the people who had taken a break from their daily routines to pay a shiva call earlier in the week had drifted back to their lives, leaving me to pick up the pieces by myself.

I showed ID and signed in at the reception desk. I was about twenty minutes early for the dedication ceremony, so I decided to wander around a bit. Off the lobby to the left, a hallway led to a number of smaller meeting rooms. A fairly new card and game room occupied the western half of the back portion of the main building; its floor-to-ceiling windows overlooked a broad court-yard where a well-tended garden sprouted in the spring.

Might as well get a preview of the main event. Sandwiched be-tween the card room and a snack machine alcove, they'd converted a utility room into the library. A poster board on an easel adver-tised the dedication ceremony, *Free refreshments,* an inducement to attend. A dozen chairs fanned out in a semicircle before two heavy, burnished wood doors. Somebody had tied a shoelace-thin blue ribbon around the curved metal door handles, creating a tiny bow. Little pomp, less circumstance. No one would confuse this dedication with the opening of a presidential library at a world-famous university.

A ten-inch square of brass hung on the wall next to the doors. *The Handleman Library*, in a neatly engraved classic font. It was weird seeing your name on a plaque, hanging on a wall. I ran my fingers along the smooth, cool surface, tracing the letters.

"Nice, huh?"

The voice startled me. A lanky man about my height, a kid re-ally, stood by my side, holding a spray bottle of Windex in one hand, a bunch of rags in the other. I couldn't place the face, but I'd seen him before. "I'm sorry, you're ... ?"

"DeRon Woodson. I started here a week before your mother joined us. She was one of the first patients I really got to know. Sweet lady."

Now I remembered. A nurse's aide. Silky baritone, crisp enunciation. Unspoken wisdom behind the words. Unnerving, coming from someone barely out of his teens. "Hey, good to see you again. How are things going?"

"Fine, just fine." Then he glanced around the lobby. "Only way it'd be better is if the patients stopped calling me a *schvartz*. But I'm not holding my breath." He grinned conspiratorially, then jutted his chin at the plaque. "Nice thing your father did, you know?"

"I guess."

He eyed me. "And it wasn't just this. There's talk of a new facility for Russians. He'd always been fond of them. Bet he had something to do with that, too. A good man."

More surprises from my father. I should be getting used to them by now, but the more I found out, the more I discovered how little I really knew about his life.

"Speaking of Russians, how's Mr. Kassian? He and your father were very close. Took him in when he couldn't stand it here at the shelter."

"He's taking it hard. At least he hasn't been drinking in a few days," I said, not sure which was worse, a drunk Kassian or a semi-comatose Kassian rocking back and forth in a chair, barely speaking.

DeRon's eyes narrowed. "He's been drinking?"

"Yes, I found him the morning after my father died, practically passed out."

DeRon lowered his head, shook it slowly from side to side. "No, no, no. Say it ain't so, Joe DiMaggio." His head continued its pendulum swing. "Mr. Kassian had been doing so well, too. Hadn't had a drink—that I heard about anyway—since your father took him in. That was the deal, what I heard. He could stay at your father's as long as he didn't touch the sauce."

"Really?" I'd assumed Kassian was a lush, but what did I know?

"Yeah. Oh, he was hitting it pretty good for a while. He'd stay at the shelter, and then there'd be some kind of dust-up, and he'd go missing for a while—back on the streets. Then he'd return and it'd start all over again. Finally, he couldn't stand it any longer," DeRon said, looking around the lobby. He lowered his voice. "I don't think the shelter director wanted him there either. They seemed to go at it pretty good."

Something didn't add up. "If Kassian hated the shelter so much, why would he come to the day programs here?"

"Kassian is an odd one, all right. Couldn't take getting locked in at night. Made a big deal about it, too. Something about being locked up back in Russia. Doesn't have any problem coming here during the day, though. In fact, I'd say he really *likes* coming here during the day. People are funny, huh?"

Kassian's a real stitch, all right. "Yeah, I guess."

"Anyway, your father stepped in and saved Mr. Kassian. Yes sir, without your father's help, Mr. Kassian wouldn't be with us no more. And that'd be a real shame. We've grown fond of him around here. Kinda like our mascot or something. Nice to see you've followed in your father's footsteps. He would have wanted you to watch out for Mr. Kassian, you know." DeRon's eyes shot over my shoulder, and he quickly turned his head and gave the brass plaque a spritz of Windex. He polished it with a rag, then sauntered off, brandishing his spray bottle like a pistol.

Footsteps came louder from behind me. I turned and saw Carol Wolfe, Director of Resident Life, approach, followed by two men and a woman, all dressed in business attire. I'd remembered her from Mom's stay, and she'd been the one who called to officially invite me to the dedication.

"Hello, Josh. I'm so glad you could make it today," she said, offering her hand.

"Thanks for inviting me. Good to see you again." I shook her hand, and she clasped the top, in a double-handed shake. Carol hadn't changed a bit that I could remember. In her mid-to-late fifties, she was tall and trim and had a welcoming face with deep-set eyes. Diamond earrings twinkled on her lobes, and she dressed well, too. When she smiled, crow's feet enhanced the total package. She was one of those women who would be attractive well into her later years.

"Good to see you, too. I'm so sorry about your father." Her eyes were moist.

"Thanks." Behind her, the two male members of her entourage set up a folding table while the woman unloaded a couple packages of store-bought cookies from a bag. From another, she produced two large bottles of Juicy Juice and a stack of paper cups. Set-up job complete, they all took their seats. A handful of residents had also gotten settled in, and a few others seemed to be closing in as fast as their walkers could bring them. Must have smelled the Fig Newtons.

Carol waved her hand at the microphone. "This isn't going to be anything terribly formal. But we did want to acknowledge Abe's contribution, even in his absence. He wasn't much for …" Carol paused. "Are you sure you wouldn't like to say a few words?"

On the phone, Carol had asked me to give a little speech about the library, or about my father, or about the Hebrew Home. I'd politely declined then, and I hadn't changed my mind. "Thanks, but I think I'll pass. I'm not much on public speaking."

Carol arched an eyebrow as she glanced at the twelve people sitting in the folding chairs. "Yes, I see. You'll at least stand up front with me, won't you?"

I felt my face flush. "Uh, sure."

She glanced at her watch. "Well, then. Let's get started."

We stood before the small gathering and Carol delivered a five-minute speech full of platitudes and gratitudes, a good chunk of it devoted to describing the wealth of activities at the Hebrew Home in minute detail. When she finished, she thanked my father again and wrapped things up to lackluster applause. Stepping to the library doors, she motioned me over to stand next to her in front of the ribbon. She draped one arm around me, pointed my head to the right, and whispered in my ear. "Say cheese."

One of her assistants snapped a couple photos, while I forced a smile. Then someone handed Carol a pair of scissors, the kind used to cut surgical tape, and she snipped the ribbon. It fell to the floor to another smattering of applause. Then the audience attacked the cookies and juice with vigor.

"Why don't you come in and take a look, Josh? See what a wonderful thing your father did." She opened one of the tall doors and held it for me. "I'll catch up to you later." She smiled, and once again, her eyes shone. "Thanks for coming. I'm sure your father would have appreciated it. He loved you very much, you know."

She held my gaze for a moment, then backed out into the hallway, leaving me alone in the library.

For the most part, the small room was simply designed. Bookshelves lined both of the side walls, and three square tables, each with four chairs tucked neatly underneath, occupied the center. A small desk stood sentry to the left of the entrance. Books filled about two-thirds of the available bookshelves.

In the back of the library, two large windows faced the courtyard, offering a view of the gardens. But it was the spectacular Star of David stained-glass panels above them that reflected my father's soul. Royal blue, deep red, and milky white sections of glass fit together like shimmering puzzle pieces. Admiring the craftsmanship, knowing how my father must have felt when he admired it, sent a shiver down my spine.

As a child, I remembered him leafing through a coffee table book with gorgeous photos of Marc Chagall's work. He'd shake his head and make appreciative noises as he flipped the pages. I guess this was his tribute to the great artist. The windows probably cost more than everything else in the library combined. My father was modest in many ways, but every once in awhile, he'd go against form and do something like this. Incredible.

I stood off to the side as a few other people drifted into the room, their hushed murmurs reminiscent of every library I'd ever been in. And every single person's face brightened when gazing upon the stained glass.

After a few more minutes of my own "Star-gazing," I left the room. My mouth had gone dry, but when I stopped at the snack table, I discovered the vultures had finished the Juicy Juice. As I crossed the lobby to the water fountain, someone called my name.

I changed course and veered toward the outstretched arm waving at me from near the reception desk.

"Josh Handleman. It's great to see you," Tamara Rosen said, as she smothered me in a hug. "How are you doing? I read about your dad in the paper. I'm so sorry." The hug continued for a moment and then she let go and stepped back, examining me up and down. "You look great."

"So do you," I said, and I meant it. Her hair was different, and she seemed more ... sophisticated. I hoped I did, too. We'd dated for most of my senior year in high school, but things fizzled shortly thereafter. Nothing dramatic, just went our separate ways after graduation.

"I thought about coming to the funeral, but ..." Her captivating brown eyes warmed my mood and got things stirring, just like they used to.

I waved her off. "Don't worry. I almost didn't go myself." I winked.

She flashed me a stern look and shook her head, then took my arm and set off across the lobby. "I've wondered about you over the years, Josh. How have you been?"

I thought about my crumbled marriage and scumbag business partner. "Okay, I guess." And then another look at her smiling face boosted my spirits. What was it about seeing an old flame that got the sparks flying? I hadn't seen her since our graduation party, but it could have been yesterday. "How about you? Married?" I blurted out, sounding way too interested.

"I'm afraid I'm taken," she said, the corners of her mouth upturned. "You?"

I hesitated. "Not anymore."

"Oh. I'm so sorry, Josh."

"Don't be. It's for the best. No kids or anything." I shrugged. If I kept saying it was for the best, then it had to be, right?

"Are you going to be staying for a while?"

"Yeah, I think." We stopped in front of the elevators that served the nursing home wing.

"We're here to visit my grandmother. She's upstairs," Tammy said. "And here comes the love of my life now." She tipped her head back toward the lobby.

Two ancient men and a striking brunette woman approached. No sign of Tammy's husband. I looked back at Tammy, puzzled. The brunette came up to her and pecked her on the cheek. Tammy turned toward me. "Josh, this is my partner, Nicole."

SEVEN

My jaw hung open.

"I haven't seen Josh since high school. We went to the prom together," Tammy said, giving Nicole's hand a squeeze.

"Hello, Josh. It's nice to meet you," Nicole said. When I didn't respond immediately, she tilted her head. "Tammy didn't tell you, did she? She likes surprising people." Nicole elbowed Tammy, and they both giggled.

I gathered myself. "No. No, she didn't." I shot a frown at Tammy, then wiped my face clean. "How long have you two been … ?"

"Almost three years," Tammy said. "Sorry, Josh. Just having a little fun."

"Yeah, sure." I probably would have done the same to her. She was always pretty good about taking a joke.

"Didn't you wonder why we never … ?" Tammy asked, arching an eyebrow. "I guess even then I knew, on some level. Don't feel bad. You were the absolute best guy I ever went out with." She and Nicole giggled again.

The elevator door opened and it took a minute for the car to unload its elderly passengers.

"Nice meeting you," Nicole said, as she got on the elevator. She held her hand over the door as she waited for Tammy.

"Well, Josh, it was great seeing you again," Tammy said. She gave me a quick hug and hopped on the elevator. "Oh, by the way. You should call my sister Rachel, she's available. You'll like her. She's fun, she's cute. And most importantly..." The doors started to close. Tammy stuck her face into the narrowing gap, talking faster so the doors wouldn't close on her mid-sentence. "...she's straight."

———

Aunt Shel answered the door in a faded pink and blue housedress that might have been fashionable in Eastern Europe—in the fifties. She caught me eyeing her ratty dress.

"Never mind this *schmatta*. It's comfortable. And it's as old as you are," she said, stretching up to kiss me.

I handed her the loaf of *challah* I'd brought and while she took it into the kitchen, I made myself at home in the living room. The shorty chairs were gone and the only reminder of our three days sitting shiva was the burned-out memorial candle still on the mantee.

Aunt Shel joined me, carrying two shot glasses and a bottle. "Peach schnapps, Josh?" One side of her mouth twitched.

"No thanks, Shel. Got any beer?"

She shook her head as the other side of her mouth twitched. "Yech. How can anyone drink that stuff? Like you're drinking liquid bread. And not even good bread. Wonder Bread." She poured herself a shot and downed it before she sat. Then she poured another and took the chair opposite the couch where I'd settled. "We should have gone to *shul* tonight."

"Don't start, Shel," I said. "Don't start." A good Jew would have gone to synagogue after his father's death to say Mourner's Kaddish. A slightly-below-average Jew went to synagogue a couple of times a year, during the High Holy Days. I wasn't sure how much lower I fell on the continuum—I hadn't been to temple since the Bat Mitzvah of an employee's daughter three years ago.

Aunt Shel took a sniff of her drink, then raised her head. "How are you doing, kiddo?"

"I'm okay. How about you? We missed you at the dedication this morning. Feeling better?"

Aunt Shel's face colored slightly. "Oh yes. Much better." She glanced away, then took a sip of schnapps.

A miraculous recovery. "Well, you didn't miss much at the ceremony. But the library is impressive. My father commissioned some amazing stained glass windows. I'll have to take you over there so you can see it."

Aunt Shel nodded. "Okay. But don't inconvenience yourself. Whenever you get around to it is fine." She sighed. "Abe liked stained glass. He always was talking about getting some for your house, but I knew he'd never really do it. He was quite the frugal one, your father."

She should talk, sitting there in her fifty-year-old potato sack. "I suppose that's how he amassed so much money," I said.

She glared at me. "You never wanted for anything. He provided for you and Judy very well. I hope you're not complaining." She leveled a finger at me and kept it pointed in my direction until I answered.

"No. No complaints here. Just curiosity. Did you know he was loaded?"

Aunt Shel ran her bony finger around the top of the shot glass. "Abe had a very good head for business. He seemed to know which deals were good ones and which ones were lemons. He offered to invest some of my money, but ..." She waved her hand. "He never liked being a show off. Even when he was a boy, he'd do well in school but he'd never brag about it. Sometimes he'd make up stories and tell his friends he barely passed a class when he got an A+."

I tried again. "So, did you know he was a multimillionaire?"

She blew her breath out. "Abe never mentioned numbers. But from our conversations, I could tell he was doing very, very well." She touched the drink to her lips, then brought it down without sipping. "Your father liked things that appreciated in value. And he liked things that you could see or hold or touch. That's why he went into real estate. Good, solid investments. I think things like stocks and bonds scared him."

That sounded like my father. Part of me wished I'd known more about him. "Did you see him much, Aunt Shel?"

"After Don died, we became closer, then after your mother died, Abe and I became a lot closer. He used to come over a couple of times a week for dinner." Her eyes glistened. "Why don't we eat? You could stand to put on a few pounds."

I'd been under the impression that Aunt Shel would be preparing one of her traditional Shabbat dinners. What I got was a jumble of re-heated leftovers—prepared dishes and casseroles people had brought over while we were sitting shiva. I loaded my plate with meatloaf, turkey, stuffing, green beans, and some lumpy greenish-orange thing. Aunt Shel smeared some chopped liver on a bagel half and poured herself more schnapps. Toasted the air in my direction. *L'chaim.*

"Where's the challah?" I asked.

Aunt Shel waved it off. "In the freezer. I've got so many leftovers, we're not starting anything new. You know how I hate wasting food." She pointed at the half dozen dishes on the table. "Eat up. There's plenty." She took a bite of her bagel.

The only thing worse than bad food is a surfeit of bad food. I settled into a steady rhythm, taking a bite out of each item on my plate, moving counter-clockwise. Chew, chew, chew, pause. Chew, chew, chew, pause. Figured it would be the most efficient way to plow through the smorgasbord. I hated to waste food, too—no matter how bad it tasted.

I plugged away, and we ate in silence for fifteen minutes until I couldn't cram another piece of dried-out fowl into my mouth. I pushed my plate away. "Uncle. I give. You can throw the rest away, for all I care."

Aunt Shel wrinkled her nose. "Don't worry. I'll put it back in the freezer. We can have it again next week."

Her straight face scared me. I'd have to come up with a previous engagement for next Friday night.

"How's Lev?" she asked.

"I don't know. I haven't seen him since he was here."

"Really? That's odd. I would have thought he'd go to the dedication. Him being a big *macher* there now and all."

"What are you talking about?"

56

Aunt Shel frowned at me. "You didn't know? He was elected to the Oversight Committee at the Hebrew Home. All fired up to get things done. Abe wasn't too keen on the idea, but Lev went ahead anyway. He's a stubborn man, you know. Lev, I mean. Although your father was plenty stubborn, too. Sweet, but stubborn. Of course, I'm not saying Lev's not sweet underneath his tough crust."

The liquor was starting to take its toll on Aunt Shel. First came the rambling. Then, if things progressed according to schedule, the tears would flow. Hopefully, I'd be long gone by then. I reached for the bottle, but she was too quick, grabbing it and placing it out of my reach. All I could do was shake my head. "So what kind of things does Lev want to accomplish at the Home?"

"I don't know. Who knows? He probably doesn't even really know." She poured herself another drink.

"Shel. I think you've had enough."

She glowered at me. "I'm an old lady. I was drinking when you were just a little *pisher*. I know when I've had enough. And I haven't yet." She winked at me, but it wasn't a crisp one. The eye stayed shut for a full three seconds before re-opening. "No need to worry about me. Besides, it's just schnapps."

Famous last words. "How about I help clean up? We can call it a night and you can get some rest." I started to get up, but she motioned me down.

"Forget it. I'll clean up. You don't know where everything goes. Besides, I want to talk to you." Her words were starting to slur. "About your life."

It had only been a matter of time before she started in on me again. I'd already told her about my breakup with Dani and brushed off her many suggestions to save the marriage, but I guess there was still plenty of fight left in the old gal.

"Okay, Shel. Go ahead." I leaned back and crossed my arms.

"You're going to be all right, aren't you, Josh?"

"Sure." I had a few flickering doubts, but I'd always survived in the past.

"Abe left you the house, right?"

She knew that already, but I guess when you get old, you want to make doubly sure of things. Especially when it came to money. "Yes, Shel. He left me the house. And the furniture. And his car. I'll be fine."

She nodded, and she seemed to be considering something. Like how to phrase her next question. "Anything else?"

"Like what?"

She didn't answer, but she stared at me, as if she suddenly expected me to remember something. "I don't know what you're getting at," I said.

"I didn't think Abe raised a dummy, but maybe I was wrong." She spoke slowly and struggled to enunciate each word, doing a pretty good job of it despite the high schnapps content of her blood. "Did you find anything else of value?"

"Well, he did leave me the key to his safe deposit box."

"Aha!" Shel said, raising a finger to the sky. She straightened up in her chair, eyes glistening. "And …"

"And it was empty." Somehow, I knew that wasn't the punch line she was expecting.

"Empty?" Her mouth stayed open slightly and her eyes seemed to focus on a faraway point. "You sure?"

"Of course I'm sure. I know empty, and that box was empty."

"*Oy vey*," Aunt Shel said. "*Oy vey iz mir.*"

"What?"

"What happened to his collection?" she asked.

"What collection?"

Aunt Shel looked me in the eyes, flecks of worry in hers. "His diamond collection."

EIGHT

TWIN AUGERS OF ANXIETY and excitement bored holes into my skull as I jousted with sleep. Forked tongues lapped at the gaping orifices, fueling feverish dreams, ephemeral and muddled. A single vivid scene remained when I awoke: Naked, I walked across a glistening beach, but instead of sand, I trod on diamonds, my soles shredded into ribbons leaving a wandering trail of crimson.

I hadn't slept well at all.

Now, with two cups of coffee in my system, I attempted to pump myself up to accept the challenge my father had unwittingly left me. If he wanted me to have his diamond collection as his legacy, then by God, I was going to find it. Maybe it was fitting that he'd introduced me to my favorite book as a kid, *Treasure Island*.

At first, I found it hard to believe my father could have collected diamonds all these years without me knowing about it. But thinking back, I quickly realized that as a child I wouldn't have cared, and once I became a teenager, the sphere of my attention only encompassed myself. To say I'd been self-focused would be quite an understatement.

Before I began the search, I called Erik to make sure he hadn't logged in the diamonds as estate assets and forgotten to tell me. He sounded as surprised as I had been. "Your father collected diamonds? How many are we talking about?"

"Not sure. Shel said he'd been collecting them for at least thirty years. He'd only showed them to her once, and only a few of them. She said he kept them in a little black velvet jewelry bag with a cute drawstring. She guessed he could have had ten or twenty. Maybe more."

Erik said, "Not bad. Could be worth something. So the safe deposit box was completely empty?"

"Completely. No diamonds, no nothing. Must be lying around the house somewhere. I'll find them," I said, trying to boost my confidence. There must be a million hiding places around here, but then again, I had nothing else to do.

"Well, if there's any way I can help, let me know, okay?" Erik said.

"Sure. Thanks." I hung up. After another quick cup of coffee and a Pop-Tart, I got started.

I hadn't gone into my father's bedroom more than a couple of times since I'd been back, unable to summon the courage to start combing through his stuff and dredging up safely buried memories. Until now. Amazing what the promise of a good, old-fashioned treasure hunt—with real treasure—can help you overcome.

I tackled his dresser first, where an array of framed photographs covered the top. A few were landscapes, but the majority were snapshots of Mom and me, ranging from my birth through high school. In the older pictures—when I was a grade-schooler—I was usually smiling, but once I reached puberty, the scowls outnumbered the grins by an overwhelming margin. Mom's smile, however, never flagged.

I found a set of Russian nesting dolls hiding behind an 8 x 10 glossy of Mom. With my palm, I wiped a thin layer of dust from the outer doll and admired the painting of a peasant girl holding flowers. The colors seemed unnaturally bright, not quite neon, but somehow it all worked. I pulled the top off the outer doll, revealing another doll within. A moment later, I'd liberated the remaining three dolls, each smaller than the one before it. I wasn't an artist, so I couldn't tell if the dolls had been handcrafted in Moscow or mass-produced in Taiwan; either way, they were pretty neat. The wooden dolls reminded me of my father, not so much because of his Russian fixation, but because of the unknown layers beneath his shell I was only now learning about.

I reassembled the dolls, stuck them back where I'd found them, and moved on to the dresser drawers. Starting at the bottom, I scooped out all the clothes and dumped them on his bed in a heap. I turned out all the pockets and made sure to shake out each garment before I tossed it into a big box I'd put on the floor. After I was through, the clothes would be donated to the Hebrew Home. It wasn't seven million dollars, but every little bit helps.

The bottom three drawers held no surprises—just clothes. Underwear, dark socks, plain white T-shirts. Old man clothes. The top drawer was a catch-all. I removed the entire drawer and overturned it onto the bed. It might have been my imagination, but I think a small mushroom cloud of dust and dirt rose up into the air. When it cleared, I took stock. Some change, some folding money, a few unmatched cuff links. A *Chai* on a gold chain. I picked up an old watch, manufactured by a company I'd never heard of, hands frozen at ten past one. I wound the little spring on the side and waited. Nothing happened. I held it up to my ear. Silence. I tossed the watch back on the bed and sifted through the detritus of my father's life.

Half a dozen pencils and pens, a bunch of paper clips. Six red plastic dice. A key chain in the shape of a stovepipe hat, no doubt kept because of my father's "Honest Abe" nickname. He was a pack rat, and I expected I'd find little piles and collections of junk all over the house, stuffed into every available nook and cranny.

A stack of photos, held together by a brittle green rubber band, poked out from under a wad of old envelopes. I picked up the pictures and pulled on the rubber band. It snapped, and I flung it across the room in the general direction of the trash can. On top of the stack, there was a picture of my father standing next to my mom, who was holding me, a little baby. Mom held one of my hands, and was waving it at the camera for me, beaming like a proud parent.

Sitting on the bed, I flipped through the rest of the pictures. Mom was in many of them, the once-vibrant colors in the pictures faded into bleached-out browns and grays and ochres. There were several photos of my father marching in protests against Soviet Jewry. In one, Mom was pushing me in a stroller and my father was carrying a placard that read, "Let My People Go." His bushy beard made him appear Russian himself.

I set the photos down and examined the bundle of envelopes. Opened one and read the letter. Written in cursive, the English was choppy and grammar-challenged, yet the vocabulary and phrasing were formal. Something about needing money to immigrate to Israel. When I was about eight years old, my father's passion for the plight of Soviet Jews was exciting and a little romantic. By the time I turned twelve, my father's long stories about strangers and distant relatives and faraway places bored me, and I secretly thought even Mom felt his "hobby" was becoming obsessive. I tossed the letters back into the pile of junk on the bed and let out my breath. No bag of diamonds here. Are diamonds still forever if they've gone missing?

I searched the rest of his bedroom, finding nothing of value—real or sentimental—except three large mugs full of quarters. Saving them to pay the tolls on the Dulles Toll Road, if I knew my father. No *E-Z Pass* for him. He was too old-school.

The bedroom between my father's and mine had been converted into a study-slash-storage area. One side of the room contained boxes, stacked three and four high. Most had descriptions of the contents scrawled on the sides in Sharpie—old silverware, family photos, Hanukkah stuff—but many were unlabeled. None were marked "diamonds."

A large, plain desk occupied the other half of the room, the "study" part. I parked my butt in the leather executive chair and started poking around. Just the usual stuff you'd find in a desk: pens, paper clips, stamps. Next to the desk were several battered filing cabinets. I scanned the contents of the closest one. Papers, papers, and more papers, hanging in well-labeled folders. All business. No precious gems—or paperwork pertaining to precious gems—to be seen anywhere.

I swiveled back to the desktop and flipped open a Day-Timer that had been pushed off to one side. Located the upcoming week, and noticed a doctor's appointment for Thursday. I guess I should call to cancel, wouldn't want to get billed for missing an appointment. Death was hardly a valid excuse for some medical practitioners. I jotted down the doctor's name, then turned the page back out of curiosity, seeing if I could learn more about this mystery man who had been my father. See if I could piece together his life by connecting the dots in his appointment book.

A single notation grabbed my eye. Tuesday, December 26, 9 a.m. Yakov Sapperstein. Beneath the name, a 212 phone number. I scribbled the name and number down on another piece of paper, then went downstairs to the front closet to retrieve my cell phone from my coat. I dialed Mr. Sapperstein, and it rang four times before rolling into voice mail. "Sapperstein Associates. You've reached the desk of Yakov—" I hung up. Probably some kind of real estate firm. I'd try again when businesses opened on Tuesday, after the three-day holiday weekend ushered in the New Year.

Next stop in the hunt: the laundry room. When Mom was around, the laundry room overflowed with clothes in various states of cleanliness, all in separate piles. There would be a pile of folded clean clothes sitting on top of the dryer waiting to be put away. Next to them, there'd be a heap of stained clothes being pre-treated with some magic elixir, guaranteed to eliminate the offending splotches. Another pile of brand-new clothes from the store would be waiting to be washed, sitting next to a hamper of dirty clothes.

My father employed a different system, although I didn't know what it was. All I knew was that the laundry room was spotless— no clothes anywhere. Which made it easier for me to determine there was nothing of interest hiding in the hamper or anywhere else.

The laundry room might have been barren, but the adjacent storage area was crammed full. Economy-sized boxes and jars—the kind you get at the warehouse stores—filled the shelving units. Tote bags and plastic grocery sacks hung on ten-penny nails my father had driven into the walls and shelf supports. The room overflowed with canned food, detergent, kitchen gadgets, cases of bottled water, batteries, batteries, and more batteries. There was even a 42-roll package of toilet paper dating back to Mr. Whipple's heyday.

So typical of my father. You never knew when a freak snowstorm, ice storm, twister, hurricane, or other Act of God would blow through, cutting Reston off from civilization for months.

I doubted my father had secreted any diamonds in there, so I decided to move on to the more likely places first. I could always come back to sift through the mountain of paper towels and toilet paper and ten-pound bags of rice.

I checked my watch: 10:30. Before I attacked the attic, I wanted to search the in-law suite downstairs. Just in case Kassian had stumbled upon a black velvet bag of diamonds and didn't know whom they belonged to.

Kassian's door was wide open and he sat in the chair reading a copy of *Newsweek*. He looked up when I entered and smiled, the first I'd seen from him. Despite his rotten teeth, it was a pleasant one. "Good morning," I said.

"Morning." He set his magazine down.

"You didn't come to the library dedication yesterday. I thought you might have been there."

"Still was feeling bad. Got a full night's sleep last night, though. I feel better today. Much better." His voice sounded stronger than it had, and the words were clearer, more precise.

"That's good. I met a friend of yours yesterday, DeRon. He says you've been doing real well since you moved in here," I said.

Kassian's face lit up for a second, then dimmed. "Mostly, I guess. Although…" He lowered his gaze.

"Hey, we all make mistakes from time to time. What's important is that we learn from them." I felt like I was the parent and Kassian the child. He nodded back at me with puppy dog eyes, reinforcing the dynamic. I wonder if my father had more of a peer-peer relationship with the old guy. It was hard to believe—Kassian didn't seem like my father's type. "Can I ask you a few questions?"

He nodded, keeping his eyes glued to mine. I sat down on the corner of his bed so I'd be at his level, not wanting to intimidate him. "Have you come across anything around the house you might consider… unusual?"

Kassian thought a minute, then shook his head. "No. I don't think so. Like what?"

"I don't know, something you think someone might have lost. And would miss." I wanted to blurt out, "diamonds, you fool, diamonds," but held my tongue.

He thought again. "No. Sorry." A frown creased his face. "Sorry."

"Don't worry about it. Just curious." I tried to appear surprised, as if I'd just been hit by a brainstorm. "Hey, would you mind if I looked here in your room? I'd like to see if I could find…" I mumbled the rest under my breath.

Kassian stared at me. Finally, he said, "Find what?"

I was hoping I wouldn't need to finish my sentence. "Find that thing I'm looking for. That someone is missing. I don't know exactly what it looks like because I've never seen it." A true statement, if convoluted. Playing the words back in my head, I realized it sounded like I was talking to a dolt. And I didn't think Kassian was a dolt, not exactly.

"Okay," he said, going back to his magazine.

If I felt weird rifling through my father's stuff, I felt really weird searching through Kassian's belongings while he was sitting there watching me. But I did it anyway. He calmly read his magazine while I pawed through his underwear. I didn't find anything, but I did feel slimy. I stopped after searching the dresser. Now that I had his "permission," I figured I could come back sometime when he wasn't there and finish checking the rest of the suite in privacy.

I cleared my throat and Kassian broke away from his reading. "Did you find it?" he asked.

"Nope. Thanks for letting me look, though."

Kassian nodded. "Okay, but you do not need to thank me. It is your house. You can look wherever you want. I've got nothing to hide."

I felt slimier as I slinked away.

NINE

THE POP-TART I HAD earlier wasn't holding me very well. I slapped together a turkey sandwich on rye with spicy brown mustard and opened a bag of chips. Grabbed a Coke and sat down at the kitchen table to enjoy my gourmet feast. Two bites in, the phone rang. I got up and answered it. The phone was one of those ancient relics, with a long cord tethering it to the wall. At least it didn't have a dial. "Hello," I said, swallowing the food in my mouth.

"Josh Handleman? This is Rachel Rosen. Tammy's sister." Her voice pitched upward, making her statement more like a question.

"Oh hi. She mentioned you were . . ." What, available? That didn't sound too flattering.

"Available?" Rachel laughed. "Yeah, she told me she said that." A pause. "Well, I am. And cute, too." She laughed again.

"I, uh, I'm sure you are." I remembered Rachel from high school. She was a few years younger than Tammy, and she'd been something of a tomboy, with a tomboy's body. Tammy was a knockout, so maybe Rachel had metamorphosed. One could hope.

"She also told me you were divorced. And she hinted you were lonely. That true?" The words were blunt, but the way Rachel delivered them made them sound gentle.

"Separated, actually. But divorce is inevitable." I stopped talking and an awkward silence rushed into the vacuum. I tried to rehabilitate the conversation. "So, you're available. What does that mean, exactly?"

"Just what you think." She left it there, as a challenge. When I didn't bite immediately, she grabbed the reins. "Would you like to go out to dinner tonight? If *you're* available, that is."

Forward, like her sister. Worked for me. "Sure. I've got nothing else planned. And a guy's got to eat, right?"

"Thanks a lot," she said, but the levity in her voice bubbled through. "I'll see if I can make it worth your while. Pick you up at seven. I know where you live."

"Okay. Sure. See you then."

"Bye, Josh Handleman." She clicked off.

Strangely buoyed, I returned to my sandwich. After two more bites, my cell phone rang. Probably Rachel coming to her senses and reconsidering. I pulled it out and checked the number. Dani. My stomach roiled, but I decided I might as well get it over with. "Hi Dani."

"Josh! My God. Why haven't you called me back? I'm so sorry about your dad." The words came out in a rush. Just like Dani. Drama reigned supreme at all times.

"Thanks. Been real busy here."

"You should have called me. Told me yourself. I had to call Erik to see what the hell was going on."

"You're right. I'm sorry."

70

"He was my father-in-law. I cared about him."

Did you cheat on him, too? "Yes. I know. I said I'm sorry."

"Goddamn it, Josh." Her tone softened. "Is there anything I can do for you? You must be a wreck."

"I'm okay." I considered telling her about Kassian and the seven million dollars and the missing diamonds, but decided not to get into it. I didn't have the energy to answer all the questions Dani would fire at me. Of course, I *was* tempted to tell her about my date with Rachel to see what she would say.

"I could catch a flight. Be there tomorrow," Dani said.

"No, that's okay. Really."

"Listen, Josh. We need to talk about things. We haven't—"

"Not now. We can talk later." We never talked while we were married, why should we start now?

"Josh, we need—"

I cut her off. "Bye, Dani." I closed the phone and set it on the table next to my plate. Picked up the sandwich, but didn't take a bite. Wasn't hungry anymore.

———

Another two hours searching through the house didn't turn up anything interesting. I decided to talk to Lev—maybe he could shed some light on my father's diamond collecting hobby.

Lev lived with his son Peter and his family in a newer subdivision on the outskirts of Vienna. It had one of those names meant to sound rich and exclusive and equestrian: Stallion Woods Reserve. The houses were large, with at least three garage stalls and lots of turrets and widow's walks and other fancy architectural gewgaws to impress the working folk. Peter the investment advisor was doing all right.

I pulled into his circular driveway and hopped out. Crunched across the gravel, up the walkway, and pressed the doorbell, activating some kind of baroque hymn. Thirty seconds later, Peter answered. "Hey, Josh. How are you?" He stepped back. "Come on in. To what do we owe the pleasure?"

He smiled at me as I entered. Peter was four years younger than I was, thirty, and he was taller and better looking, too. For some reason, his sinewy build and short blond hair—streaked with highlights—always reminded me of a foreign Olympic hockey player. Except for the teeth. Peter's were perfect.

"Do I need a reason to visit?" I clapped him on the back. "How's Jenn?"

"Good. She and the boys are at the mall. Where else?" He laughed. "Want a beer?"

"Sure." I followed him through the large entryway, down a long hall, and into an enormous kitchen, with twelve-foot ceilings and two refrigerators. I pulled up a stool at an island counter as big as the entire kitchen in my father's house.

Peter got us a couple beers and leaned across the counter. "So. How are you doing?"

Like everyone else who had asked me that question during the past week, Peter's tone was subdued, yet caring. Everyone's compassion was grating on me. I wondered how much time had to pass before people related to me as a normal person again. "Fine. Getting better every day."

"Good to hear. Coping with the death of a loved one is never easy." He took a sip of beer and pushed himself up to a standing position. "If you need help handling any estate issues, give me a call." I'd known Peter a long time, through my father's friendship with Lev, and I often wondered how he could be so friendly while his father was so gruff. Maybe he'd been switched at birth by gypsies.

"Thanks, but Erik drew up my father's will, and he's been helping out. Thanks for offering, though."

"Sure." Peter went back to the fridge and opened it. "Hungry?"

"No, not really."

He closed the refrigerator and opened a cabinet, coming back with a jar of peanuts. "Always need something to snack on with my beer." He shook out a handful of nuts. "You know, your father came to me for some investment advice a few years ago."

"Oh?"

"Yeah. Routine stuff mostly. I had an inside line on some hot opportunities. He could have done real well."

"Could have?" I asked.

"Yeah. He decided he wanted to go in a different direction. Something more, um, traditional. I wasn't involved."

The way Peter said it made it sound like there had been some disagreement. "Like what?"

Peter waved it off. "I don't know. T-bills or CDs. Something safe. And a little boring. Whatever. He got the last laugh. I heard he did quite well with safe and boring." Peter's eyebrows lifted.

"Yeah. He did pretty well all right." I drank some beer. Enough small talk. "Is your dad around?"

"Oh. Sure. Hang on." Peter took three steps to his right and pressed the button on an intercom set into the wall. "Pops? Josh is here. He wants to see you." He turned to me. "He'll be down in a minute or two. Sure I can't get you something to eat?" He popped some peanuts into his mouth and chased them with his beer.

I shook my head and gazed through the large bay windows into the backyard. A two-level deck surrounded a covered pool. On one side of the deck, a gleaming stainless steel grill, big enough to hold fifty burgers, stood next to a brick fire pit. Peter and Jenn must entertain a lot. I had a hard time picturing Lev in a Hawaiian shirt and flip-flops.

"Hey, Pops," Peter said, as Lev entered the kitchen.

Lev nodded to his son, then to me. "Hello, Joshua. How are you?"

"Fine, Lev. You?"

He glared at me. "I believe you know how I am." He shot a sideways glance at Peter. "What is it you wished to see me about?"

"I have some questions about my father."

Lev drew in a breath. "Yes?"

I glanced at Peter and hesitated. I didn't want to make my father's missing diamonds common knowledge, but since my father had asked Peter for some advice about his investments, maybe he knew something that could help me. "Were you aware he owned some diamonds?"

There was the tiniest flicker in Lev's eyes, and then it was gone. "Yes. I knew he collected diamonds. He liked their beauty. And their value."

"Diamonds? Your father collected diamonds? He never mentioned that to me," Peter said. "How many did he have?"

"Well, that's one of the things I'm trying to find out." I turned to Lev. "Do you have any idea how many he had?"

"You do not have them?" he asked.

I bit my lip. "Actually, they're … misplaced at the moment."

"Misplaced?" Peter asked. "What does that mean?"

Lev answered. "It means he does not have them." The old man slowly shook his head. "Abe had been collecting diamonds for many years, since you were a baby. Every so often, he would tell me about one he'd seen or one he'd purchased. He was quite proud of them."

"You were his best friend. He didn't tell you more than that?"

"We were very close, but he didn't tell me everything. A man must have some secrets. Large ones, small ones. It does not matter. Otherwise, he is like jellyfish. Transparent and spineless. Looking to sting someone to justify its existence."

Lev's analogy must have lost something in the translation. "Do you know where he got them?"

"No, I do not. From the usual places, I would expect. Diamond merchants, jewelry stores."

I hadn't run across any receipts for diamonds, but I hadn't really been looking for them. And there were a lot of papers and boxes to go through.

"Let me get this straight," Peter said. "Your father collected diamonds for years and now you have no idea where they are? Or even how many he had?"

I nodded slowly, feeling bad, although their disappearance wasn't my fault. "Lev, how many do you think there were? I mean, are we talking five diamonds, or twenty?"

Lev frowned and looked up into space. "I should think that by now, he would have bought at least forty diamonds. But that is just a guess on my part. I did not ask him many questions. A man's private business is his private business. Whatever he told me, I listened, but I did not pry."

Peter let out a low whistle. "How much are loose diamonds worth? Three thousand bucks, on average? Five? That's at least $120,000, maybe more. And they're missing."

With math skills like that, it was easy to see how Peter flourished. "Not missing. Just not found yet," I said, trying to be a glass half-full kind of guy.

Peter tilted his head. "He could have sold them all and spent the money," he said. "Maybe there aren't any diamonds anymore."

Not likely. "Nah. They're around. I just have to find them."

For the next ten minutes, we tossed out ideas about what might have happened to the diamonds, but in the end, it was all talk. The bottom line: unless they turned up during my house search, I'd need more information to track them down.

Peter took a long swig from his beer and wiped his mouth with the back of his hand. "Good luck, Josh. And if you need any help with your treasure hunt, you know who to call. I'm good at finding things, especially valuable things."

I said my goodbyes and walked out to my car. Just as I reached the driveway, the front door slammed and Lev called out, "Joshua. Please wait."

He glanced back at the closed door and came nearer. Lowered his voice. "Joshua. You see what this means, don't you?"

I was tired of his guessing games. "What?"

He fixed me with his evil eye. "This is the evidence you require. Kassian murdered your father for his diamonds."

TEN

"Jesus Christ, Lev. Will you give it a rest?" I stepped closer, until I was almost standing on top of him. "I've heard enough of your ridiculous theories. Kassian did not kill my father. He fell. He tripped and fell down the stairs. It was an accident." I shouted the words at him.

Lev's expression didn't change. "Do you believe your father's death and the disappearance of his diamonds is a coincidence?" he asked, voice level.

I licked my lips. I didn't usually believe in odd coincidences, but... "Yeah, I guess it is. Sometimes things just happen and they seem related, even if they're not. I mean, Kassian? Come on. Have you ever spoken to him?" I inched away from Lev.

"Yes, of course. He claims he is from a town near where I was raised. In Russia. We have spoken on many occasions. That is how I know he is guilty."

"Why do you dislike him so much?"

Lev's features tightened. "He does not reflect well on Russian Jews. And he is an unscrupulous liar."

Tell me what you really think. "We've been through this before. Just because you don't like someone doesn't mean he's a murderer." I fished the car keys out of my pocket. "I've got to get going."

Lev grabbed my arm. "Joshua. Please listen to me. Your father and I were cut from the same length of cloth. He would do this for me, if our positions were reversed. His death was not an accident. You have the criminal living under your roof. You must do something. If not for yourself or for me, then for your father. He was a man of justice."

I thought of all the Soviet Jewry marches he went on. He always had been a staunch advocate for justice. Sometimes to the exclusion of his family. "I'll talk to Kassian again, Lev. I don't know what else to do about it."

"Go to the police. Explain the situation. They will see. You are too overcome with grief to see things clearly. They will see. You must go to them."

"Why don't you go to the police? You're a lot more passionate in your beliefs than I am."

He shook his head. "No. You are his son. You must go. They will believe you. Me, all they will see is a senile old Russkie with crazy ideas."

Would they be that far off?

Lev continued. "Besides, I have too many bad memories of dealing with the police. Back home, I had many run-ins with our authorities. Of course, your police are different here. Not corrupt. Not vicious. In your country, they do not throw you in prison for what you believe."

I held my hand up. "I said I'll talk to Kassian again. But I still don't think he could have done it. It doesn't make any sense."

"Madmen often don't make sense," Lev said, point made.

I left him on the driveway and drove off. Kassian killing my father *didn't* make sense, any way you sliced it. But I didn't really believe in coincidences, either.

———

I stopped at the Giant on the way home and stocked up on groceries. Got plenty of fresh fruit and vegetables, a few packages of boneless chicken breast, and a couple of pounds of salmon. One of my New Year's resolutions was to eat better and get into shape. Since I'd left Dani, most of my meals had come wrapped in paper and been accompanied by fries and a shake.

As I put away the food, I noticed movement out the window in the back. Someone was crossing through the yard toward the woods. My father's house backed up to an expansive wooded area bisected by hiking trails, part of the county-owned park system. The trails weaved through the trees and connected with other trails and paths, providing those inclined with a means for getting around by foot. Every time a proposal to develop some of the parkland surfaced, it was shot down. Reston was a town full of exercise- and nature-loving liberals, and they fought like cornered animals when it came to protecting their natural environs.

I moved closer to the window to get a better look. The small hiker had an odd gait, but one I recognized. Kassian was going for a stroll in the woods.

I thought about following him and grilling him, but I was exhausted. Listening to Lev's wild-ass accusations was draining, and I'd bored myself silly tearing the house apart looking for the phantom diamonds. Maybe it was all some kind of ruse. Perpetrated by I-don't-know-who, for I-don't-know-why, but intended to drive me nuts. If so, it was working.

I let Kassian enjoy his nature walk while I got ready for my date with Rachel.

———

At two minutes to seven the doorbell rang. I opened the door, and there she was, dressed in black jeans and a green blouse, hands clasped in front of her like a proper schoolgirl. She didn't look like any tomboy I'd ever seen. With her dark complexion, model-like cheekbones, and curly, shoulder-length hair, I had a hard time believing she was "available."

"Hi, Josh Handleman," she said. "I'm Rachel." She stuck her hand out as if she were running for office.

I gave it a little pump. She had a small hand, but a firm grip. "Hello, Rachel. It's nice to see you again." I opened the door wider. "Come in."

"Thanks." She smiled, and a couple of crooked teeth broke the illusion of perfection she'd been casting. "But why don't we pretend we've never met before? I don't think knowing me when I was fourteen counts as *knowing* me."

"Fair enough. You look…" I stepped back and made a show of checking her out. "Fantastic. Tammy was right."

She chucked me on the shoulder. "Shut up," she said, but her grin widened. She was a happy girl and I could feel the energy radiating from her, in waves. "Hungry?"

"Sure. Didn't have much lunch."

"And a guy's got to eat, right?" she said, smile not faltering in the least. "Let's go. I'll drive."

She drove us—in her blue Prius—to a little pan-Asian place in a strip mall in Sterling. It wasn't crowded. "Trust me. This place looks dead, but it's got great food. A friend of mine turned me on to it last year," Rachel said as we were seated. "You like spicy food, right?"

I nodded. "The spicier, the better."

We examined the menu, which ran to ten pages. Chinese, Thai, Vietnamese, Korean. I wondered how many chefs were back in the kitchen, but judging by the size of the place and the lack of diners, I figured it was probably just one guy from West Virginia armed with a few cookbooks, winging it. I shut the menu. "Why don't you order for us? You've eaten here before. You know what's good."

Her face lit up. "Okay. My pleasure," she said, and she reached across the table and touched my hand. "Sure you trust me?"

Sparks ran across the back of my hand. "Should I?"

"Of course. I'm very trustworthy. Just ask my Girl Scout leader. You'll have to wait until she gets out of prison, though," she said, straight-faced. She removed her hand and studied the menu a little longer. The hairs on my hand still tingled where her fingers had rested.

The waiter came and Rachel ordered. Soup, appetizers, main course. Instead of writing down our order, the waiter repeated it back to us, in broken English. I wondered if we would get anything we actually ordered. I wondered if we would even be able to tell.

"So, what do you do?" I asked, after the waiter disappeared into the back. "Besides stalk your sister's old boyfriends?"

"I don't do that much anymore. Too many restraining orders." She made a face. "I'm a third-grade teacher."

"Oh, really? They let you near children?" The banter came easy and natural.

"I'll have you know, I'm the most popular teacher at the school. The kids are always chanting, 'We heart Miss Rosen.'"

"You sure it's not 'We hate Miss Rosen'?"

"Funny," she said, scrunching up her nose.

"Well, I don't remember many teachers like you back when I was in elementary school."

She furrowed her brow. "You can remember back that far?"

"Hey, I'm only a few years older than you."

"Really? I would have guessed you were older than that," she said.

"Funny," I said, scrunching up my nose.

"Nice comeback. I'm guessing you're not a stand-up comedian."

I tried to remember the last time I flirted like this. When Dani and I sniped at each other, it was the real deal.

Rachel glanced around the restaurant, and I followed her eyes. A few more people were being seated. She turned back to me. "Tammy said you have your own business, but she wasn't too forthcoming with the details."

"I owned a liquidation firm. You know, when a company goes out of business, we come in and find buyers for their stuff. Furniture, computers, inventory, whatever."

"Like vultures?" she asked, giving me a look of mock horror.

That's what my father used to say, too, only there was nothing mock about his derision. "Not quite. We work to get as much value as possible for these companies. We don't drive them out of business. We just help them as best we can. In fact, that's why we're so competitive. Because we aren't vultures, like some of the other firms. I try to be as compassionate—and fair—as possible."

"Okay. I believe you. Sounds depressing though, being around all that failure."

"Yeah, I guess it is, a little. We got a lot of business from the dot-com bust. And many of the guys we worked with weren't losing their own money—it was venture capital. Almost like play money. It was a weird time, all right." I clammed up, not wanting to run on too long and put Rachel to sleep.

She hadn't taken her eyes off me. "You said 'owned,' like in past tense. What happened?"

"Technically, I'm still part-owner. Except I haven't gone in to the office in the past two months."

"Sounds like a great gig, if you can get it," Rachel said, but I could tell she was trying to be nice. She must have sensed there was some unpleasant explanation from my tone.

"My partner and I had a falling out. A big one." I shook my head, sorry to put a downer on things. "I'll let my lawyer sort things out."

Luckily, I was saved by the arrival of the soup. Followed by the spicy vegetables and spring rolls, and then our main courses. And Rachel was right, the food was terrific.

While we ate, we talked about small things, probing and testing, trying to figure out how to pigeon-hole each other. Likes, dislikes, similarities, differences. Seeing if any deal-breakers breached the surface. Typical first date stuff. But Rachel wasn't your typical first date. She was someone worth the effort, at least as far as I could tell right now, right there, sitting in a restaurant in a strip mall in Sterling.

When the check came, I reached out to grab it, but Rachel beat me to it. "My treat. I asked you out, remember?"

"Okay. Thanks. But next time it's on me."

"If there is a next time, you mean," she said, and I could hear the "wink" in her voice. "Let's go." I liked the fact that Rachel was a take-charge woman. Dani often played the part of the damsel in distress, and she'd been pretending she'd been in distress far too often in the latter stages of our marriage.

Rachel drove me home and pulled into the driveway. "Here we are."

I turned in my seat to face her. "Can I ask you something?"

"Sure."

"How come you *are* available? I'd think you'd have to fight guys off with a stick. A large one."

In the dim light, I thought I detected a blush. "I just got out of a relationship. Ended kinda badly. So ..." She perked up. "Now I'm available."

Sounded logical. "Want to come in? Have a drink?"

Rachel smiled. "I had a great time tonight. Really. But if I came in, one thing would lead to another, and ..."

Yes?

"... well, I may be fun and I may be available, but I'm not easy." She flipped her hair out of her face and leaned over. Our mouths connected in a nice, lingering kiss.

She broke it off. "Besides, technically, you're still married." She straightened up and hit the button to unlock the doors. "Good night, Josh."

I got out and waved goodbye. Trudged up the path to the door. I thought things were going great. Then reality came into focus. What would a great girl like Rachel see in me, especially in my current guise of Depressed Josh? I dragged myself inside and found the phone ringing. I snatched it up. "Hello?"

"Josh?"

It was Rachel. "Yeah?" I went to the front window and pushed the curtain aside with my finger. Her car was still in the driveway.

"I don't have any plans for New Year's Eve. Would you like to go out with me?"

"I, uh, tomorrow night?" My heart beat faster.

"That's New Year's Eve, isn't it? Come on, we'll have fun."

"I thought I was technically married," I said.

"Life's too short to get hung up on silly technicalities. What do you say?"

I'd talked to Erik about going out with him and Katy, but I'm sure they wouldn't mind if I brought a date. Katy never liked Dani anyway. "Okay. Sounds great. We can catch up with some friends of mine, if you're game."

"Think you might need some help to 'crack me'?" She laughed. "Wise move. Although I..." She stopped talking.

"What?" I squinted at the car, but couldn't make out anything in the darkness.

"I may not be easy, but I'm not all that hard either."

My kind of girl. "I'll pick you up around eight. Sound good?"

"Looking forward to it. Bye, Josh Handleman."

I watched her car back out of the driveway and zoom off. Maybe I wasn't as much of a downer as I thought. My prospects for a Happy New Year were looking up.

ELEVEN

THE NEXT MORNING, I joined Kassian at the kitchen table for breakfast. He was working on a couple of toaster waffles drenched in syrup. I had a pouch of Pop-Tarts on my plate. Still one more day before I had to take my resolutions seriously. "How are you doing?"

Kassian nodded as he swallowed. "Okay. I am doing okay." He stared at me for a second, then returned to his waffles. If Dani were here, she'd have a fit—breakfast with two brilliant conversationalists.

"Well, that's good." I took a sip of my OJ. "What are you going to do today?"

Kassian shrugged and chewed.

"How about tonight? It's New Year's Eve. Got plans?"

Another shrug. I figured there was something going on at the Hebrew Home. Maybe he could join in the festivities, although he didn't seem like the party animal type.

Kassian concentrated on his food. Cutting it precisely and chewing it thoroughly. Must be hard to have your only connection to the real world taken away from you so suddenly. "Listen, Kassian, I'd like to ask you some questions."

One eyebrow shifted on his clean-cut face. He gave me a curt nod and put his knife and fork down. All ears.

"On that day. When my father died. I'm trying to piece together what happened." My mouth was dry so I took a couple gulps of juice. "Can you tell me again what you did?"

"Of course. I woke up. Got dressed. Had something to eat. I do not remember what." He shook his head apologetically, and I got the feeling that Kassian was exercising great patience, perhaps knowing how important this was to me. Like if I asked him to repeat his story fifty times, he would do so, each time as deliberately as the first.

"Go on."

"I went back downstairs to use the bathroom. Then I left for the Home." He stopped talking and kept his eyes on mine. Finished.

"From what door?"

"From my door. Of course."

"And you locked it?"

"Yes. Always. Abe was the most trusting person I have known, but even he wanted the doors locked," Kassian said.

"What time was that? About?"

"Lev always came over to play chess with Abe at around ten. So I was sure to be gone by 9:30. He is ..." Kassian frowned and shook his head, but didn't describe Lev any further. He didn't have to.

"How did you find out what happened to my father?" I asked. The first time I'd asked Kassian, he'd been vague about some of the details.

"They told me at the Home."

"Who told you?"

Kassian tilted his head upward and consulted the ceiling. After a moment, he leveled his eyes. "Miss Carol. She told me about your father's accident. That he had fallen down the stairs and died."

"Okay. Then what did you do?"

Kassian closed his eyes. "I do not feel well. I think I should lie down." He opened his eyes. "I have told you what I know."

I put kindness in my voice. "I talked with DeRon. He told me about your progress over the past six months." I leaned forward and put my elbows on the table.

"Yes?" Something flashed across Kassian's face. Pride, if I had to guess.

"Don't let one mistake, one backslide, ruin all that," I said. Kassian glanced away. When he looked back, a film of sadness covered his face.

"My father was a good judge of people. If he wanted to help you, that meant he saw something in you that moved him, something that told him you're a good person. I know it's difficult to talk about, but I need to know what happened. So I can begin to heal. You—of all people—know what I mean. Please, Kassian, return my father's favor and help me out here."

Kassian stared at me. Unblinking. Sizing me up. Was I as trustworthy as my father? After twenty seconds, he nodded, as if I'd passed muster. "What did you do after you heard about my father?"

"I walked to the liquor store, bought some vodka, and returned here. I had no other place to go." His lip trembled.

"And you drank your vodka?"

"Yes. I drank. I am not proud of that. But it is what I did." He bowed his head. "And one very small part of me is glad Abe is not here so he would not have seen me do this."

"You're only human. You had a big shock. It's okay."

"It is not okay. I did not have enough courage to even come up the stairs to look at the spot where he died. I am a weak person. Very weak."

I leaned back in my chair. This version matched the earlier account Kassian had given me. Except for his topple from the wagon. But I could understand his reticence to open up about that. "Okay. Just a few more questions. Did you notice anything unusual during the week before it happened? Weird people hanging around? Did my father seem out of sorts?"

Kassian glanced at the ceiling again. "No. Just the usual."

"And what's that?"

"Abe seemed happy. Busy. He had visitors. Mostly people for business. But I am not always here. I walk a lot and go to programs at the Home. I do not know what happened when I was not here, of course."

Of course. "Did you recognize any of the visitors?"

"No. When Abe had visitors, I stayed in my room."

"Then how do you know they were people for business?" I asked.

Kassian's eyes flitted around. No one would ever need a lie detector for this guy. "I assumed. Sometimes I would hear a car drive up and watch out the curtains. They looked like people for business. I do not know for sure, of course."

Of course. "But nothing seemed out of the ordinary?"

"No. Nothing."

Now for the $120,000 question. I focused on Kassian's face. "Did you know that my father collected diamonds?" I asked.

His eyes dilated. "Diamonds?" Kassian said, almost unable to get the word out.

"Yes. Did he ever show them to you?"

"I do not remember," he said.

My ass, he didn't remember. I squinted at him, but decided I wasn't going to get any useful information if he didn't want to tell me. I wondered if Kassian had done more than merely see my father's diamonds. Had he gotten his hands on them? "Well, if you remember something about diamonds, let me know, okay?"

"Yes, of course."

Of course. One last avenue to explore. "Why don't you and Lev get along?"

"I have nothing against Lev. He does not like me."

"Why?"

"I do not know. Maybe he was jealous of my friendship with Abe."

Finally, Kassian said something that made sense. "Why would he be jealous?"

"I do not know. Abe was a supporter of us," Kassian said, pointing at himself.

"Us?"

"Russian Jews. I am a Russian Jew. Abe wanted to build a place especially for Russian Jews at the Home."

"But why would Lev be jealous of that? He's a Russian Jew too."

Kassian fixed me with his eyes. "Yes, he is. But he does not wish for a new building to be built. I heard him and Abe arguing about it. On more than one occasion."

"So why would Lev dislike you because of that?"

"I do not know. It is just a feeling I have that Lev does not like me and it has something to do with our heritage. You will have to ask him." Kassian pressed his lips together.

My head hurt. Ever since my father's death, I hadn't gone more than six hours without getting a headache. But I think talking to Kassian, with his warped logic and nutty secrets, exacerbated my pain.

I excused myself to get some Motrin.

TWELVE

AFTER MY TALK WITH Kassian, I decided to resume my treasure hunt, expanding my search to look for a paper trail that might lead me to the diamonds. I headed up to my father's study, but stopped on the staircase, leaning forward so I could inspect the top step. I'd been walking on it for more than a week now, and I'd noticed the bare spot, but I'd never really *examined* it. A three-inch square of honey-colored wood shone through the threadbare gray carpet. Had my father's cane caught on this spot, causing him to tumble down the stairs? Did the bottom of his smooth leather slippers hit the wood patch and send him skidding? Why hadn't he spent a few of his millions to get new carpet? Why hadn't he moved to a condo after Mom died, like we'd all begged him to?

I straightened and tried to put the what-ifs behind me. Tried to erase the image I had of my father lying at the base of the stairs, neck twisted at an impossible angle. If I could just focus on the present, the bad memories would fade. The past was irreversible.

Painful, but gone forever. Forward, forward, forward. I forced myself forward. I had work to do. I had diamonds to find.

First stop: the filing cabinets in my father's study. Three four-drawer, battleship gray filing cabinets stood shoulder-to-shoulder-to-shoulder. I'd peeked in them earlier on the off chance the jewelry bag was laying on top, just waiting to be discovered. It hadn't been. The filing cabinets actually held files.

In the first cabinet, all the folder tabs had similar, real-estate-sounding labels: Alliance Properties, Dunn and Hill Holdings, Reston Towers, Property Development Associates, Ring and Forster Commercial. Inside the thick folders were all sorts of official documents—or at least copies of official documents. Lease agreements, appraisals, contracts, invoices, memos of understanding, property deeds, miscellaneous letters. Hundreds of companies and individuals and lawyers were referenced in the papers, and I was thankful my father had the foresight not to make me executor of his estate. Maybe he did love me more than he let on. Erik would work with my father's real estate attorneys to get everything squared away. He'd take his share of the fees, and the Hebrew Home would get the lion's share of the assets. And I wouldn't have to get involved. Just like my father wanted.

The contents of the second filing cabinet were similar to those of the first, except for the dates on the documents, which predated the records I'd already looked at. A few of the project names were familiar, but most were simply that: names on paper. Like my father, I preferred working with things that were tangible, things I could put my hands on. That was one of the aspects that attracted me to the liquidation business. Desks and computers and boxes of machine screws all had weight and could be touched, pointed to, or carted off in a moving van.

It was obvious my father kept meticulous records. So where were the receipts or appraisals or GIA certificates for the diamonds? Valuables like that didn't simply appear out of nowhere. Every time I bought a book or pair of shoes, I got receipts, in duplicate or triplicate. Where was the documentation for the diamonds? I sifted through the rest of the cabinet, but my enthusiasm was waning. More of the same.

I slid the bottom drawer closed with a little too much oomph, and the sound echoed in the small study, sending another shock wave through my brain. The Motrin had done a decent job dulling the pain, but every so often a bolt would shoot through my head, catching me right behind my left eye. Served me right for slamming the drawer shut.

I moved on to the last gray cabinet, and at first, I was heartened by the lack of real estate papers. But the feeling was short-lived. The top drawer held household bills: phone, electric, credit cards. Each had its own folder, and the bills were all filed by date, oldest in the back. Very organized. When I paid bills, I threw all of the paperwork into a paper grocery bag. Every year I changed bags. That was the extent of my filing system.

I opened the second drawer and my interest perked up again, if only a little. It held things of a more personal nature. There was a folder containing some brochures about cruises, and another with a few articles my father had clipped from the paper touting European vacation packages. A fat folder held dozens of greeting cards, but I didn't have the stomach to go through and read any of them, afraid of what emotions might get triggered. There would be time to deal with all of that later. Behind the greeting card folder was one marked "Josh," in my father's precise handwriting.

I removed it from the drawer and set it on my lap. I wanted to put it aside, to jam it back into the filing cabinet and slide the drawer shut, but I couldn't, the tug too great. I flipped it open and suppressed a chuckle. All my grade-school report cards stared back at me. Most recent on the top, all the way back to kindergarten. Hey, you never knew when these might come in handy. You never knew when you might get into a throwdown with a buddy and have to pull out your kid's thirty-year-old report cards to prove your worth as a parent. I shoved the folder back into the cabinet. My father amused me sometimes. Would I amuse my children after I died?

The doorbell rang and I was glad for the interruption. Maybe it was a Jehovah's Witness, and I could engage him or her in a lengthy discussion about some esoteric religious symbol or the meaning of life. Or whatever it was they espoused. That would distract me for a couple hours.

My visitor wasn't a Jehovah's Witness—it was Carol Wolfe from the Hebrew Home. "Hello. Please, come in," I said, stepping back.

"Hello, Josh." She entered, and I noticed her glance linger on the floor of the foyer. Was it my imagination?

"May I take your coat?"

She shook her head. "No thanks. I won't be staying long."

"Okay." I had no clue why she was here. Maybe she had some pictures from the dedication ceremony she wanted to show me.

She stood in the foyer, hands in her coat pockets. Her face remained impassive as she searched for what she wanted to say. Negative vibes floated through the air.

"Sure you wouldn't like to come in? Have a seat?" I smiled, trying to put her at ease. Clearly, she had something on her mind. And if I had to guess, it was something I didn't want to hear.

Her veneer cracked, and a smile appeared, but it wasn't a happy one. "Josh, I haven't been completely forthcoming with you. Your father was a wonderful man…"

I braced for the "but."

She reloaded. "He was a wonderful man, and we'd gotten to know each other quite well during the past two and a half years. We…" The basement door slammed, and she paused, looking around.

"That must have been Kassian leaving." No surprise registered on her face, but I clarified it for her anyway. "He lives here. In the basement."

She nodded slightly. "Yes, I know. This is difficult for me," she said, talking faster as if she were being timed and only had a few seconds to say what she wanted to. Needed to. "Your father and I were in love. He wanted to keep things discreet because he didn't want his philanthropic activities at the Home to be misinterpreted. I went along. Maybe I shouldn't have, but I did. I wanted to tell you a long time ago, but…" She searched my face for a reaction, but I'm sure my shock was obvious. "I'm sorry, Josh. So sorry."

"I…I don't know what to say." *My father had a girlfriend?*

"We were going to be married. In the spring."

Another jolt to my solar plexus. "You and my father were engaged?" I glanced at the diamond ring on her finger.

Carol brought a hand out from her coat pocket and dabbed her nose with a tissue. "We were going to tell you. You have to believe me."

I stared, dumbfounded.

"Like I said, he wanted to be discreet. But he was going to tell you. He promised me."

The way she kept saying it made me suspicious. "Uh huh."

"Your father loved you Josh. He might not have shown it in traditional ways, but he loved you. You have to know that."

I wasn't sure what to believe. My headache returned, pounding its hello. Jumbled thoughts jostled to gain purchase. "How long did you say you've known my father?"

Carol jammed her hand back into her pocket. Stood up a little straighter. "We met when your mother was with us. At the hospice."

"Oh. And when did you start 'dating'?" An edge had crept into my voice, and I knew it, but was powerless to change it. Not that I wanted to.

"Josh, please. It wasn't like that. Abe was devastated by your mother's illness and he needed someone to talk to. We went for coffee a few times and I listened. Helped him cope. That was all. It wasn't until after..." She stopped and her face flushed. It was a long moment before the red tinge ebbed.

I narrowed my eyes on purpose. "Until after she died that you swooped in?"

She stepped back and removed her other hand from her pocket. Held it out to me. "Here's a house key. I thought you might want it back." She left the key in her outstretched hand for me to take, but I made no move for it. I knew I was being a jerk, but I couldn't help myself. It was as if I were watching the scene unfold from above through the wrong end of a telescope.

Carol's lips squeezed together as she held the key out to me, arm stiff. After a moment, she relaxed her posture. "I'll just put it back on the hook with the spare." She moved past me into the kitchen. I followed, but stopped at the entrance and watched her slip the key ring onto the empty hook by the telephone.

She noticed me observing and didn't say anything, but her features tightened. She walked back toward me and I moved aside, giving her a clear path to the door. When she reached it, she turned back. "Josh. I'm sorry that you found out this way. We should have told you much sooner. But I'm not sorry about loving your father. He was a wonderful man and I will miss him dearly."

As she opened the door to leave, the sunlight sparkled off her diamond earrings.

THIRTEEN

CAROL'S VISIT PUT THE kibosh on my diamond hunt. Wasn't in the mood anymore. I spent the next few hours putzing around the house, telling myself I was doing necessary chores, but mostly just wasting time, procrastinating until it was time to get ready for my date with Rachel. She'd called, running late, and asked if I could pick her up at the Hebrew Home where she was visiting her grandmother.

I put on the only suit I'd brought with me. I'd had it cleaned, of course, but I wasn't sure that was enough to prevent me from thinking about the last time I'd worn it. My father's funeral. Hopefully, Rachel would take my mind off all the unsettling things I'd been learning about my father's life.

When I got to the Hebrew Home, I found the parking lot much more crowded than it had been for the dedication. Maybe they *were* having a big New Year's shindig for the residents. A stab of guilt struck me—I should have asked Kassian if he needed a ride before I left. I opened my phone and started to call home, but I knew Kassian wouldn't answer, even if he were there. Instead, I called Rachel. She answered on the second ring and told me to come up to room 438. I showed my ID and glanced around the lobby to make sure Carol wasn't lurking about. No need to reprise this afternoon's awkward encounter in a public place.

Following the signs, I located room 438 and knocked on the doorjamb, even though the door was wide open. "Come on in," Rachel said, and I obeyed, entering the small room. Rachel leaned against the wall next to a large blue vinyl chair that practically swallowed her elfin grandmother. Rachel pushed herself off the wall and came over to kiss me on the cheek. Then she introduced me. "Nana, this is Josh Handleman. Josh, this is my nana."

Alert eyes tracked me as I walked over to shake her hand. She was smaller than tiny, and sitting in that large chair with a blanket covering her knees made her seem almost microscopic. If she were a tad bigger, she could have fallen off the same cake as Kassian. A thin layer of gray-white hair covered her light-bulb shaped head. Her papery skin felt cool, but her bony grip was stronger than I'd imagined. Not strong, exactly, but I could detect life. "Pleased to meet you."

She nodded and opened her mouth to speak. I leaned down so I could hear her better. "Happy New Year," she bellowed, and I jumped back.

Rachel laughed. "She may be ninety-six years old, but she's still got her voice." Rachel wore a gray and black low-cut short dress, with an ornate necklace dipping into her cleavage. Spiky high heels with lethally pointed toes completed her outfit. Dressed to party. I'm not sure it went with my funeral suit, but I certainly wasn't complaining. Besides, nobody would be looking at me.

A shrill whistle emanated from her grandmother. Nana fiddled with her hearing aid and the noise subsided. "Are you Rachel's boyfriend?" she said, voice loud enough to be heard down the hall.

Rachel intervened. "Nana, I only met Josh yesterday. I'm not sure whether I'm going to keep him or throw him back into the pond." She grinned, and her crooked smile hinted she was going to enjoy finding out.

"Well, give it your best shot, sweetie. I don't want two lesbian granddaughters. Great grandchildren would be nice." She pointed one of her bird claws in my direction. "I'm not getting any younger, you know."

I gave her a half-shrug, half-nod, and caught Rachel's eyes. *Save me.*

Rachel said, "Okay, Nana. I'll work on it. But leave Josh alone." In a stage whisper almost as loud as her grandmother's voice she added, "He's very sensitive. You have to be extremely gentle with him. Like a frightened kitten."

Nana nodded solemnly as she glanced at me. It wasn't often I got pity from a ninety-six-year-old.

"Okay, Nana. Happy New Year. Josh and I need to get going. I'll see you next Sunday." Rachel bent over and kissed her grandmother goodbye.

"Bye, sweetie," Nana said to Rachel. Then she swiveled her head to me. "Bye, John. Nice meeting you." The skeletal finger reappeared from under the blanket and wagged at me. "Be good to my Rachel."

Rachel didn't say a word, but her eyes danced with laughter.

We left Rachel's car at the Hebrew Home and I drove to the Ritz-Carlton in Tysons Corner, where we were meeting Erik and Katy for the three D's: drinks, dinner, and dancing. I left the keys with the valet and tried to ignore his look of disdain as he got behind the wheel. To her credit, Rachel hadn't said anything about the Taurus, but I think I agreed with the valet. The car screamed "geezer."

The party was some kind of pseudo work-related thing of Erik's and when he'd invited me, he said it would be more drinking and partying than business. At the time, I'd just been happy that I wouldn't have to spend New Year's Eve alone wallowing in self-pity. Now, I had a chance to show off Rachel, which was more than enough to boost anyone's spirits.

At the door, I gave my name to an underfed guy in an extra-large tux gripping a clipboard with white knuckles. He checked his list, and finding what he was looking for, waved us in with a look of great relief, past a huge red banner that read, "Welcome Elite." Leave it to Erik to get me—and a date—into an exclusive bash.

Hundreds of people milled about the large ballroom, all with drinks of various sizes and colors in their hands. The guys wore tuxes or suits and the women were dolled up to the max, but Rachel managed to outshine them all. "There they are," I said, as I scanned the crowd. Erik and Katy were off to my right, talking with another couple. I grabbed Rachel's hand and we weaved through the crowd in their direction, ducking and dodging the other partygoers, careful not to bump anyone's drink hands.

Erik must have seen us coming, because he was saying goodbye as we got there. "Hey buddy. You found us," he said, giving me a quick guy-hug. I kissed Katy hello, then introduced Rachel.

"I'm so glad to meet you. Josh has told me all about you," Rachel said. "Some of it was good, too." She kept a straight face for a second, then smiled.

Erik pointed at Rachel, but spoke to me. "Hey, I like her. She's got some spunk."

Katy and Rachel complimented each other's outfits, while Erik whispered in my ear. "That's Tammy's little sister? Wow." He glanced around, and still in a whisper said, "Listen, I should give you a heads—"

"Hey there," Brandon Flannery said, stepping out of the crowd, buxom blonde draped on one arm like a sommelier's napkin. "Nice to see you again." He sported a broad, shit-eating grin.

So much for a pleasant evening. "You too," I lied. "This is Rachel Rosen."

Rachel shook his hand, and Brandon held on way too long. Then he let go abruptly, remembering his date. "This is Layla. Layla Richards."

Layla growled a low-pitched hello—a two-packs-a-day growl—followed by a sip from her martini glass. Properly introduced, our little gang commandeered one of the dining tables in the back, close to the buffet lines. The cocktail reception was winding down, and the clanging of the large chrome chafing dishes as the chefs prepared the food stations punctuated the sounds of conversation around us.

"So what party is this?" I asked Erik.

"It's put on by a group called the Northern Virginia Business Elite. Lawyers, real estate types, bankers, venture capitalists, lobbyists—they're the ones with the oily hair. Those kinds of people. But I told you, tonight is more party than business. You could try to network, but it'll be pretty hard as the night wears on."

"All these people are 'business elite'?"

"Self-anointed." He shrugged. "Don't worry, you won't get busted. I know one of the organizers. Told him you were Abe Handleman's son. You got a gold pass." Erik lifted his wineglass and took a sip as he checked out the crowd.

Next to me, Rachel smiled and patted my arm. Moved in close. "I'll give you a gold pass *and* two gold stars. With a cherry on top," she said, quietly, so only I could hear. People were starting to get into line at the buffet tables. "Why don't we get some food?"

Our little group got in line, and ten minutes later we were back at the table with our meals. Rachel and I chowed down on a variety of delicacies, both of us steering clear of the Brussels sprouts and hollandaise sauce. Something else we had in common. Erik and Katy ate mostly in silence, and across the table, Brandon and Layla spent more time pawing each other than eating. Every few seconds, I noticed, Brandon's eyes wandered down to examine Layla's prodigious chest. The way she kept working it, she didn't seem to mind in the least.

In my ear, Rachel whispered, "Layla doesn't seem like she's one of Northern Virginia's elite businessfolk."

"Maybe Brandon is." I had no idea what he did. When we'd played poker, the topic never came up. Or if it had, I'd been too steamed to notice.

The next time I saw Brandon checking out Layla's top shelf, I called out, making sure my voice was heard above the loud background chatter. "Hey, Brandon. I never caught what you do for a living."

He hit me with the insincere smile again. "I'm an entrepreneur. A little of this, a little of that. I even worked with your father on a couple of development things. Nice guy." He turned to Rachel. "And what do you do? Fashion model?" His smile broadened, slipping slightly when Layla landed an elbow in his ribs.

To my surprise, Rachel didn't unleash her sarcasm howitzer. "Schoolteacher. Third grade."

"I bet your students have a crush on their teacher, all right. I know I did." While he spoke, Layla tugged on his arm. She whispered in his ear. "Listen, my girl here wants to ditch this place. We got a room upstairs." He paused and undressed Rachel with his beady eyes while he addressed me. "Would you and your date care to join us?" All that was missing was the exaggerated wink. I wondered if Erik and Katy felt left out of the fun.

"No. But thanks for the offer." Maybe in an alternate universe. I glanced at Rachel. She hadn't verbally responded to Brandon's "offer," but I could guess what was running through her mind. And it probably had something to do with the creative use of steak knives.

Brandon and Layla said their goodbyes, and Rachel and Katy excused themselves to go to the ladies' room, giggling. I moved over a chair so Erik could hear me better. "You think Layla charges by the hour?" I asked.

Erik grinned. "He's been dating Lay-ya for a couple of months. Don't like her much, but she does have her good points, I suppose." He glanced around the room. "Like the party?"

"Sure. Fancy. How much do I owe you for the tickets?"

"My treat. Told you, I know a guy. Besides, they're a business expense. It'll come right out of the Hebrew Home's pocket." When I didn't fall for the bait, he smiled awkwardly. "Hey, just kidding." He turned serious. "Did you find your father's diamonds?"

"Nope. And I've searched damn near everywhere. Maybe he sold them."

Erik shook his head. "I don't think so. I would have known. If they were worth anything, that is. I suppose it wouldn't have hit my radar screen if they were only worth a few thousand." He shrugged. "Of course, if you knew they weren't worth much, you could stop searching. Not worth the aggravation you're putting yourself through."

"True. But I haven't found any receipts or paperwork or anything. I got nothing else to do with my time, so I guess I'll keep looking." Sad, but true. And—more to the point—if I kept focused on this task, I wouldn't have to worry about the larger picture yet. Where to live, what to do. Who to spend time with. My life, the mess.

Erik gripped my shoulder. "Hey, I really like Rachel. You two seem good together."

"Thanks. Yeah, she's … she's a lot different than Dani, that's for sure." Dani was critical and liked things her way, or no way. Rachel was more of a go-with-the-flow girl.

"Just take it slow, my friend. If it's meant to be, then it will be."

"Thanks for the Zen," I said. At the other end of the ballroom, a band started to warm up. I leaned closer to Erik. "What do you know about Brandon's dealings with my father?"

Erik sighed. "Look. I know you and Brandon didn't hit it off. But he's not such a bad guy. Really." He held my eyes for a moment. "I hooked them up a couple of years ago. Brandon was looking for some property to develop, and I knew your father was a player. They got a few things going since then. Nothing earth-shaking. Why?"

"Just curious. You know much about my father's other 'deals'?"

Erik swirled the drink in his glass while he thought. "Why?"

"Just curious. I'm trying to learn as much as I can about his business. Ironic, isn't it? When he was alive, I never cared that much."

"Don't be so hard on yourself. You're not as big a jerk as you think you are." Erik squeezed my upper arm.

I nodded, not sure if I'd agree with Erik's characterization. "Who handled his real estate stuff?"

"Guy named Teresywzki. Terry 'Terrible' Teresywzki. Why?"

"Thought I might want to talk to him."

Erik shook his head. "Your choice, but wear a hard hat. He doesn't take any prisoners. I'm working with him on your father's estate. If you're real nice to me, I'll get you in to see him. He's a tough ticket." Erik cocked his head to one side. "Come to think of it, I hooked them up, too. What would Honest Abe have done without me?"

Rachel and Katy returned just as the band started playing in earnest. Rachel pulled me out of my chair by my hand. "Care to dance, sailor?"

I got up but didn't move toward the dance floor. "I'm not much of a dancer."

"So? Neither am I. Come on." She dragged me out to one corner of the large wood parquet square that had been laid over the ballroom carpet in front of the band. They were playing a slow song, so I gently took her hand and drew her close. Swayed to the music as best I could. She swayed back and put her head against mine and I could feel the heat from her skin on my cheek and her warm breath tickled my ear. I held her swaying firm body against mine and inhaled her heady perfume. My pulse quickened and things began to rev up within me.

"I think you're a good dancer," she said, above the music. She pressed her pelvis against mine. "And I see you're very enthusiastic. Which is nice."

I responded by hugging her tighter.

"Let's go," she said.

And we did.

FOURTEEN

THE SUNLIGHT STREAMED IN through the blinds. Rachel lay two-thirds on top of me, one arm and one leg wrapped around my naked torso. When we got back last night, we rang in the New Year privately with some champagne. Then we'd managed pretty well—and energetically—on my single bed and drifted off to sleep. Sometime in the middle of the night, we woke up and managed again, then fell back asleep for the duration. My back was a little stiff, but I didn't want to move and risk waking Rachel up. She deserved her rest.

It was weird making love in my childhood bedroom, in the same bed I'd slept in since I was ten years old. Not bad, just weird. I'd gotten over it quickly.

My back's protestations got louder. If I shifted a bit…

Rachel's arm slid off me. Then her leg. "Hmm. You awake?" she asked, without opening her eyes.

"Good morning," I said.

"Hmm," she said.

"Hungry?" I asked, brushing some of her hair aside so I could see her entire face.

She opened her eyes and grinned at me.

We managed one more time on my narrow twin bed.

———

After we'd worked up an appetite for breakfast, we dressed. I loaned her some sweats and a T-shirt, and she looked a whole lot different than she did in her party duds. Not worse, just different. More girl-next-door. If the girl next door had a ferocious case of bed-head.

We padded barefoot down to the kitchen and rummaged through the cabinets for some chow, finally settling on Cheerios. My head was in the refrigerator getting the milk when I heard Rachel let out a surprised, "Oh!"

"Good morning, miss," I heard Kassian say. I'd neglected to tell Rachel about my basement boarder.

"Hey, sorry about that," I said, putting the half-gallon of milk on the table. "Rachel, this is Kassian. Kassian, this is Rachel." Kassian hung back in the doorway, neat and tidy in his customary outfit: black slacks, white shirt, gray cardigan.

Rachel stared at him, eyes wide. I tried to remember if I'd seen her surprised before, but couldn't recall. She was cute when startled, even in my old baggy clothes.

"Kassian lives here. In the basement suite. My father took him in." I got us bowls and spoons. All three of us. Cozy.

"Oh. Sure." She recovered nicely. "Nice to meet you."

Kassian shuffled farther into the room. "Happy New Year, Miss Rachel. And you, too, Joshua."

"Thanks, Kassian. Same to you." I distributed the bowls and spoons, setting a bowl down at an empty seat. "Please, join us." I motioned him over.

He studied Rachel and she smiled at him, as if she were encouraging a shy child to join the playgroup. He nodded and sat at the table. "All out of your usual Pop-Tarts, Joshua?" he asked, making what might have passed for a wink at Rachel.

I made a little face and poured Cheerios for all. Score one for Kassian.

After breakfast, Rachel said she needed to get going. She collected her clothes but didn't change into them, choosing to remain in my old sweats, even if they didn't go with her spiked heels. It was quite a look.

I drove her back to her car at the Hebrew Home. I was sad to see her go, but I believed the unspoken sentiment was mutual. We didn't want this thing to flame out because we screeched off the starting line too fast. I promised to call her and our goodbye kiss was long, lustful, and a terrific incentive to call her soon. Not that I needed one.

I got back home and, over my internal objections, unpacked my workout clothes. It was warm for New Year's Day, about fifty degrees, so I threw a sweatshirt over my T-shirt and donned some running shorts. Up until about three years ago, I worked out with some regularity, not thinking twice about running four or five miles. Since then, though, my discipline had diminished as my waistline had increased. Time to get back into shape.

I laced up my New Balance shoes and tucked a key and five bucks into my sock. Went around back to pick up the trail going east. I'd decided that the arboreal path would be more relaxing—

and healthier—than running in the gutters, inhaling the exhaust fumes of the cars whizzing by.

Before I began, I jogged in place for a few seconds to make sure all the parts still worked, then I pressed the start button on my watch timer and set off, ignoring the cracking sounds from my ankles. It took me a couple minutes to find the right pace. Not too fast to get winded, not too slow to feel like a running fraud. My stiff back had loosened, and my lungs drank in the cool fresh air. The sweat gathering on my skin felt great.

During the first five minutes, the only humans I passed were a couple of kids on bikes, pedaling with some effort on the asphalt path. Somewhere along the line, this path hooked up with the W&OD bike trail, which ran from Leesburg to Alexandria. It was a favorite of those with long-distances in mind—both bikers and runners. I doubted I'd get that far today, but if a marathon was in my future …

I fell into a rhythm and my mind entered that zone where you're able to shut out the environment and concentrate, where the thoughts and ideas flowed freely, interconnecting and synthesizing and opening up new horizons. But instead of anything positive and enlightening, my thoughts centered on Lev's accusation. Was my father murdered? I tried to put myself into the shoes of an objective observer. Who would benefit from my father's death?

Those mentioned in his will would benefit financially. But the only individuals named were Aunt Shel and yours truly. The Hebrew Home was the greatest beneficiary, by far, but it seemed improbable anyone there would knock off my father simply to get a hefty donation.

Carol's tight-lipped face appeared before me. She had a key. She could have killed my father and locked up behind her. The Hebrew Home was her baby. Was the story about her engagement to my father a clever cover-up? And those diamond earrings … My concentration wavered as I broke stride to avoid a few large roots cracking the path's surface. I checked my watch. Twelve minutes had elapsed. Almost time to turn around.

The more I thought about it, the more it didn't feel right. Carol, the Hebrew Home, murder. I was an analytical guy by nature, but when it really came down to it, I trusted my gut. And my gut was telling me Carol wasn't involved.

What about his real estate cronies? Did any of them stand to benefit from my father's death? Could my father's murderer have been one of the tux-clad business elite I'd rubbed elbows with last night? What about that asshole Flannery? I didn't like him, but as I'd been telling Lev, disliking someone wasn't grounds for suspicion. Thinking he was behind my father's death seemed far-fetched. Of course, *anyone* murdering my father seemed far-fetched. I made a mental note to ask Terrible what's-his-name about it when I talked to him.

I felt like a giant loser, an outsider. Why didn't I know more about my father's life? Why hadn't he felt he could have trusted me? Had I been that cold to him? Did he interpret my moving to the West Coast as abandonment?

Since Mom died, conversations with my father had gotten rarer, petering out to once a month, if that. When we did connect, we only talked about trivial things. Sports, weather, the stock market. He'd always ask about Dani, but that's as far as he'd ever venture into my personal territory. On the flip side, I'd often ask about his health or his personal life, but he seemed to take great delight in pooh-poohing me. Eventually I'd stopped asking him directly, instead getting most of my information from Aunt Shel. But, as I was finding out now, she'd omitted a lot of stuff. A lot of important stuff. She'd never mentioned Kassian, for instance, and there'd been no mention of Carol whatsoever. I wonder if *she* knew of my father's engagement.

And what about Kassian? Why did Lev believe he killed my father? Did being a Russian Jew factor into this in any way? Maybe I should have another talk with Lev to see what his position on the Home's Oversight Committee was all about.

Checked my watch again. Fifteen minutes. About a mile and a half, maybe a little more. Three miles was enough for the first run of the year. I turned around and headed back. The spring in my step was starting to fade, and the running began to feel more like plodding. I wiped some sweat from my forehead. Did runners truly like the act of running?

My mind returned to the diamonds. Since Aunt Shel told me about them, my mind had been returning to the diamonds frequently. I didn't even care so much about their monetary value. My father had wanted me to have them, and I think that was driving me. His final gift to me. His legacy.

But my attitude was beginning to scare me. I felt like one of those obsessed collectors who can only think of their porcelain cats or their antique automobiles or their bottle caps with Elvis' picture painted on them. *Diamonds, diamonds, diamonds, oh where can you be?*

I knew where they weren't. They weren't in the safe deposit box. Or the study or my father's bedroom or my room. There were still places in the house I could search. But did I really think the diamonds would be there? Could he have given them to someone?

I slowed as another kid on a mountain bike came at me. He smiled and waved and I returned the greeting. Happy kid. I felt like yelling after him, "Just wait until you're older. And your wife runs off with your business partner. And your father dies. And you can't find the fucking bag of diamonds he's left you." But the kid didn't deserve that. Nobody did.

The surroundings began to look familiar. I checked my time: thirty-one minutes. Done. I slowed to a walk and shook out my legs, one at a time, like I'd seen the long-distance runners do on TV. Found a large tree to lean against while I stretched my calves. Started to head for the house when I heard the back door slam. I ducked behind a tree and watched Kassian walk through the backyard and turn west down the path, in the other direction.

He walked out of sight.

I followed.

FIFTEEN

I STAYED WELL BEHIND, ready to dive off the path into the woods if Kassian suddenly whirled around. I wasn't exactly sure why I wanted to stay hidden, but it felt like the right thing to do. Actually, it felt weird, as if I didn't trust him, but I guess I'd have to get past that. After a few minutes, I realized I didn't have to worry about being spotted—Kassian was oblivious. He strolled along, eyes front, seemingly without a care in the world. Made sense, why would he suspect he was being followed? As he walked, he tapped a rolled-up magazine lightly against the outside of his thigh.

Most likely, Kassian was going to the Hebrew Home. You could get there, and to the synagogue three blocks beyond it, by continuing on the trail for a couple miles west. On pleasant Saturday mornings—and Friday evenings in the summer—you would often see families walking to services, yelling at their children to stay on the path so they wouldn't mess up their dress clothes tramping through the thorny underbrush.

New Year's Day wasn't a big deal on the Jewish calendar, but the Home had a dedicated TV lounge, complete with a large-screen, and there were plenty of college football bowl games to watch. Kassian didn't strike me as a big USC fan, but you never knew. On the other hand, maybe he just wanted the free popcorn.

A middle-aged couple overtook me from behind. I smiled at them as they passed, and it seemed like they were really motoring. Then I realized that I'd barely been moving forward, thanks to Kassian's dawdling pace.

Up ahead, the path forked. The Hebrew Home to the right, more residential neighborhoods to the left. To my surprise, Kassian veered left.

Was Kassian on an exercise walk? I wasn't sure walking at this speed even counted as exercise. But Kassian seemed to be in pretty good shape for an old guy, so I guess he got his workout somehow. By maintaining a counter-clockwise bearing and switching paths, you could walk in a giant circle and arrive back at the house. I'd never measured it, but it had to be at least five miles. And it wouldn't surprise me, with all the twists and turns of the path, if the distance were closer to ten miles. As a kid, I'd spent many afternoons exploring the wooded paths of Reston, but most of the time it had been on my bike and "getting my exercise" hadn't ever occurred to me.

We walked for a mile or so, then skirted the back of a small shopping center that contained a 7-Eleven, a Chinese take-out place, and a dry cleaners. The pungent smell of garlic tempted me from my surveillance, but I fought it off, mentally making a note to come back soon for some Kung Pao Chicken. Ten minutes later we meandered through a townhouse development. The path crossed a street, then resumed alongside the tenth hole of Reston Hills Golf Course. Here, more people walked about, hurrying this way and that, and a foursome waiting to tee off eyed Kassian, but he continued along without distraction. I followed from a distance, trying to seem as inconspicuous as possible.

At the tenth green, the path took a ninety-degree jog to the right, plunging into the woods bordering a neighborhood of pricey single-family homes. It ran behind their properties, parallel to the street they fronted, and most of the yards were buffered from the trail by split-rail fences and dense evergreen shrubbery.

Up ahead, Kassian slowed and concentrated on something to his left. I stepped off the asphalt and crouched, taking refuge behind a low-growing pair of holly trees. I still had line-of-sight with Kassian, who had stopped cold. He glanced behind him, in my direction, then spun in a complete circle. No one else was around.

Moving faster than I'd ever seen him, he hustled off the path to his right, scrambling up a slight incline into a patch of thicker woods. I had to shift positions to keep a bead on him, but he was too far away and doing enough of his own rustling to notice me. He disappeared for a moment, then I picked him up again as he crawled onto a small rock ledge in a cleared-out space, about fifteen feet above the path. I edged a few steps into the woods to get a better angle. He'd maneuvered himself into a cross-legged sitting position on the ledge, with his back up against a tree trunk. Settled in.

He'd been there before. Many times, if I had to guess.

I checked my watch, pressing the mode button so it would toggle over to real time from the stopwatch function. A few minutes after noon. I stared at Kassian for a couple minutes, while all sorts of questions ran through my mind. But I didn't have any answers to the most fundamental: What the hell was going on?

A trio of teenagers approached from the direction of the golf course. I bent over and untied and retied my shoe. Then did the same to the other one. They passed, not giving me a second thought, and I refocused on Kassian. He hadn't moved, but I doubted if the teenagers would even notice him, the way he'd tucked himself away, off the path and above eye level. With his black and gray outfit, he blended in like a raccoon.

I burrowed into my own hidey-hole where I could keep an eye on Kassian, careful to stay hidden from anyone who might come along the path. I don't know what kind of excuse I'd give if someone happened upon me; searching for a contact lens seemed pretty lame. At least Kassian had a magazine, although I'm not sure who would believe he'd climbed up on a ledge in the woods to catch up on his reading. I stretched out my legs. Getting a cramp now would be embarrassing.

A woman rode by on her bike, pumping, then coasting, pumping, coasting. A couple minutes later, another woman—I think it was a woman, it was a little hard to tell from my angle, with holly branches obscuring my view—walked by pulling a dog on a leash. She sang a little tune, way off key. The dog whimpered, and I couldn't blame him. I covered my ears and did my best not to whimper myself.

I watched Kassian. He didn't move from his perch. What was a reasonable length of time to spy on him? I didn't have much espionage experience, so I figured if he didn't move in half an hour, I'd give it up.

In half an hour, I gave it up and headed home.

My muscles ached and my legs felt like two-by-fours as I trudged back, following the same maze of trails in reverse. A few people waved as they passed. I didn't know them, just amiable folk being friendly on the sunny start to a new year. I returned the greetings, wondering if they had a mysterious little old man living in their basement, too.

When I got home, I wanted nothing more than a nice long shower and a nap. Instead, I took the opportunity—with Kassian still in the woods—to search the in-law suite more thoroughly.

I paused at the threshold. I'd lived in this room after my sophomore year at school, when I'd dropped out to pursue my own business interests. Before my father's daily nagging had forced me to flee to the West Coast. But I'd never kept it as tidy as Kassian did.

His room was immaculate. Bed made, furniture dusted, trash can emptied. From the doorway, you couldn't tell anyone lived there. I didn't know how long Kassian would be gone, so I didn't waste any time. I searched the entire dresser again, then under the bed, in the closet, in the bathroom. Went through everything with the proverbial fine-tooth comb. Found absolutely nothing. No cryptic notes. No bus station locker keys. No treasure maps. In fact, except for the photograph of Kassian with a woman and a little girl on the bureau, there was nothing of a personal nature whatsoever. Nada.

I made sure everything looked like it had when I started and hit the showers.

After standing under the hot water for fifteen minutes, I felt better. I skipped the nap and resumed my search for the diamonds. It took forty-five minutes to give the kitchen pantry an "all-clear," and another twenty minutes to rummage through the hall closet and linen closet. Pushing through was getting harder, knowing to an al-most certainty that my efforts were futile. Why would my father re-move diamonds from a safe deposit box and hide them in the house? As much thought as I'd given to that question, you'd think I would have come up with at least *one* plausible explanation.

I dragged a step stool upstairs into the hallway and set it be-neath the trap door leading to the attic. I climbed the steps and pushed the door up and into the attic itself, setting it off to one side. A shower of dust and pieces of insulation fluttered down, lit-tle bits of fluff floating to the carpet, as if I were in a life-sized snow globe full of fiberglass. I shook the crap off my head, and flashlight in hand, ascended into the attic. As my head cleared the attic floorboards, the cold air hit me first, followed by a stale, musty odor. The smell of years gone by. Balancing on the top step of the stool I flicked on the light and shone it around. Wall-to-wall cardboard boxes.

A thick layer of dust covered the closest box. The blown-in in-sulation had accumulated around its base, like a mini-snowdrift. I played the light across the rows of boxes. Each one like the first. Smothered in dust, surrounded by insulation. No one had been up there in years.

I decided to keep it that way and ducked out of the attic. Plopped on the stool and took a deep breath. Wasn't sure if I felt disappoint-ment or relief. I'd held out the smallest speck of hope that the dia-monds would be in the attic, in the last place I'd look. Now that I knew better, I felt a little deflated. On the other hand, I could stop this ridiculous hunt I'd been on. Since I began, I'd felt greedy and materialistic, tearing apart my father's house, looking for the dia-monds. Sparkling pieces of rock. My father had just passed away, and I was worried about finding a velvet bag full of rocks. Yes, it was his last "gift" to me, and that meant something, but still … I'd given it a good try and come up empty. There was only so much I could do.

Maybe I should concentrate on something a little more important. Like how my father died. Accident or murder? I'd been so sure it was an accident, but if you added everything together—the missing diamonds, Kassian's odd behavior, Lev's insistence coupled with the feeling I got he was withholding something—it made the case for murder stronger. And then it hit me, clear as today's sky. Maybe I wanted to find the diamonds, not for their monetary value, nor to keep his legacy "alive," but so I could dismiss the idea that my father could have been killed for them. I'd *wanted* to believe his death was an accident. That he had no enemies, certainly none vicious enough to kill him by pushing him down a flight of stairs.

I owed it to my father to find out the truth.

Who would murder him? And why?

SIXTEEN

What was Kassian doing in the woods? There were better—and closer—places to commune with nature, and reading a magazine sitting on a rocky ledge in the woods didn't seem very comfortable. Was he waiting for someone? Not tucked away like that, he wasn't.

He was observing something. Something specific.

I fetched my laptop and booted it up. Pulled up MapQuest and played around until I got an aerial image of Reston Hills Golf Course. Found the tenth hole. Kept re-jiggering the map until it showed the area in the woods where I figured Kassian and I had been playing our warped version of Spy-vs.-Spy.

Two houses on the nearby street, Palmer Way, backed up to the area, but I couldn't determine the addresses. Even though there must be some way to get them via the wondrous Internet, it would probably be easier—and quicker—if I hopped in the car and drove over there. I closed the laptop and decided to break for food. It was dinnertime, and I hadn't eaten since sharing Cheerios with Rachel many hours ago.

I opened a can of soup, dumped it into a bowl, and stuck it in the microwave. Thought about calling Rachel to tell her what a great time I had last night, but held off. It wasn't that I was afraid she'd come to her senses and realize I wasn't the right guy for her. I could tell we had some serious chemistry going. But I didn't want to suffocate her. Back when Dani and I were first dating, it seemed like we were together every minute of every day. In retrospect, maybe that hadn't been such a good thing—although at the time, we couldn't keep our hands off each other.

The microwave dinged and I retrieved my food. The soup was too salty with soapy undertones, but at least it was hot. I wolfed it down, accompanied by a handful of crackers. So much for eating better this year. I dumped the dirty dishes into the sink and wiped my hands on the striped dishtowel hanging on the oven door handle.

I needed to have another talk with Lev. See if he was willing to be a little more specific about his suspicion of Kassian. I called over there and Peter answered.

"Hey, Josh. How's it going?" he asked, voice still infused with sympathy.

"Fine, Peter. You?"

"Great. Had a couple days off, ready to get back at it tomorrow. January's a busy time for me. People always resolve to get their money matters in order."

"I bet. Something I should do, too." I paused. "Hey, is Lev around?"

"Naw. Went to the Hebrew Home. Board meeting, I think."

"On New Year's?"

"That's what he said. Who knows with him? Especially lately. I'd give you his cell phone number, however ... I bought him that phone last year, but he never turns it on." Peter sighed and lowered his voice. "Find those diamonds yet?"

"No." I suppressed my own sigh. "I'm beginning to think there aren't any."

"Well, ever since you mentioned they were missing, I've been thinking about it. Your father selling them makes the most sense. I mean, *no one* misplaces a bag of diamonds," Peter said. "I'm sure he sold them and donated the money where it could do some good. That would be like your father, right?"

"Yeah, maybe…"

"It's certainly logical. Your father was always looking out for the little guy, wasn't he?"

I nodded, though nobody was around to see. "You're probably right."

"Josh?" Peter sounded tentative.

"Yeah?"

"My dad has been ranting about how you should go to the police. Tell them your father was murdered."

"Yeah, he's been after me pretty good about that, too."

"I just wanted you to know, I've been doing my best to dissuade him. I agree with you one hundred percent. It was a tragic accident. But my dad won't let it go. He's making himself sick with it and I'm getting worried. He's a tough old guy, all right, but this thing… this thing has him… I'm afraid he'll have a stroke or something. Jenn wants me to send him away on vacation. That'll be the day."

I couldn't remember the last time Peter had been worked up about something that wasn't business related. "Relax, Peter. I'm going to talk with him right now. I'll try to get him settled down."

Peter exhaled into the phone. "Okay. Thanks. And good luck."

Before I left, I checked to see if Kassian had snuck in when I wasn't looking. No sign of him. Hopefully, he was someplace safe and warm. I'd never signed up to be an eldersitter, and I didn't think it would make the list of my top ten ideal careers. Neither would "diamond detective."

I grabbed a pad of paper and a pen as I left.

On my way to the Hebrew Home, I took a detour. Past the golf course to Palmer Way. I drove slowly down the street and flipped on my high beams so I could read the addresses on the mailboxes. I crawled by, jotted them down as I passed. At the end of the street I U-turned and cruised down the row again, looking for any sign of what might have interested Kassian. Unless he was drawn to a trampoline in one of the house's side yards, nothing struck me.

Ten minutes later I pulled into the Hebrew Home's mostly empty parking lot. New Year's Day was pretty quiet everywhere, I guess. On my way into the building, I spotted Lev's Lexus SUV with the personalized plate, STOX3—third in Peter's mini-fleet of "rolling write-offs." I wondered how my Beamer, with generic plates, was doing back in Santa Clara. The Taurus got me around okay, but I missed my baby.

At the reception desk, I signed in and asked where the board meeting was being held. An old guy with a bushy beard and one eyelid at half-mast seemed puzzled. "There is no board meeting today," he said with a thick Old-World accent. "Next Monday." Then he turned away as a ringing phone captured his attention.

I waited patiently for him to finish his call. He set the receiver down in the cradle, then seemed surprised I hadn't left. "There still is no board meeting tonight."

"Yes, I get that. Do you know Lev Yurishenko? I believe he's on the Oversight Committee."

"Yes, I know him," the man said. I could barely see his mouth through all the hair.

"Is he here?"

"Yes."

Like pulling teeth. "Where can I find him?"

"I didn't realize he was missing," the man said, and I thought I could detect the hint of a smile. It vanished quickly. "He is with Mrs. Wolfe. In her office, I believe." The phone rang again, and the man turned away to answer it.

Leaving the old guy to find another straight man, I wandered off to locate Carol's office. I hadn't realized that Lev and Carol knew each other, but it made sense, both professionally and personally. Lev was on the committee here, and being my father's best friend, he must have known about their relationship. Why he'd neglected to tell me, I didn't have a clue. Except that Lev was mysterious about most everything, a trait he shared with Kassian. Maybe it was a Russian Jew thing.

A sign that read "Administration" pointed down one of the hallways radiating from the lobby. I headed in that direction. Offices lined both sides of the corridor, nameplates on the doors. But the nameplates only announced the functional titles, no actual names. Probably so they wouldn't have to keep replacing them when the personnel turned over.

The door to the office at the end of the hall swung open and Carol and Lev emerged, discussion still going on. They took a few steps in my direction, stopping when they realized I was standing there.

Carol spoke first. "Hello, Josh. Nice to see you." Her words were warm, but the tone chilly.

Lev painted me with his usual scowl. "Joshua. What are you doing here?"

"I need to talk with you," I said to Lev. Next to him, the tension in Carol's face eased.

"Well, I'll leave you two alone. Nice seeing you, Josh." She turned to Lev. "Think about what I said. We'd love your support on this." With a parting smile she walked away.

Lev stared silently at Carol as her footsteps echoed down the hall. Then he turned to me. "Joshua. I hope you have come to tell me you've gone to the police."

I didn't want to have this conversation standing in the hallway. "Can we sit down or something?"

"This way," Lev said, and he started off down the corridor. We found seats in one corner of the almost vacant lobby. He straightened himself on the chair, coat folded in lap, hat on head. Waiting for me to speak.

"I didn't realize you knew Carol."

"Of course. She is a director here. I am on the Oversight Committee." He brushed some lint from his coat. "And Carol was a friend of your father's." His eyes searched mine to see if I knew exactly how good a friend she was.

"You can relax. Carol told me about their relationship. You won't have to betray any confidences." I glanced around the lobby. On the other side, two residents shared a couch, reading to themselves. The old hairy guy was still at the front desk, waiting for his next visitor to annoy. "Peter said you were at a board meeting."

"Peter was mistaken. Carol wanted to discuss something with me."

"On New Year's Day?" I asked.

Lev shrugged. "She has no family in town. It was convenient for both of us. Quieter than a normal day." He stopped talking.

"What did she want to discuss?"

"Their proposal to start a Russian Unit. Carol wishes my support in the matter. She is very persuasive. And charming. I can see why your father cared for her."

"How come you're against the proposal?"

Lev sucked in some air. "Russians must take care of their own. We are strong. We do not need charity. We do not need a place where children can cast off their parents and forget them. We do not need to be singled out as being weaker or more destitute than others." He paused and glanced around, tone becoming more urgent. "I do not wish to be exclusionary. The Hebrew Home should expand its facilities for *all* to use. Why should only Russian Jews be let into the new unit? I am proud of my people, but I do not wish to be labeled racist."

"Wasn't my father behind the Russian Unit?"

"Yes. He was a major proponent of this idea. I loved your father, though I did not agree with him on this."

I had a hard time picturing my father and Lev on opposite sides of the fence. "But he had the money."

"Yes." Lev licked his lips. "Your father had the money."

"So what's going to happen?"

Lev sighed. "The proposal will be revised and changed and discussed. And discussed some more. Then there will be a vote. I expect it will be approved, even without your father's vocal support." One eyebrow rose. "After all, they have his money now."

I never cared much for politics. National, local, whatever. Too many egos, too many people digging their heels in. Too many petty people protecting their fiefdoms.

"So what is it that brings you here to talk with me?" Lev leaned forward slightly. "Have you found Abe's diamonds yet?"

I shook my head.

"As I thought. And you will not. Because Kassian has stolen them. Why do you not see that?"

"Peter's worried about you. He thinks the stress over my father's death is affecting your health."

He leaned back and a tight grin appeared. "When our children are young, we take care of them. Worry about them. Then, when *we* are old, they take care of us and worry about us. That is the way it should be. Peter is a good boy. His mother—God rest her soul—and I raised him right. But he worries needlessly in this case. My health is fine. I am still strong. And Kassian killed your father."

Stubborn as a mule, too. "Peter thinks it was an accident."

"Peter does not know Kassian as I do," he said.

I wondered if Lev knew about Kassian's Daniel Boone impersonation. "Tell me again why you are so convinced."

"You have doubt now?" He licked his lips once more. "I knew it was only a matter of time. Kassian is a taker. He is soft. He is not what he appears to be."

"He appears to be an old guy who can't take care of himself. That's why my father took him in. If there's more to it than that, you've got to tell me."

Lev considered my request. Then he shifted in his chair and moved his coat from his lap. "Back in Russia, I was what you would call a dissident. I spoke out against the government. Wrote articles. Things that you can do freely in this country, but were not so free there. They warned me, but I was young, headstrong. I did not listen to their threats. After some time, they got tired of warning me so they threw me in jail. Called it a psychiatric hospital and they would not let me leave. It was worse than jail. My parents were destroyed by this."

My father had told stories of the imprisoned dissidents, but he'd never mentioned that Lev had been one of them. I'd never been absolutely sure if the stories were real, or if my father had been exaggerating to make a point as I thought he often did about other things. "I never knew, Lev. I'm sorry."

He pulled his shoulders back. "I do not wish your pity. I did not cow to them. I stood up to them proudly. After a few years, the political climate changed—thanks to many men like your father—and they felt it better to let us go. Of course they charged us money to leave. They said it was to pay them back for the education they had given us, a 'diploma tax.' Those who could afford to, got out. Many could not. I left many friends and family behind." He averted his eyes, and I was afraid to ask about the unfortunate ones. My father had told me stories about them, too. "In 1973, they flew us to Vienna, Austria, first. Then on to Israel." Lev paused and gazed over my head, lost in the past.

I waited for him to continue, not sure what this had to do with Kassian.

Lev wiped his nose with his handkerchief, and back in the present, went on. "Some did not wish to go to Israel, but came here directly instead, with the assistance of the American Jews. Many in Israel called them dropouts and were not pleased."

"And?"

"And Kassian was a dropout."

I guess I didn't see what the big deal was. I'd pick the U.S. over Israel too. "Did you know him then?"

"No. He left Russia many months after I did. In Israel, I met my wife and we came here a few years later, with others from her family. Some years after that, we became friends with Abe and Judith."

I pictured Lev's wife, Anya. Jet-black hair and dark brown eyes full of compassion. "So what does this have to do with Kassian?" I asked, as gently as I could.

"Kassian claims he was imprisoned. Abused by the authorities. We were a small community, and while I did not know everyone, I think I would have heard of him."

"Lev, it was a long time ago. And from what my father said, things were chaotic, confusing. Why would he lie about it?"

"To get your father to provide him with money."

"Why would Kassian think something that happened so long ago would influence my father now?"

Lev shook his head. "You are misunderstanding me, Joshua. Kassian wrote to your father asking him for money back in the early 1970s. Somehow, he got the letters through and received Abe's. It was not always easy."

"What?" I closed my eyes. In addition to marching in protests and peppering newspapers and magazines with strident Letters to the Editor, my father donated money to various Soviet Jewry organizations back in the day. I often heard him discussing it with Mom. "Are you saying my father sent money to *Kassian*, thirty-some years ago?"

"Yes. Now you understand." Lev stared at me. "Your father paid for Kassian to exit Russia and come to the United States. I'm not sure how he got him the money, but your father was a clever man. And persistent."

"You're putting me on."

"No, I am not. You knew your father. It was his way."

"So what happened with Kassian?"

"According to your father, Kassian settled in New York City. Got married, started a family, but had trouble with the vodka. Many of us did, it is no secret. Some of us were strong enough to get control of it. Others wound up like Kassian. In shelters or on the streets. Drunk. Destitute. Or worse, dead. Somehow, Kassian survived. Your father said he lost contact with him. Until this past year, when Kassian contacted Abe. And moved here. You know the rest." Lev finished and sat back, arms folded across his chest.

My brain struggled to absorb Lev's story. I tried to collate the new information with what I already knew to judge if it made any sense. Kassian and my father knew each other for thirty-five years? They were corresponding while I was *in utero*? I remembered the dozens of letters in my father's dresser, written in Russian. "My father wrote to many persecuted Jews. Did he send money to all of them?"

Lev pondered this. "I do not believe so, although it is possible. He was a selfless man. He only told me of Kassian."

"So why would he pick Kassian to 'save,' out of all of them?" I asked.

Lev's tight grin reappeared. "That is an easy question to answer." He paused, eyeing me as if I were a subject in a psych experiment. "Because Kassian claims he is your father's cousin."

SEVENTEEN

As I drove home, I tried to come to grips with what Lev told me. *I was related to Kassian?* I'd asked Lev how Kassian said he was related to my father *exactly*, but Lev didn't have any details. He said every time he asked my father, he got some kind of vague answer that seemed to change from time to time. In other words, Lev didn't believe Kassian's claim, and he doubted my father did either. The one time he'd confronted my father directly about it, my father had told him to mind his own business, blood was blood.

I pulled up to the dark house and glanced at the dashboard clock: 8:35. Was Kassian still out on the prowl? I hoped not—I had a few things I wanted to discuss. The door to his bedroom was open and the room was dark. I flipped the light on and there he was, asleep in bed. I turned the light off and drew his door shut. As much as I wanted to find the truth, I didn't have the heart to wake the old guy up. My interrogation could wait until morning.

Back in the kitchen, I reached for a Pop-Tart, but remembering my resolution, grabbed a banana instead. Got my laptop off the counter and started it up. When it was ready, I unfolded the scrap of paper with the Palmer Way addresses and got ready to Google them, hoping something of use would pop up.

I typed in the first address, 11242 Palmer. A page with about a dozen results materialized from cyberspace. Scanning the results, I found two listings with the same name associated to the address: Roger Davis. I clicked on the first one, and the minutes from a three-year-old zoning hearing came up. I paged back and clicked on the second listing. Google took me to the "references" page of a LawnPro landscape service website. Roger Davis, Resident of 11242 Palmer Way, satisfied customer. One down, one to go.

I repeated my search procedure with 11244 Palmer Way and found the name of the homeowner with ease: Stephen Wentworth. And there were a ton of Google hits. Turns out Wentworth was a corporate V.P. at Digitelex. I clicked on a link and was directed to a page advertising a business luncheon where Wentworth had been the keynote speaker. The meeting's sponsor: The Northern Virginia Business Elite. I wondered if I'd met him at last night's soiree.

I picked up the phone and called Erik.

"Hey, man. Katy and I missed you when the ball dropped. Too bad you had to cut out early," Erik said, a little chuckle in his voice.

"Yeah, well, thanks for inviting us to the party. We had a lot of fun."

"Any time, my friend. Any time," he said.

"Ever hear of Stephen Wentworth?"

"Honcho at Digitelex. What about him?"

I figured Erik would know him. He knew everybody. "Know him well?"

"Not really. Met him, but never really talked to him. Why?"

"Was he there last night?"

There was a moment of silence. I imagined Erik pulling on his chin as he parsed his memory. "Nope. Don't recall seeing him. You got a beef with this guy?"

"No. His name came up and I wanted to find out more about him. That's all."

"Married. Couple of rugrats, I think." Erik laughed. "That help?"

"That helps about as much as you usually do," I said. "Thanks anyway. I don't suppose you know someone named Roger Davis, do you?"

Another pause. "Nope. He in the Elite, too?"

"Don't have a clue. If you haven't heard of him, probably not," I said. "Well, thanks for nothing, bud."

"Any time. Glad to be of no help."

"You get what you pay for. Say hi to Katy, will you?" We said goodbye and I hung up.

I folded down the top of my computer with the nagging feeling I'd just wasted the better part of an hour, no closer to an answer to my question. What was Kassian doing in the woods behind those houses?

———

I didn't wake up until ten o'clock the next morning, catching up on the sleep I'd missed entertaining Rachel. I threw some sweats on and went downstairs to talk to Kassian. Too late. His bed was neatly made and there was no trace of him—the little man was an expert at covering his tracks. Had he returned to his surveillance post in the woods? I was tempted to go find out, but I was tiring of the bullshit. When I saw him, I'd ask him flat out. He might not tell me the truth, but that's where I was planning to start.

I ignored the cinnamon-brown sugar Pop-Tarts calling my name, opting for a bowl of bran flakes and skim milk. Threw some raisins on top, determined to eat healthier even if it killed me.

After breakfast, I called my father's doctor to cancel his appointment. When the receptionist asked if I'd like to reschedule, all I could squeeze out was a hoarse, "No thanks."

My next call was to Yakov Sapperstein in New York.

"Hello, Sapperstein Associates." A person, not a recording.

"Uh, yes. May I speak with Mr. Sapperstein?" I asked.

"Which one?" the voice replied.

"Yakov. Yakov Sapperstein."

"Please hold."

Ninety seconds later, the line was picked up. "This is Yakov. How can I help you?"

"My name is Josh Handleman. I'm calling on behalf of my father, Abe."

"Oh, yes, yes. How are you?"

"Fine thanks. I'm calling about—"

"Let me apologize again for last week. My son broke his arm so we had to cancel our trip at the last minute. I'm very sorry," Yakov said. "We have rescheduled our trip, so I can reschedule my appointment with your father. How is Friday morning?"

"Mr. Sapperstein, I'm—"

"Please, call me Yakov."

"Okay, Yakov. I'm … Why were you going to meet with my father? Are you a friend of his?"

Yakov let out a small laugh. "He is a friendly man, but we've never met. We've talked over the phone on several occasions. He wanted to discuss some business. First an appraisal, then..." He trailed off.

As I thought, real estate. "Unfortunately, Yakov..." I got choked up. Maybe I should practice saying the words, "my father is dead," fifty times a day until my throat didn't tighten anymore.

"Mr. Handleman?"

"Yes. I'm here." I gathered myself. "Unfortunately, my father passed away."

"Oh no," Yakov said. "That is terrible. I am sorry for your loss."

"Thank you." Dead air filled my ears. "So... Well... I guess..." I waited for Yakov to say something. When he didn't, I muttered, "Goodbye then."

"Mr. Handleman?" Yakov said.

"Yes?"

"What will you be doing about the, um, assets?"

Life goes on. "A lawyer named Erik Nolan is handling my father's estate. He can put you in touch with my father's real estate attorney. He'll be able to help you. Let me give you his numb—"

"Real estate?" Yakov asked.

"An appraisal? Isn't that what he wanted from you?" I felt the first faint beats of my headache returning.

"An appraisal yes. But not of real estate. Of diamonds."

"You were going to give my father an appraisal for his diamond collection?" My wisp of a headache receded.

"Yes, that's right. He got my name from a mutual friend and called me up. Said he had some diamonds he wanted to get appraised. It was my impression he was considering selling them."

Finally, finally, finally, someone who knew something about the diamonds. My pulse quickened. "What can you tell me about them?"

Yakov hesitated. "How did you find my number?"

I explained about the entry in my father's calendar. He thought for a moment. "What do you wish to know?"

"Did my father explicitly say he was going to sell them?"

"No, he didn't. But I can read between the lines."

Dozens of questions bounced around my brain, like balls in a bingo hopper. "When did you call to cancel?"

"Friday morning." He paused. "Friday, the 22nd. Early."

The fateful morning. "And you spoke to my father?"

"Yes," Yakov said. "I remember he seemed in a very good mood."

"Do you think he would have sold them before he met with you?"

"No. When I told him I had to cancel and reschedule, he didn't seem very upset, like he wouldn't mind waiting another week or two. He did say that he'd have to return to the bank, but it didn't sound like he cared much about that either. I asked him if he already had an appraisal, and he said he didn't, not on the entire collection. Your father seemed much too shrewd to sell his diamonds without knowing exactly how much they were worth. Besides…" Yakov paused, clearing his throat. "I told him I would give him a very good deal, should he wish to divest himself."

"Did he say how much he thought his collection might be worth? In general terms?"

"No. Not really. He did say it would be worth my effort to come down, however."

I plucked another question from the swirl in my head. "Did he tell you how many diamonds he had?"

Yakov was silent for a moment. When he spoke, the words came out deliberately. "No, he did not. He was a little hazy with some of the details. But I am used to that. Many people act differently when they are talking about diamonds. I don't know why, but it's something I've found to be true."

"Yeah, I'm not getting many straight answers, either," I said. People act differently when someone dies, too.

"Mr. Handleman?"

"Yes?"

"If you don't mind *me* asking *you* a question?"

"Sure," I said.

"Why don't you know how many diamonds your father had?"

I explained to Yakov about the missing diamonds, wondering how many more times I'd have to go through it. When I was finished, he had little to say, and I detected no small measure of displeasure squeezing through the phone line.

Join the fucking club, Yakov.

EIGHTEEN

YAKOV EXPRESSED HIS SYMPATHY again, and I told him I'd get back to him if the diamonds ever resurfaced. His "I look forward to it" dripped with sarcasm. I hung up, and my growing frustration threatened to bubble out of control.

I now knew for sure the diamonds actually existed. Lots of them. My father hadn't sold or given away his collection. He'd taken the diamonds out of the safe deposit box in preparation for Yakov's appraisal and when his appointment got cancelled, he'd planned to take the diamonds back to the bank. But he hadn't done that—he'd been killed before he had the chance. So whoever killed my father had his diamonds. *My* diamonds, if you wanted to be precise.

Lev was right. It was time to go to the police.

Conveniently, the Fairfax County Police Department had a station near Reston Town Center, across from the public library. I didn't know whether that meant Reston was a hotbed of criminal activity or whether there had just been an empty taxpayer-funded building. At the front desk, I waited for the uniformed officer to get off the phone before I dumped my problem into the authorities' hands.

"Hello, Officer. I'd like to report a murder. And a robbery. And I—"

The officer, a young woman, held up her hand. "Hold on. Hold on. A murder?" She eyed me suspiciously. To her, I must have been another walk-up crackpot, spouting wild tales of mayhem.

I took a deep breath. Started from the top, more calmly. "Yes. I'd like to talk to somebody about a possible murder." I emphasized the word "possible."

She sighed and shook her head, like she must do to all the nut jobs. "Just a minute," she said, as she picked up the phone and nodded to a set of three molded-plastic chairs off to the side. "Have a seat."

Instead of sitting, I paced around the small lobby. Several people came and went. I could overhear their conversations with the desk officer and none of them sounded serious. Certainly no one had anything as important as murder. Yet they got their questions answered without having to cool their jets in the lobby. I suppose handling a murder required a specialist.

A glass display case held certificates and citations from other local agencies, recognizing Fairfax County's finest for various achievements. Several trophies from police-sponsored Boys Club athletic events stood in a line on a glass shelf inside the case. A plaque, commemorating the Department's involvement in a September 11 anniversary function, hung proudly on the wall next to the display case.

"You the one with the murder?"

I spun around and my head slowly tilted upward. A tall man, shaved bald, stood before me, hands on his hips. Six-six, at least. Nicely tailored suit. "Yes, that's right," I said. "I'm Josh Handleman."

"Detective Morris." He stuck out his hand and I shook it. Like shaking hands with a catcher's mitt. Not only large, but leathery, too. "This way." We got buzzed into the back, and I trailed him through a couple hallways into a large cubicle-filled room that looked more like an IBM office than a police station.

Morris pulled up short and I jammed on my brakes to avoid ramming into him. "Here we are," he said, gesturing to his cubicle. "Please." He nodded at the chair alongside his desk as he lowered himself into his and steepled his hands together. "Okay. Let's hear it."

On the drive over, I'd rehearsed how I'd tell my story. I couldn't remember a word of it now, so I just let fly. "I think my father was murdered. They found him on the floor, dead. Said he'd tumbled down the stairs. But I don't think so." I stopped for air and stared right into Morris' impassive face.

I waited for him to say something, but he simply nodded. *Go on.*

"I assumed it was an accident. Then I come to find my father's diamond collection missing. Two plus two …" I don't know why I said that, I never speak that way. My jangled nerves were getting in the way.

Morris picked up a pencil. "Spell Handleman."

I did and he jotted it down, then ripped off the sheet of paper from the pad and stood. "Back in a minute."

He left and I followed his head and shoulders above the half-height cubicle walls as he zigzagged through the room before disappearing through a doorway. Several cops glared at me as they passed Morris' cubicle, but maybe they weren't really glaring, maybe I just felt guilty of something. Maybe that's how everybody felt, sitting in the police station talking to a detective.

Morris' disembodied head appeared again, and I tracked his progress through the cubicle maze. He sat and flipped open a file he'd retrieved. Began reading in an even tone. "Abe Handleman. Died December 22. Unattended death. Ruled accidental." He looked at me. "That right?"

I nodded, then shook my head. "Except the accidental part, that is."

Morris closed the file and leaned his chair back until it touched a filing cabinet behind him. With the tip of a shoe, he pulled out a desk drawer and extended his long legs, resting them on top of the drawer. "Why do you think so?"

"Someone killed him to get his diamonds."

"Diamonds, huh?" Morris nodded at the closed folder on his desk. "Says there he tripped down the stairs. Doors were locked— dead bolted, too. Lived alone. My guy said the carpet on the stairs was threadbare. And that your father was … how did he phrase it? Handicapped?" He made no move to consult the file. Evidently, he'd read it and committed it to memory before he returned to the cubicle.

"My father used a cane, but he wasn't really handicapped." I'd found a handicapped hangtag on the rearview mirror in his car, and I'd ripped it up on my way to the funeral home. "I know it appears to be an accident, but I don't think it was."

"So you've said. But we need some evidence." His expression remained neutral. If he thought I was a crackpot, he wasn't letting on. At least not yet. "What about these diamonds?"

"My father owned a diamond collection. And it's been stolen."
I looked at Morris. "Don't you need to write this down? File a report or something?"

The beginning of a smile tugged at the sides of his mouth. "Why don't we talk things over first? Then we can file a report if we need to." The smile persisted, but it was ornamental only. No warmth. "Tell me about these diamonds. How many are missing?"

"All of them," I blurted out, then stopped to take a breath. "I mean, I don't know exactly."

"You don't know? How many diamonds did your father own?"

I swallowed. This wasn't going like I'd hoped. "I don't really know."

"You don't know?" Morris' brow furrowed. "Have you ever seen these diamonds?"

"No."

"Father talk about them a lot?"

"Uh, no, not really."

"Ever?" Morris asked, like he knew the answer to the question already.

"No, but he—"

"How do you know they exist?"

"People have told me. People who have seen them."

"Recently?"

I thought back to my conversation with Aunt Shel. She probably hadn't seen the diamonds in decades. "No, I don't think so."

Morris nodded. "Okay. What makes you think they were stolen and not lost, or given to someone, or sold? Or accidentally thrown in the trash?"

"He had an appointment with an appraiser on the day he died."

Morris' eyes flashed for an instant, then returned to their normal state. "And he'd seen them?"

The room was getting warmer. "No, he hadn't seen them yet. My father took the diamonds out of the safe deposit box the day before, and then he was killed on Friday and now they're missing. That's what makes me think they were stolen. By the murderer."

"Do you have receipts for the diamonds?"

I shook my head.

"Photos? Authentication certificates? Appraisal reports? Insurance papers?"

I shook my head again.

"Do you have anything *whatsoever* that proves the existence of these diamonds, besides the word of a few friends and relatives?" He pursed his lips. "And the appointment with the appraiser, of course."

"No. Unfortunately, I don't."

"Don't you think it's odd that your father had these diamonds, but that there's no paper trail?"

I wiped some perspiration from my forehead. That question had me stumped, too. "Look, I know there were diamonds."

"Mr. Handleman. Are you aware that stolen diamonds usually don't have paper trails?"

"They were not stolen, Detective. My father bought them over the years. I'm sure of it," I said.

He held up his hand. "Okay, assuming there are diamonds, how do you propose we go about searching for these diamonds without any documentation?"

I shrugged. "All you have to do is find his murderer."

Morris smiled. "That's a good plan." He wiped the smile off his face. "Let me ask you something, but please think before you answer it, because accusing innocent people is not something I tolerate." He stared at me. "Got any theories who might have done this? Father have any enemies ruthless enough to kill him?"

Kassian hardly fit that bill. Not ruthless. And if he did steal the diamonds, what was he still doing in my basement? My first instinct had been right. This was a mistake, a huge one. "No. None that I can really think of."

Morris picked up his pencil and spun it around in his fingers while his eyes bored into me. Then he kicked the desk drawer in with his feet, tipped his chair down, and sat forward. "Mr. Handleman. In no way do I wish to be disrespectful or to upset you. But I'm a straight-talking guy. So please do not be offended. Okay?"

I gave him a quick nod and he opened the file and removed a few photos. Slid them across the desk to me. "These are pictures from the scene."

In front of me was a picture of the carpet on the top step I'd been examining the other day. Close-up and in color. Morris spoke while I looked at the photos. "The report theorizes that your father's cane caught on the jagged edge of the carpet, throwing him off-balance. It probably didn't take much for him to fall. We see it a lot in the elderly." Morris stopped talking and gave me a look brimming with reproach. "Were you aware of the dangerous condition of the carpet in your father's home?"

I pressed my lips together. I'd brought it up on at least one occasion since Mom died, but it had fallen on deaf ears so I'd given up pestering, knowing how stubborn my father was. If only I'd been more persistent.

Morris flipped to the next page in the report. "The responding officer notes that the two EMTs concur in his assessment. The officer took a look around and found nothing out of the ordinary. No one in the house—the responders had to break in through a side door. No sign of a struggle. Nothing seemed to be amiss. Nothing obvious was missing. Per our procedures for an unattended death, the officer took some photos and made a few sketches. He attempted to contact next of kin, but the victim's—your father's, excuse me—sister did not answer her phone. Your father's friend..." Morris glanced at the report. "Lev Yurishenko provided the information."

I nodded, seeing where this was going. I guess I'd known it was a long shot, but...

"I'm sorry, Mr. Handleman. Truly."

I recognized a blow-off when I heard it. "So now what?" I asked. Part of me—the masochistic part—couldn't let it rest. Wanted things to go my way.

"Now?" Morris' eyebrows rose. "Now, I guess we'll see if any evidence turns up. And if it does, you be sure to get back to me, okay?"

"You're not going to do anything, are you?"

"I didn't say that," Morris said. He picked up the file and slid it into a gap on the computer table next to him, between the monitor and cubicle wall, along with about a dozen other folders. "I'm going to keep this file handy, right here. Where I can reach it real quick, just in case."

He couldn't have been any more patronizing if he'd winked as he said it.

NINETEEN

I NEEDED TO CONFRONT Kassian about his lies. Deception didn't sit kindly with me, and I wondered what other things he'd been lying about. Maybe, with a little persuasion from me, he'd remember something about my father's last moments and a little velvet bag of diamonds. If Detective Morris wanted evidence, I'd do my best to come up with some.

On my way home from the police station, I swung by the Hebrew Home to see if Kassian was there. A young woman with much less facial hair had replaced the old guy at the desk. She waved me through, barely glancing at my ID.

I checked the TV lounge and the card room, but came up empty. On my way to the snack bar, I bumped into DeRon, pushing a mop bucket down the hall. His face brightened. "Hello, Josh. How you doing today?"

"Fine, DeRon. You?"

"Dandy." He kicked the bucket with the toe of his work boot. "Just cleaned up some puke. Couldn't be better."

I flashed him a little smile to show I felt his pain. "Have you seen Kassian today?"

He shook his head. "Nope. Last I saw him was day before yesterday, in the evening. Had a special New Year's program a lot of the residents enjoyed. Showed some old Lawrence Welk and Guy Lombardo tapes. But I haven't seen him since."

Probably back in the woods on stakeout. "Okay, thanks." I turned to leave, but stopped. "Do you remember the day my father died?"

DeRon screwed his face up. "I remember Ms. Wolfe being upset. And Kassian too, when she told him. Tough to forget that."

"Right. The last time we talked, you said Kassian had been here all day, for some activities," I said, trying to prompt his memory.

"Yup. Fridays are music and movie days. I don't remember what we showed, though."

"Do you remember what time he got here?" I asked, trying to be casual with the question. Not sure I was pulling it off very well.

DeRon thought a moment. "Well, we show the movie at one. Before that was lunch, and before that we had some type of music program and then either Rabbi Roundtable or some arts and crafts project. That Friday was..." He ran a hand over his hair. "I think we had the Rabbi in. Yes, that's right, Rabbi Cohen."

"And Kassian was here for that?"

"Yes. He likes to sit up front. Even asks a question or two. He's not as uneducated as he lets on."

"So you're positive Kassian was here the entire day?"

DeRon cocked his head at me. Lifted his chin. "As far as I remember. What are you getting at?"

"Would someone else also remember seeing him?"

DeRon squinted at me.

"I'm not saying you don't remember. But it was probably busy, lots of people coming and going, and..."

"Sure it's busy. But if I said he was here, he was here," DeRon said, eyeing me as if I'd called his mother a round-heeled schvartz. "If you don't take my word, feel free to ask around." He grabbed the mop handle with both hands. "Bye, Mr. Handleman." He pushed the mop bucket down the hall, not looking back. I certainly wasn't trying, but I seemed to be pissing off a lot of people lately.

On my way out, I stopped in the lobby and called Rachel. It was after three-thirty, so I figured school had already let out and her little charges had scattered to the four winds. I composed a cute greeting in my mind while I waited for her to answer, but when she did, all I eked out was a glum, "Hello."

"Hi Josh Handleman," Rachel said, and I perked right up. Funny how small things can have such a large impact.

"I was thinking about you."

"I would have been thinking about you, too, but I've got a class of very active third-graders that command my attention." She laughed, and I could picture her crooked smile and scrunched-up nose. "Where are you?"

"At the Hebrew Home."

"What are you doing there? Checking out your father's library? Making sure the overdue fines are being collected?"

"Every quarter helps," I said. "Actually, I'm not doing much of anything."

"Say hi to Nana while you're there. She really likes you, *John*." More laughing. "Tell her we got married and I'm pregnant. That'll make her day."

"I tell her that, it might be her *last* day. Anyway, I was wondering if you'd like to go out to dinner tonight." I needed a rational shoulder to lean on. Kassian's lies and my visit to the police station had unnerved me. I felt as if my life had spun into the Twilight Zone.

"Oh, I'd love to, but I can't. Going to yoga class with a friend."

"Oh. Okay." My mood dipped again. I needed to get off this emotional roller coaster.

"But I'm free tomorrow night."

Back up the incline. "Great. It's a date." After some more innocuous flirting, I clicked off. I still needed to talk to Kassian. That should deflate my mood again.

The balmy weather we'd enjoyed the past couple of days had given way to a typically frigid January, and I jammed my hands deep in my pockets as I walked through the parking lot. Parked two cars away from mine was STOX3, Lev's SUV.

Maybe he'd like to hear about my discussion with Detective Morris. At least I could get him off my back. I marched back into the lobby and signed in again. Wondered if Carol pored through the visitor logs to see who was coming and going, and I wondered if there was some kind of limit to the number of times you could enter in a week. Getting barred from the Hebrew Home would be quite an accomplishment.

I expanded upon my earlier search and found Lev playing chess in the game room. As soon as he saw me, he hit the chess clock with the palm of his hand. Then he whispered something to his opponent, sprang up, and strode my way.

"Hello, Joshua. Have you been thinking about my plea to you?"

I held up both hands, palms out. "Relax, Lev. I went to the police today. Talked with a detective."

Lev's eyes got large. He grabbed my arm and pulled me out into the hallway. Then he glanced around and led me to an alcove in front of the men's room. "You told him about Kassian killing your father? What did he say?"

"I told him I thought my father's death wasn't an accident. That it was murder."

"And that Kassian killed him?" Lev eyed me.

I took a deep breath. "Actually, I don't believe I mentioned Kassian."

Lev's scowl deepened. "What did the detective say?"

"He showed me some photos. They are sure it is an accident. And I'm inclined to—"

"What about the diamonds? Did you tell them Kassian stole them after he killed your father?"

"I mentioned the missing diamonds. But I don't have any proof—receipts, insurance papers, anything—that proves they even exist. I'm not—"

"I will tell him. I have seen these diamonds." Lev tapped his chest with a finger.

"When? Ten years ago? My father could have sold them since then. You can't..." I broke it off. It was no use. Going to the cops had been a mistake, but I wouldn't be able to convince Lev of that.

"But they must investigate. They are the police. Please tell me it is not like in Russia. Where the police do only what the corrupt officials tell them. This is America."

"Evidence, Lev. Evidence. They're not going to spend time and money investigating just because the grief-stricken son of the victim and the victim's best friend have a *feeling*. They need something tangible."

Lev stared at me, face of granite.

I felt bad. Lev's last hope dashed. "Well, the detective did say he'd keep the file open on his desk, in case something came up. So …"

Lev's stare intensified and the muscles in his jaw rippled.

"I'm sorry, Lev. It's time for you to let go. It's time to let my father rest in peace." As I left, I glanced back over my shoulder at Lev. He watched me go, eyes narrowed to slits, body inert, fists clenched by his sides.

TWENTY

THE DARKNESS ENVELOPED ME, pressing against my skin with a palpable weight, threatening to suffocate me. I sat still and controlled my breathing, forcing my mind to avoid certain thoughts, certain alleys I'd rather not wander down. Emulating some mysterious type of Eastern philosophy I'd read about once, where you flushed all thoughts of the past and visions of the future from your mind so you can exist only in the now. But it was hard with four or five beers in my system, with death and diamonds having been front and center for so many days. I tried chasing away the nasty thoughts with mind-photos of Rachel. Her lopsided smile, the crooked teeth. The cascade of dark hair on her shoulders. Other senses got into the act. The sweet smell of her shampoo, the silkiness of her smooth skin against mine.

Those sensations proved to be temporary, replaced by the ugly pictures that had been seared into my brain. Kassian's face. Lev's scowl. The cane on the floor, the death-scene photos of the frayed carpet. I hadn't seen pictures of my father's body, lying in a heap, but I knew they existed. Detective Morris had been considerate in not showing them, even if he was a patronizing son-of-a-bitch. I could envision the stark photos, my father's eyes wide open, mouth twisted in the last throes of a desperate scream for help. Or mercy. I gulped down the rest of my beer and reached for another. I didn't need any light, I knew where the six-pack was, next to me, my only true friend, keeping me company in the dark.

I sat motionless in Kassian's room, all notions of controlling my thoughts like some kind of swami gone to shit. I thought about Dani and tried to remember how she smelled, with little success. I thought about Handleman & Stutz, Liquidators, and felt nothing but contempt. Kassian, Lev, diamonds, that asshole Brandon, secrets, Carol, all marched past the reviewing stand in my parade of thoughts. Even the hairy guy behind the desk at the Hebrew Home made a cameo. I gulped more beer.

My gloomy reverie was interrupted by the sound of the key in the lock. The door creaked open and the room exploded in light.

"Good evening, Kassian," I said, shielding my eyes from the sudden brightness.

Kassian jumped back. When he saw who it was, he let out his breath. "Hello, Joshua." He shut the door, but didn't come forward. His hand remained on the doorknob.

"I've been wanting to talk to you, but you're a hard man to track down, you know?" The words sounded different now that I was saying them aloud, rather than thinking them as I had been for the past two hours. I was pretty buzzed and wondered if Kassian could tell. When I realized he was speaking, I focused on his lips.

"What?" I said.

"I said I've been around. Nowhere special, really."

"Uh huh. Right. Been in the woods?" I pointed my can of beer at him.

"The woods?" The little man's gaze didn't settle on anything. Suspicious eyes bounced around the room.

"Don't lie. Not anymore. I followed you. To your hideout in the woods. By the golf course. Come on, Kassian. Spill."

He swallowed and his Adam's apple danced. "I like the solitude. No one bothers me there."

I closed my eyes and pictured him yanking the door open and dashing off into the night, never to return. When I opened my eyes, he was still there, cowering by the door. "I do not believe you."

"It's the tr—"

"Cut the shit. You're full of lies. You told my father you were his cousin. What about that?" I held out my beer again.

Kassian looked down at his shoes. Mumbled something.

"Speak up. And the truth would be nice for a change." Part of me felt like getting up and squeezing his little neck until the truth popped out. Part of me felt like going to sleep and waking up when the nightmare was over.

"I am your father's cousin. One of his uncles was my father."

"Yeah, I know how cousins work. But I don't believe you."

Kassian shrugged. "It is the truth. I am sorry you do not believe me."

"Listen up, Kassian. Something's going on around here. And I think you know more than you're telling me. I plan on finding out. Everything." I hoisted myself out of the chair. Turned around and set my can of beer down on the seat. Waited a second for a wave of dizziness to settle. Kassian hadn't moved, but his eyes had grown, and I could smell his fear. I walked toward him, and as I got closer my anger blossomed.

I stopped two feet in front of him. Looked down. Glowered at him. He stood his ground, but his face tightened. "Goddamn it. I want some answers."

He recoiled as if I'd struck him. But he didn't speak.

I reached out and grabbed his chin, tilted it up at me. "Did you steal the diamonds?" I asked, the voice in my head screaming.

He shook his head, as best he could with my hand holding it. I squeezed harder. "Did you kill my father?"

This time, Kassian shook his head more forcefully, and I let go. "No. Do not say such things. I loved your father."

I stepped back, breathing heavy. What was I doing? My face flushed and I knew it was more than the beer. "I'm … I'm sorry, Kassian."

The fear in his face had morphed into something else. Pity. Anger. Defiance. Sadness. I wasn't sure what it was exactly, but it pierced my alcoholic haze. He smoothed his sweater. "Maybe I should go. Leave. Find someplace else to live where I would be more welcome. You are clearly not your father's son."

I eyed him, thinking. After a long moment, I gave him my reply, someone else's words using my voice. "Maybe you should."

After all, I *wasn't* my father's son, was I? He'd told me that himself plenty of times.

———

The next morning, I slept until ten o'clock. Again. Last night's drinking binge hadn't produced a restful sleep, and I knew if I wanted to, I could sleep another four hours. But excessive sleeping was a sign of depression, and I didn't want to believe that I was getting more depressed than I already was.

My head pounded as I maneuvered myself to the edge of the bed and replayed my encounter with Kassian. I wasn't a particularly happy drunk, and on the few occasions in my past when I'd imbibed to excess, I usually had some mess to clean up. Nice to know some things hadn't changed.

I threw on some clothes and clambered downstairs to apologize. Kassian was plainly keeping secrets, but I didn't really think he could be involved in anything more serious than that. It just didn't add up. My accusations had been out of line, fueled by frustration and alcohol. I hoped he would forgive me for manhandling him. And for suggesting that maybe he should move out. Despite his furtiveness and odd habits, I'd started to become attached to the old guy.

Too late. A neatly made bed greeted me. The elusive old Russian had slipped out again. I checked his drawers and they still contained his clothes, so he hadn't taken off for good. I'd have a chance to apologize later.

Instead of a big breakfast, I popped two Motrin and gnawed on half a slice of plain bread, cringing with the knowledge that I'd be eating lunch in a couple hours with Matt and Goose. They'd invited me over to check out their company's new digs and talk about "something exciting." As long as exciting didn't mean painful or uncomfortable or shocking—in a bad way—I would be all right.

I killed an hour at Target looking at "storage solutions," then drove over to a mixed-use office/industrial park in Herndon. A utilitarian sign, "VidGamZZZ, Inc.," was the only thing that distinguished their office from the other fifty or sixty housed in five boxy warehouse buildings on the west end of the park. Half a dozen restaurants—of varied ethnicities—occupied another building in the middle, and a mid-rise traditional office building anchored the east end of the complex. Judging by all the empty spaces in the lot as I drove by, Herndon's commercial real estate market was as depressed as I was.

I pushed the door open to a jingling bell overhead. But it was so noisy, I'm sure no one heard. A dozen people chased a red rubber playground ball, playing some unique form of basketball on a mini-court in the middle of the high-ceilinged converted warehouse. The baskets looked like they were about eight feet high, rather than the regulation ten feet.

Computer geeks cum jocks, wearing jeans and shorts and skirts and suits, ran and jumped and jostled for position. One woman rolled along the sidelines in an office chair yelling instructions, metal casters screeching. A short guy on the team in yellow "pennies" broke free from his defender and drove to the hoop. His attempt at a tomahawk dunk failed, and players on both teams jeered. He retrieved the ball and pegged it at the guy heckling loudest, hitting him in the chest. The two squared off in a mock fight, much to the delight of the on-lookers.

Goose saw me and blew a whistle hanging from his neck. "Okay, everybody. Break's fini. Back to it." The players drifted off and Goose ambled over. "Hey, man. What do ya think?" He swept his arms at the court. "Had it custom designed for our space. Nice, huh? We had to come up with something to match Google's perks. Did you know they have on-site massages?"

"I didn't realize you were in Google's weight class." I looked around. "It's nice, though. Where's Matt?"

"He'll meet us at lunch. Come on, let me give you a little tour."

I followed Goose past a couple rows of desks. A computer and two sleek side-by-side LCD monitors rested on each desk next to game consoles. Video games played on every one, a choreographed ballet of motions, colors, and looped soundtracks. "Must be pretty swell, getting paid for doing what you'd do anyway," I said.

Goose looked hurt. "Hey, there's a lot of work involved here. It's not all fun and games." He frowned, then his face lit up. "Fuck that. It's awesome. Sometimes I have to remind myself I have a life to go home to." His grin faded. "Don't tell Carla I said that, okay?"

"Don't worry. I've never even met Carla."

Goose continued the tour, and we entered a large room in the back. Pushed off to one side against the wall, a foosball table gathered dust, a dinosaur from the pre-electronic age. Mounted on one wall was Goose's *pièce de résistance*, a 100-inch hi-definition plasma screen. In front of it, four gamers reclined in specially built chairs, working controllers furiously as a quartet of armor-clad mutants battled on screen for supremacy of some sci-fi fantasy world.

As I watched, one of the mutants sliced off the head of another with a futuristic, three-bladed laser machete. A fountain of crimson blood spurted through the vanquished creature's neck-hole. "Cool, huh?" Goose asked, eyes transfixed.

"It's something, all right." And it *was* mesmerizing. I could see how millions of teenagers—and older kids-at-heart—got addicted. I'd played some Madden Football over the years, but Dani hadn't been too keen on me wasting time in front of the screen.

"Come on, let's go. I'm hungry. If we don't get there soon, Matt will demolish all the breadsticks."

Tutti Frutti's was some slacker's idea of an Italian restaurant. Dave Mathews Band blared from the speakers, and red and white plastic pennants festooned the walls. Four giant plasma screens showed YouTube-style clips. The male waiters all sported long sideburns and the females displayed a variety of face piercings. Considering the crowd of twenty- and thirty-somethings scarfing down their lunches, the brains behind the Tutti Frutti facade knew what they were doing when it came to concept dining.

"You guys eat here often?" I asked, as a hostess with multi-hued hair showed us to our table. We'd found Matt in the lounge area, playing Golden Tee, the video golf game.

"Couple of times a week," Matt said, opening his arms. "We are amongst our own. A lot of the tech guys from up and down the corridor come here." Dozens of high-tech companies—heavy in telecom, software, and defense—had erected outposts along the Dulles Toll Road. This was just one of many hangouts they flocked to.

The hostess handed us our menus and left. "So what's good here?" I asked.

"I always get a cheeseburger," Matt said.

"And I always get fish and chips," Goose said.

"At an Italian restaurant? Why did we come here?"

"We like the breadsticks," Matt and Goose said in unison.

Our server came and we ordered. The usual for them, lasagna for me. When she left, they both made faces. "Dude, seriously, the Italian food sucks here," Goose said. "Except for the cannolis."

"I'll risk it." I set my menu down. "So—"

"Did you find the diamonds yet?" Goose said, leaning forward across the table.

"Jesus, Goose," Matt said, shaking his head. "Give the guy a break."

I looked from one to the other. "How do you know about the diamonds?"

The brothers exchanged glances. "Erik might have mentioned something about it," Goose said.

So much for a lawyer's—or a friend's—confidentiality. "He did, huh?"

"Don't rat on us, Josh. He's worried about you," Matt said. "We all are."

"So? Did you find them?" Goose asked. Matt shot him another dirty look.

I shook my head. "Nope. But ..." A grin made its way to my lips. The questions about the missing diamonds were getting to me. I'd give Erik's chain a yank, courtesy of the Spoletti gossip connection.

"What are you going to do?" Matt asked.

"I went to the cops yesterday to discuss the case." Both sets of eyes were glued to me. "And the detective said they were this close ..." I held my thumb and forefinger an inch apart. "... to solving the case and nailing the scumbag who stole them. I should have my diamonds back before the end of the week." I leaned back, smiling to myself, thinking about Erik's face as Goose or Matt relayed my tall tale. It was a policy of mine—never pass up a chance to tweak Erik. I wondered how long it would take for him to get back to me.

"That's great," Goose said. "Congrats." He clinked his water glass against mine.

"Thanks." I took a sip of water. Maybe I could put the diamonds behind me now. "So, tell me about this 'exciting opportunity' you wanted to let me in on." It sounded like an Amway pyramid scheme or something.

Goose looked at Matt and Matt nodded.

"Okay," Goose said. "We want you to do some consulting for us." He paused to gauge my initial reaction.

What did I know about hard-core video games? Seeing their set-up, I was convinced I'd be a stranger in a strange land, struggling to keep from having my head chopped off. "What kind of consulting?"

"We thought you could help us out with the launch of our new product, *Siege and Conquest*. On the business end of things. You know, create some publicity, smooth out the distribution problems," Goose said.

"Problems already? I thought it hadn't even launched yet," I said.

Goose's eyebrows came together. "There are *always* distribution problems. On-line, bricks and mortar, wholesalers, retailers, it doesn't matter. Screw-ups are inevitable."

Matt interjected. "You can be our firestopper. Our secret weapon in the never-ending war against incompetence." The server returned and set a basket on the table. Matt's hand darted underneath the folded white napkin and pulled out a warm breadstick. He took a bite. "What do you say, Josh? Interested?" he said around the food in his mouth.

"Why me? There must be more qualified guys around."

"Come on, Josh. Don't sell yourself short. You started a business and grew it. That takes the kind of talent we need. Besides . . ." Goose said. He glanced at Matt, sitting next to him, munching on another breadstick. "Your father was good to us. We want to repay the favor."

"What do you mean he was good to you?"

Matt swallowed. "Your father invested in us. Listened to our plans for expansion and lent us a hand. And a chunk of capital. Without your father's help, we'd be at the mercy of the venture guys. You'd be eating lunch with one of them right now. And it wouldn't be at Tutti Frutti's. It'd be at someplace where they have linen napkins and serve food you couldn't pronounce, let alone digest."

"He invested in your business?" I asked.

"Yeah. He really came through for us," Goose said.

Matt grabbed my forearm. "We owe your father a lot. Let us help you out, just until you get something else going. It's not a handout. We know you'd be good at it. We need you."

The bullshit was getting deep and I'd left my galoshes behind. "How much did he invest?"

Goose glanced at Matt, who shrugged. "He owns—owned—eight percent of the company."

I tried to get my head around this latest revelation. My father had a stake in a video game company owned by my friends. My father. Video games. My friends. The surprises kept on coming. "So what happens to my father's stake in your company now?"

"It's part of the estate. The lawyers will figure it all out. But I guess, technically, the Hebrew Home owns it." Goose shrugged, glancing again at his brother. Matt shrugged back.

I shook my head and smiled, thinking of the irony. *Siege and Conquest*, brought to you, in part, by the aged and infirm of the Reston Hebrew Home. I wondered what Rachel's Nana would think of three-bladed laser machetes.

Our lunches came, and the Spoletti boys were right. The lasagna sucked.

TWENTY-ONE

I LET RACHEL PICK the movie, and she chose some chick flick with a name that sounded like every other chick flick: *Hearts in Love*, or *Forever Together*, or *All Guys Are Gaseous Goofs*. It starred the latest sensations, whom I didn't recall seeing before. She liked it. I didn't, but I liked the fact she liked it.

We stopped at Wisconsin's Best Frozen Custard on the way home despite the arctic temperatures. According to Rachel, it was never too cold for frozen confections.

"Thanks for the movie," she said. "I wasn't sure you'd like it." She licked her chocolate cone around the side, creating a spiral trail in the custard.

"Had a great time." I nodded, adding a sincere, "Really." We were the only two people in the store, except for the girl behind the counter. I took a big bite of my cone, also chocolate.

"Well, even if you didn't *really* like it, thanks for going with me. I needed a relaxing evening."

"Kids get you down today?"

"No. I love my kids. It was the parents. They're the ones you have to watch out for." She took another lick, and some custard smeared on her chin. I reached over and wiped it off with a napkin.

"Thanks," she said, and her face brightened. "I really love kids. I'd like to have a whole brood of them." Her eyes caught mine.

"Yeah, kids," I said. Dani and I had talked about having them, but neither of us was one hundred percent behind the idea. Luckily, we didn't pursue it. I took a couple bites of frozen custard. Tasted like ice cream to me.

"What? You don't like kids?"

"I didn't say that. I like kids just fine."

Rachel worked on her cone. After a minute of diligent effort, she came up for air. "So, tell me about your childhood. What warped you so much you don't like kids?" She smiled when she said it, but it had a different quality than her other unadulterated smiles.

"I didn't say I didn't like kids." My decibel level rose.

Rachel stared at me. "So, about your childhood?"

"Just the usual, I guess. My father was pretty hard on me. Wanted me to make something of myself. Wanted me to live up to my potential."

"Don't all parents want that?"

"I think my father went over the top. He was always so forgiving, so considerate to others. My friends, other relatives, complete strangers even. With me, though..." I'd finished the custard off the top, so I bit into the cone. Like cardboard, stale cardboard. "Even in his death, he managed to..." The words just stopped. I cleared my throat. "Bottom line: In my father's eyes, I was never good enough."

Rachel took my hand, squeezed it. "I think you're good enough." She smiled, and it was back to the old version. The thousand-watt smile. "Just barely good enough. So there's plenty of room for improvement."

"Thanks." I squeezed her hand back.

"I'm a good talker, Josh," she said. "But I'm a *very* good listener. I'd like to hear more about your father."

She knew my father had died, of course, but I hadn't told her any details of the past two weeks. I'd wanted to keep all that unpleasantness—Lev's insistence the death wasn't an accident, the missing gems, my berating of Kassian, the shafting my father gave me in his will—out of my relationship with Rachel. I wanted what we had to be untainted. But I guess I realized that was impossible and ultimately lethal to any hope of something good evolving between us. Trust was paramount.

So as we sat in the deserted shop eating the last bites of our frozen custard, I filled her in on the crazy, mixed-up world of Josh Handleman.

As I talked, she mostly nodded and touched my shoulder, letting me get it all off my chest without interrupting. Like I was another of her nine-year-old students telling a painful story about some playground transgression. I'm sure she was a great teacher.

Wanting to change the subject and not sound like such a whiner, I told her about the game of telephone I was playing with Matt, Goose, and Erik. It didn't help; I still felt like a little kid with a skinned knee. Emotions were such pesky things.

My cell phone rang in my pocket. I ignored it, but it rang again. And again.

"Aren't you going to answer that?" Rachel said. "Maybe it's Erik getting back to you." She smiled, getting into the little joke almost as much as I was.

I hesitated and the phone rang again.

"It's okay. Go ahead." Rachel held her hand out.

"Okay. Just a sec," I said, pulling out the phone and flipping it open. I didn't recognize the number, although it had a Northern California area code. I shook my head at Rachel and mouthed, "not Erik." Into the phone I said, "Hello."

"Josh. I need to talk with you."

Dani. She'd switched phones on me. "Look, now's not—"

"Heath and I broke up. I'm…" Sniffling in the background. "I need to talk."

Heath was quite the life-wrecker. Mine, now Dani's. I turned away from Rachel and lowered my voice. "Can I call you later? I'm in the middle of something." I glanced over my shoulder. She was concentrating on her cone.

"Oh, Josh. I really fucked up. We made a mistake. I need to talk with you. Please." Dani sounded like she'd had a couple gin and tonics, her reliable stand-by. I shielded the phone even more, as best I could without giving Rachel my entire back to gaze at. "Look, I'll call you later. Okay? Call one of your girlfriends in the meantime. Yvette's good to talk to."

"Josh, don't—"

"I'll call you later. Bye." I disconnected and turned my phone off. Twisted back to face Rachel. "Sorry about that." One more pain in my side.

"Everything all right?"

"Just … nothing. Not important," I said. "You still eating?"

Rachel's features tightened. "Josh. Whoever you were talking to sounded upset."

My mouth had gotten dry. "Yeah, listen, that was my ex. She's—"

"Oh. You don't need to explain," she said, holding up her hand. "It's none of my business. I mean, you had a life before you met me, right?" She glanced at the big clock on the wall, with ice cream scoops as the hands. "It's getting late and I have to get up early. Let's call it a night, shall we?"

I drove her to her townhouse, which she shared with a couple of fellow teachers, and walked her to the door. She didn't invite me in. I kissed her goodnight and she kissed back, but it was more chaste than exciting. "I'm sorry, Josh. I'm kinda tired and I have to wake up early. A girl can have an off night, can't she?"

I wasn't sure if she meant a "night off" or a sub-par night, but I didn't ask her to explain. "Sure. Sleep well. Pleasant dreams and all that." I turned to go, but she called out.

"Josh. I'll phone you. Okay?" Something flashed across her face.

"Sure," I said, not sure if I was getting blown off for good. "Sure."

I guess nobody likes a whiner.

———

I drove home, wondering what the hell had just happened. Rachel and I were really hitting it off. Common interests, same values, physical attraction. Most importantly, she laughed at all my jokes. And then, splat.

Was it the capricious nature of budding relationships? Or was it something more personal? Something about me she didn't like? Maybe it really was my whining that turned her off. I reviewed the topics of our last discussion. Kids, my father, suspicions of murder. The phone call from Dani. Could Rachel be jealous? If so, it was an easy fix. I'd just explain that I had absolutely no more feelings for Dani. Piece of cake.

I came up with a romantic plan involving flowers, candy, and a passionate Handleman original poem to chase away her green monster. I was home before I knew it, hope rekindled.

When I pulled into my driveway, the kitchen light shone through the front window. I knew I didn't leave it on, so that meant Kassian must have returned. A wave of relief washed over me. I'd been worried that he'd followed through on his threat to leave, driven out by my obnoxious—and intimidating—behavior. Now I had a chance to apologize.

When I opened the front door, the foyer was dark—no light spilled in from the kitchen. Strange. Was the old Russian playing some kind of hide-and-seek game? "Kassian?" I called out. Something tickled at my nose. Not a smell really, but a sense. A sense that somebody had been there, in my house. A sense that something was different.

I flipped on the foyer light. "Kassian? You here?" I went to the top of the stairs and peered down. No light on there. The hair on my forearms tingled. Was I letting my nerves get the better of me? Or had someone broken in? With everything that had happened, I didn't want to take any chances.

I slid open the door to the hall closet and my eyes fell on my father's cane, hanging on the rod. I remembered the day I'd first

172

heard Kassian rustling in the basement, but this time I eschewed the cane for a more formidable weapon. I reached around the frame of the closet to where my father used to keep an old wooden baseball bat—left over from my Little League days—tucked away for just such an emergency. I let out a breath as my fingers closed around the handle. I pulled it out, thankful my father hadn't been a complete pacifist.

I hefted the Louisville Slugger in my hands and called out again, emboldened. "Anyone here?" After a silent moment, I added, "I've called the cops. They're on their way. And I've got a weapon, too. Don't make me use it."

Slowly, I inched toward the stairs, convinced I heard the floorboards creaking from above. Holding the bat tightly, I took the stairs one at a time.

A sound behind me sent my heart racing. The lights went out as I spun around, and something hard and heavy smashed into the side of my head, knocking me off balance. I collided with the wall, then lost my footing and tumbled down a few stairs onto the floor of the foyer. The front door banged closed as the intruder fled into the night.

I scrambled to my feet and ran to the door, but didn't see or hear anything. After a couple fruitless moments staring into the black night, I turned the hall light back on. On the floor, in the same spot where I'd found my father's cane, were the baseball bat and a slightly dented can of pineapple juice. The object I'd been whacked with. My head smarted where I'd been struck, but it had been a glancing blow. The attack had startled me more than anything else. I'd also banged my right elbow on something as I fell, but I'd live. Nothing a little ice wouldn't relieve.

I picked up the can of juice and went to the kitchen. The pantry door hung wide open. Evidently, the intruder heard me come home and hid in there, then busted out and assaulted me after he heard me mention the cops. I placed the juice back on the shelf and closed the door. I guess I needed to report the break-in to the police, but the thought of talking to another skeptical officer wasn't very comforting.

Maybe a beer first would help. I started to the fridge, but did a double take when I saw a surprise waiting for me. There, in the middle of the old oak kitchen table where I'd done my homework as a kid, was a present.

A black velvet jewelry bag.

TWENTY-TWO

THE BAG SAT THERE, mocking me. *Here I am. Can you find me now? Open me up, c'mon, open me! Open me, Josh. See what's inside.*

Slowly, I walked to the table and picked up the velvet bag. Lighter than it looked. Shook it and heard a barely audible clicking. I wedged one finger into the opening, wiggling it to loosen the drawstring.

I held the bag with a trembling hand and tilted the contents into my other palm. A few diamonds tumbled out. Clear, cut, sparkling diamonds. I stared at them, tilting my hand back and forth to catch the light until a chilly draft distracted me. The piece of cardboard that had been taped to the broken windowpane by the kitchen door was hanging by a lone piece of tape.

Someone had broken in to return the diamonds. I put the diamonds back in the bag and pulled the drawstring closed. Set off to search the house to see if anything else was missing. Or if anything new had materialized.

Satisfied everything seemed normal—at least under the circumstances—I returned to the kitchen table with my booty. Got a dark colored dishtowel and spread it out. Then I dumped the contents of the jewelry bag onto it, spreading the diamonds with my fingers. There were dozens of stones, but I counted the entire lot, one-by-one. Twice. Exactly fifty.

I ran upstairs to get a magnifying glass and dashed back to the kitchen, not wanting to leave them alone for more than a few seconds. Now that I had them, I didn't want to take any chances. I examined some at random. They all looked about the same size, not small but not gargantuan, and I couldn't discern anything about the other 3 "c's"—cut, clarity, or color. To me, they looked like diamonds.

I pawed over them for another hour and a half, concentrating on the natural beauty of the diamonds themselves and waiting for the adrenaline rush to subside. Now that I'd gotten over the one-two shocks of being assaulted and then finding the diamonds, I felt depleted. It was late and I was tired. And I didn't have the energy to wrestle with the three-hundred-pound alligator that had crawled into my brain, asking the same question over and over: What the hell was going on?

———

I woke up the next morning, head resting on a lumpy pillow, not sure what was reality and what was the stuff of dreams. I reached under my pillow and pulled out the bag of diamonds. Question answered. Not the larger question, but at least I knew I wasn't going crazy.

Thankfully, no knot had risen on my head where I'd been "juiced." Just a little tender. And my elbow didn't hurt at all. I'd been lucky and knew it, but I also knew relying on luck was a risky long-term strategy.

I dressed and checked to see if Kassian had returned. He hadn't. I needed to track him down. To apologize for what I'd said and done to him, and to find out if he knew anything about the returned diamonds. I hoped he hadn't fallen off the wagon again, and I felt like a total shit for lashing out at him like I had. I wonder if my father had felt this level of responsibility for the old guy, too.

I continued my new breakfast regimen of bran and bananas with skim milk. Maybe after a few months, I would actually learn to like the taste, but I considered crumbling up a Pop-Tart and throwing it in the bowl, at least as a stepping-stone. Then I heard Kassian's voice in my head, razzing me about my breakfast pastry and vowed to stay the course.

As I shoveled in the tasteless glop, I thought about the break-in. I had a lot of mental discipline, but I could force myself to ignore what had happened for only so long. I wasn't sure what to call the incident. Could you call it a burglary if the intruder *left* something of value?

Who would steal diamonds and then return them? I figured if you were dishonest enough to take something like that, then you would follow through and sell them. It wasn't like shoplifting a CD or something. Fifty diamonds had to be worth some serious cash.

After I forced down the final mouthfuls of cereal, I pulled out my cell phone and flicked it on. Six messages waited. I retrieved them and wasn't too surprised that five were from Dani. What with all the gemology I'd practiced last night, I'd forgotten to call her back. I glanced at my watch, but it was too early now, especially if she'd had a late night drinking. Her breakup didn't really make me feel good—I wasn't the vengeful type. Of course, it didn't really surprise me either. Heath had been a good *business* partner, but he had his share of personal foibles, lack of commitment and false loyalty being high on the list. Maybe that's what attracted Dani—two peas in a pod of deceit.

The sixth call was from Aunt Shel. Her toilet was clogged and she wanted me to come by and fix it. At least somebody wanted me for something I could actually accomplish.

I clicked through my list of outgoing calls until I found the diamond guy. Hit the send button. After a moment, the receptionist answered and put me through to Yakov Sapperstein.

"Hello, Yakov? This is Josh Handleman."

There was a slight hesitation, then Yakov said, "Yes, yes. Of course. How are you?" Salesman-friendly, with a tinge of the famous Big Apple impatience.

"Fine. I was wondering if you were still planning on being down here this week?"

A pause. "Yes. I am taking my son to the museums. His school doesn't start until next week and he's been dying to see the Air and Space." Another pause. "Why do you ask?"

"My father's diamonds have, uh, resurfaced. I was hoping you could come by and give me an appraisal."

"Yes, of course." A little more verve found its way into Yakov's voice. "We are taking the train this evening. How about tomorrow morning, around ten? I have the address and directions already. I look forward to it."

I marked it on my calendar and started a to-do list on a piece of notepaper I got from the junk drawer. Fix Aunt Shel's toilet, find Kassian, call Dani, call people to tell them I'd found what I'd been searching for. I stopped writing, knowing these action items would be all I could tackle without having to reshuffle the priorities and add new tasks to the list. Stuff always changed.

———

The security chain rattled from behind the thin door, followed by the thunk of the dead bolt. The door cracked open and Aunt Shel's face poked out. She squinted at me from inside her darkened house.

"Morning, Shel. You need a plumber?" I hoisted the plunger onto my shoulder and jangled a small bucket with a few wrenches and screwdrivers I held in my other hand.

She eyed me for a second, then swung the door open. "Don't you call first?" She turned her back to me and receded into the house, like an ebb tide.

I followed her into the darkness. All the lights were out. From somewhere in the back, I heard the frantic tones of some morning talk show on TV. "Have you morphed into a vampire? How about turning on some lights?" I flipped the switch for a nearby lamp. It cast wan shadows across the living room, the light barely reaching the far wall. What was in there, a 10-watt bulb?

Aunt Shel flopped onto the old couch, her housedress billowing around her knees. Today's schmatta had a different pattern than the last one I'd seen, but it was of the same vintage—ancient. In the dim light, she looked every bit of her many years. My father's death had accelerated her march to join him. I set my stuff down and went over to kiss her hello, to see up close what kind of shape she was in.

I bent over, and a vaguely medicinal, peachy smell rose up to greet me. I stepped back before completing the kiss. "Shel, have you been at it already?"

She waved me off, as if it were no big deal. A warning sign right there. "Just a little eye-opener. Haven't been sleeping well."

I scanned the room for the bottle, but she must have hid it when she heard the doorbell. "Schnapps isn't the answer. I'll take you to see someone, if you want."

She shook her head in that way she did when she thought you were spouting foolishness. Then she studied me. "Looks good on you."

It took me a second to realize what she was referring to. I was wearing my father's old parka. Since I'd been back, I'd been too stubborn to put it on when it had gotten really cold, but today ... Maybe I was coming to terms with things.

"Abe always used to wear that coat, all winter long." Her wizened face had a wistful look. Nostalgia and schnapps, a potent combo. "*Zitsen.*" Sit.

I took the wing chair opposite her. "Can I ask you a question?"

"Of course. Ask away." She scooted up on the couch a little.

"What do you know about Kassian?"

Aunt Shel frowned. "What do you want to know? How your father took him in like he was family? Treated him like a king?"

"Kassian says he *is* family."

Again with the hand wave. "I know what he says. And it does not matter what I think. Since Abe started helping him, he had been much happier." She leaned toward me. "Abe liked to help the needy and I don't suppose there are too many needier than Kassian."

"You think my father knew Kassian was lying?"

"Maybe, maybe not. It doesn't matter. You know his determination to help Russian Jews, no?" She stared at me, waiting for a response. I nodded. "He would do almost anything to help a persecuted Jew. So when Kassian tells him he is a cousin, Abe wants to believe him, even if he knows in his head it is a lie." She licked her lips. "What harm is done? Abe gets to help someone and Kassian gets food and a roof over his head. Everyone wins."

"But could he be related to us?"

Aunt Shel leaned back on the sofa. "Ach, what does it matter?"

"It matters to me," I said. "It matters to me a lot." I was getting tired of the runaround. If my life was going down the tubes, at least I deserved to know the truth about things.

"There is no need to get hostile, Joshua." She glared at me for a second, then settled back. "You know we had relatives in the Soviet Union?"

I'd heard generalities, but no details. "That's what my father used to say. But I never heard names."

"Our father—your grandfather, who you never met—used to tell stories to Abe and me. When we were children. About great thinkers and inventors. Big machers. We never knew whether they were true or not, and we did not really care. He told them with so much excitement it made our family seem special." She looked at me. "Do you know what I mean?"

I nodded, remembering the passion my father had when he talked about his support of Soviet Jewry.

"When we got older, Abe tried to track down some of these relatives." She stopped and examined her hands clasped in her lap.

"And what happened?"

"Your father was a persistent man. He discovered many interesting things about our family."

"Like what?" Interesting or alarming?

"Most things you would not care about. But..." she paused and smoothed out her dress. "I believe I heard Abe mention the name Kassian. A long time ago."

"So Kassian *is* related to us? I wish you'd just tell me the truth, Shel. You owe it to me. You owe it to my father." Sometimes you just had to pull out the big guns.

"*Oy gevalt*, Josh. Settle down. I will tell you, although I did not even tell your father. I didn't want to make him feel like he'd been fooled. Now that he's passed..." She looked up at the ceiling and her lips moved in a short, silent prayer. She met my eyes. "How about a little drink first?" She started to get up, but I motioned her back onto her cushion.

"We can have a drink later. Tell me what you know first." I softened. "Please?"

Aunt Shel sighed. "Years ago, I got a letter from my Great Aunt Ina in Poland. She had stayed behind when the rest of her family—our family—came to this country. She had some distant relatives in Russia, but I don't remember exactly how they were related. Anyway, she tells me that one of her cousins is married to a man named Kassian." Aunt Shel stopped and looked at me to see if I was paying attention.

"Go on, I'm listening."

"Good, because I do not think I could repeat this story," Aunt Shel said, giving her head a little wiggle. "Ina says that this Kassian was very ill. But before he died, he 'sold' his name to another man. Then this man used his new name to leave Russia and come here. And hook up with his cousin Abe."

Kassian was an imposter? "Are you telling me that our Kassian, the one living in my house, is a fake?"

Aunt Shel shrugged. "I do not know. Aunt Ina was old and her Yiddish was not so good. The facts might have been lost. Or twisted. But I do not think Abe's friend is who he says he is."

"So who is he?" I asked.

"What does it matter? Your father befriended him. And he is a harmless old man, no?"

"Don't you want to know the truth, Shel?" I asked, feeling that the elusive truth was drifting out to sea, never to be recovered. "Why didn't you ever tell my father about this? Surely he would have wanted to know."

"It would not have mattered. He would have only felt poorly about his judgment. Sometimes your father was too kind. I used to say he never met a man he couldn't help." She smiled. "Even as a child, he would be nice to the neighborhood urchins. Of course, he was a bit of an urchin himself."

I stood and paced across the room. Letting it sink in. It was unlikely something that happened so long ago had any bearing on the events of the past couple weeks. If Aunt Shel and her Great Aunt Ina were right, my father's boarder *became* Kassian more than forty years ago.

Surprising as it was, Aunt Shel's history lesson led me no closer to finding out what Kassian was up to, in this decade, in this country. When I found him, though, I'd be sure to ask about his lineage.

I glanced at Aunt Shel. Her eyes were glued to me as I paced the floor. "What?" I asked.

"I'm worried about you, Josh. I'm old and I have enough money to last until … to last as long as I do. But you're so young."

"I can get a job, Shel. I'm employable, you know." I didn't elaborate about my big future in video game consulting.

She looked at me like I had just fibbed about breaking a window playing baseball in the backyard. "I just wish …"

I cut her misery short, pulling the velvet bag out of my pocket.

TWENTY-THREE

"OH MY GOD. YOU found the diamonds." The crushing weight seemed to have lifted from Aunt Shel's shoulders.

"Here they are," I said, holding the bag from the top and shaking it like a velvet bell. Except there was no ringing, only tiny clicking sounds.

"Where were they?"

"Never mind the details. Here they are." And I wasn't planning to let them out of my sight until after they got appraised tomorrow. Then it was into a safe deposit box at Virginia Central.

Aunt Shel tapped the side of her head. "Smart boy. I'm so glad you found them." She exhaled, the tension draining from her face. Then she pointed at me. "You should still get a job. Make something of yourself."

"Relax. That's what I plan to do." Once I figured out a few things. Now that I had a little cushion to play with, I might not have to jump at Matt and Goose's offer.

"How about that drink now, Josh? To celebrate."

"I'm all for celebrating." I got up. "Be right back."

I returned with two glasses of orange juice. I had a resolution to uphold and Aunt Shel had her liver to think about.

"What's this?"

"Drink it. It's good for you." I held up my glass and made a big show of drinking mine, elbow raised, pinky out. Licked my lips. "Ahhh. The elixir of the gods, if they'd lived in Florida. Now where's that backed-up toilet?"

Aunt Shel gave me her famous backhanded wave. "Forget it. Got my neighbor next door to do it last night. What, you think I can wait around forever for a busy man like you to come over and help me out?"

I pleaded for Aunt Shel to lay off the schnapps and left her to follow her conscience—or not. When people got to a certain age, or to a certain level of crotchetiness, they were on their own.

At the car, I called Erik, who answered on the first ring. Before I could even say hello, he started in on me. "I heard you went to the cops. And they found the guilty party."

"Oh? Who told you?"

"You forget, I'm connected," Erik said. "Well? Who did it?"

I laughed, although the prank had been funnier in my head than in reality. "I was just putting you on. Getting you back for spilling your guts to Matt and Goose. I thought lawyers were supposed to be discreet."

"If you were my client, yes. But you're just my best friend, so I can say whatever I damn well please," he said. "So what's up?"

I explained about my run-in with the intruder and the appearance of the diamonds.

"Jesus, are you okay?"

I touched the sore spot on my head. "Yeah, sure. Good thing for him it was dark or I'd have laid him out."

Erik said, "What kind of numbskull does something like that?" He paused. "Well, at least you got your diamonds back. But it doesn't make much sense, does it?"

"I think a conversation with Kassian might shed some light on things. I just have to find him."

"Where is he?" Erik asked.

"If I knew, I wouldn't have to find him. Haven't seen him in a couple of days. Since our argument."

"Maybe he's the one who gave them back. You guilted him into it. And then he skipped town out of shame."

"Could be," I said, although Erik's theory didn't sit right with me.

"Forget him. You've got what your father wanted you to have. That's the most important thing. Hey, I gotta run. Catch you later."

I clicked off and contemplated calling Rachel. She was in school now, teaching, but I could leave her a message. She said she would call me, but did it really matter who called whom? I pondered it a little longer, feeling as if I were back in high school trying to interpret the signs from a girl I was hot for. It didn't escape my memory that I'd been hot for Rachel's sister, Tammy, back in school. I closed the phone.

I started the car, but didn't put it in gear. Instead, I opened the phone and called Rachel. Waited for the beep and spoke in a ridiculous French accent. "*Bonjour, mon petit chou*. Would you like to go out *avec moi* this Saturday night?" I hung up, an instant later wondering if I could call her cell carrier to get them to delete the message before she got it. *C'est la vie. C'est la mort.*

After Aunt Shel's, I swung by Virginia Central Bank to see about exchanging safe deposit boxes. I wasn't exactly superstitious, but box 112 had left a decidedly bad taste in my mouth. A fresh start would be good, and there wasn't a much fresher start I could think of than a bag of sparkling diamonds. I asked for Cyndi, but she was out on a break so I spoke to Earl about renting a different box. He said he'd have to check with Cyndi about any "new availabilities," and made sure to tell me—with a little gleam in his eye—that he'd mention my request to Cyndi *the instant* she returned. The way he said it, I couldn't tell if he was making fun of me or shooting for a gold star in customer service. I flashed him my noncommittal smile and left to hunt for Kassian.

First stop, Hebrew Home. I checked all the common areas and asked around. Flipped through the sign-in sheet. No Kassian. On the way out I bumped into DeRon. He glared at me as if I smelled like a skunk rancher. "Mr. Handleman."

"Hi, DeRon. Have you seen Kassian?" I tried to sound pleasant and friendly. Didn't want a repeat of my last conversation with DeRon.

The smallest flicker of expression, before the switch flipped and the coldness returned. "No, sir."

"Well, if you do, could you call me? Please?" I found a scrap of paper in my pocket and scribbled my cell number on it. Handed it to him.

He stared at it for a second, then at me. Nodded. "Sure, Mr. Handleman. Sure."

Disappointed, I stopped at home and found no sign that Kassian had returned. I didn't know very much about his day-to-day routines, so I had no idea where he might be hanging out. I'd only heard him speak of the Hebrew Home, and he never mentioned any friends except for my father. There was one other place I could think of, and the thought of Kassian huddled under a tree in the freezing woods disturbed me. Darkness wasn't too many hours away. I grabbed a couple old blankets, threw them into the back of the Taurus, and took off. Couldn't let the old guy freeze to death.

Reston Hills Golf Course boasted a large Victorian clubhouse where it hosted many swanky charity events throughout the year. I'd attended one many moons ago, and I remembered the small army of uniformed valets parking the expensive cars as the party-goers pulled up to the front entrance. I drove around the side, past a sign marked "Bag Drop." There were only about five cars in the side lot. Even though golfers are masochistic by definition, there weren't too many out today. Not with a wind chill in the single digits.

I parked at the far end of the lot, away from the clubhouse, and tucked the blankets under my arm. Set out on the cart path toward the tenth hole. The wind whipped leaves around my legs as I walked, swirling them into little piles before the next gust sent them scattering. To my right, a couple squirrels played tag in the bare oaks bordering the hole. Spiraling up and down the tall trunks, the clicks of their claws a staccato beat. Above, the gray January sky threatened many more weeks of depressing winter, the smell of snow emphasizing its message. I wondered what happened to the sunshine we'd enjoyed on New Year's Day. Was that our allotment until spring? Maybe I should just head back to California and forget about tracking down old Russians.

At the tenth green, I turned right and followed the path into the woods. As I approached the place where I'd hidden the other day, I slowed, trying to spot Kassian's perch. It took me a few moments, eyes scanning through the trees, until I found the rock ledge. I didn't see him sitting there, but I wasn't absolutely sure I had identified the right spot. I inched closer, holding the blankets tight to my body as protection against the bitter wind. I wanted to shout out, to tell him I was here to take him home, but I felt self-conscious disturbing nature with my urgent calls. And besides, I didn't want to scare my prey away. It was possible he'd found another hidey-hole nearby. One that was warmer or more advantageous to whatever mission he was on.

I moved slowly down the path. My father's heavy winter coat was warm, but my face was uncovered, inviting the wind to take a few bites as it whistled past. I continued down the path until I'd gone fifty yards beyond the ledge and the only sign I found of a human—Kassian or otherwise—was an empty silver-green Sprite can, half covered with moldering leaves.

I blew out my breath and a plume of white fog dissipated before my eyes. Was Kassian's visit to this particular spot random? Had he known I was following him and decided to stop here until I left him alone? Could his real destination have been farther down the path?

The cold made my decision easier. Walking would get my blood flowing. I turned and continued along the trail, picking up the pace until I was moving at a pretty good clip. The path remained behind the row of houses, then branched off to the right. Two minutes later, I'd come back to the golf course, somewhere on the back nine. But the path looped back toward the clubhouse. Which meant that if Kassian had been interested in something farther along, he would have taken a different route to get there. The object of his attention had to be back in the woods.

I retraced my steps, telling myself that something would turn up if I searched hard enough. With the dense clouds and the low ceiling, I didn't have much daylight left, but I thought I'd make one more pass and examine the rock ledge more thoroughly.

I set the blankets down on the path and climbed up the slope, both hands grabbing saplings to keep me from slipping on the leaves. When I reached the ledge, I found that part of it extended into a little sheltered area. It looked like some kids had dug themselves a cave to play in. Inside the cave, a magazine laid on the dirt, the *Newsweek* I'd seen Kassian carrying. I picked it up, a photo of a soldier graced the cover. The address label read Abe Handleman. I rolled the magazine up and stuffed it into the pocket of my father's coat.

I plopped down on the ledge, sheltered from the wind, and leaned back against the tree trunk as I'd seen Kassian do. From my vantage, I could lean forward and observe Wentworth's backyard through some branches. The height of the ledge allowed me to see right over the fence into his backyard. A bay window—no curtains—faced the yard, and if there had been a light on inside the house, I'd be able to see what they were eating for dinner.

A molded plastic playset stood in the yard next to a small, seashell-shaped plastic sandbox. A solitary red bucket rested upside-down in the sand, waiting for a warmer day when its playmates would return. Erik had said he thought Wentworth had kids. Evidently they were still on the young side.

I tried to see the Davis' house next door, but a couple holly trees blocked my view. I shifted position, but could barely make out the roofline. If Kassian was indeed spying on somebody, it had to be Wentworth. But why? What in the world could Wentworth's connection to Kassian be?

I picked my way down the slope and retrieved the blankets. Tucked them back under my arm for the walk to the car and glanced at my watch. School had been over for some time. Still holding the blankets and with heavy gloves on, I managed to dig my phone out of my pocket and flip it open. I was hoping to see the message icon displayed, but nothing appeared on the screen. Rachel hadn't returned my call.

I needed to work on my French accent, for sure.

TWENTY-FOUR

A LONG HOT SHOWER boosted my core temperature back to normal. A couple of cold Redhook Ales boosted my core temperament back to merely depressed. Nothing was on the tube. Usually, that wouldn't prevent me from surfing the channels, anesthetizing myself with thirty-second snatches here and there, until I'd snap out of my TV trance and realize I'd wasted hours of my life. Tonight I preferred to wallow in self-pity without the video anesthesia. Just me and my ale and my problems, which rolled before my eyes in black and white like the closing credits on an old sitcom.

My father was dead and I was officially a thirty-four-year-old orphan. Someone who claims to be related to my father may have killed him and hasn't been seen for days. The police think I'm a crackpot. And Rachel hadn't called back all afternoon or so far this evening. My few other friends were with their families or their girlfriends or out on the town looking to strike up new friendships. I suppose I could have gone over to Aunt Shel's, but I'd rather drink Redhook alone than schnapps with her. Too much nagging.

On the plus side, I did have a bag of diamonds.

I held it up to my right ear and shook it, the now familiar clicking sound comforting. My father hadn't completely forgotten about me—he hadn't purposely left me an empty safe deposit box.

Tomorrow morning, I'd find out exactly how much they were worth, although I'm not sure to what extent it would matter. I didn't have any plans for the money. I had a place to live and enough money for the time being to be able to eat and fill up the car and buy new underwear. Maybe I'd donate some of it, just like my father had. Maybe I could get the Hebrew Home to open up a unit dedicated to jilted husbands who got screwed by their business partners. I popped open another bottle and tilted it back, savoring the cold liquid as it gurgled down my throat.

The doorbell rang. I made no move to get up. It rang again, followed by a rapping. Insistent. I swung my feet off the coffee table and hoisted myself off the couch. Went to the door. Flung it open without bothering to check the peephole. If it was the diamond man come to give me more diamonds, than I would welcome him with open arms.

It was Cyndi from the bank. "Hello, Josh. How are you this evening?" I resisted the urge to shield my eyes from her blinding smile.

"Okay. You?" I asked.

She maintained her smile as she looked past me into the house. "Fine thanks. Sorry to drop by like this. I hope it's all right."

"Um, sure. Why not?" Just doing a little wallowing is all.

"Do you mind if I come in?" she asked. In her hand, she carried a leather briefcase.

"Oh. Forgive my lack of manners." I opened the door fully and swept my arm. "Please, *entrez-vous*." Might as well try the French again. Maybe my accent would sound better with a few beers in me.

She giggled and entered. "Nice house. Nice and warm. Your father lived here, didn't he?"

"That's right. Where I grew up."

Cyndi began unbuttoning her coat.

"Can I take that for you?" I asked.

I hung it up in the hall closet, and when I turned around, she'd migrated to the living room. From behind, she looked Stairmaster-fit in a tight black skirt that accentuated the positive. Shiny black leather boots gave her an extra two or three inches. I turned on a couple lamps as I joined her in the living room. I got a good view of her from the front, in a clingy gray turtleneck, and she looked positively spectacular from that angle, too. She could have stepped from the pages of *Elle*.

"So, what brings you out on such a cold night?"

"I have something for you," she said, tapping her glossy tapered fingernails on her briefcase.

"Oh?"

She pointed to the bottles of Redhook on the table. "Having a party?"

"No, not really. Care for one?"

"Sure, that would be great." She sat on the couch and placed her briefcase next to her.

I opened a bottle and handed it over. Picked up the one I'd already started and lowered myself onto the couch beside her. Watched with a great deal of interest as she took a long sip, ruby red lips parted slightly to allow the amber liquid in. She set the bottle down on the coffee table with a little thud. "That hit the spot," she said, as she hit me with another one of her blazing smiles. "Shall we?"

I stared at her, not sure what she was asking.

She reached into her briefcase and pulled out a manila file folder. Opened it with a graceful turn of a slim, tanned wrist. "Earl told me you came by today. Wanted a different safe deposit box." She reached over and patted my arm. "I can totally understand. I think it's the right thing to do. You don't need anything at all reminding you of your terrible tragedy."

"Thanks." I wondered if she made house calls to all the bank's customers. Seemed a bit unusual, but maybe that's how she got to be branch manager at such a tender age.

Cyndi angled a piece of paper my way, keeping a fingernail on one corner, anchoring it. "Here's the rental agreement."

I leaned in close to read the agreement, and caught a whiff of something floral. Perfume or shampoo. Something delicate and … inviting.

"It's just a standard agreement. Here," she said, keeping her finger on the agreement and offering me a pen with her other hand. "Sign right there." She reached over to indicate where my John Hancock belonged and brushed her arm against mine. Her firm thigh pressed along the length of my leg. Any closer and we'd be slow dancing.

I scrawled my name and leaned back, just a bit.

"Excellent," she said, as she slid the agreement back into the folder and the folder back into the briefcase. As if by magic, she produced a little envelope with the number 245 on it. "Here's your key. Box 245. My lucky number." I could have sworn she winked at me as she said it, but it vanished too quickly to be sure.

"Thanks."

Cyndi rose and took a few steps farther into the living room, leaving her briefcase on the couch. "This really is a nice house. I can see your father living here," she said, admiring one of the few pictures on the wall. She nodded at it. "This totally seems like your father's taste." It was a picture of the Wailing Wall in Jerusalem that he'd brought back from one of his trips there.

I left the couch to get a closer look, although I'd seen it so often I didn't even notice it anymore. "Yeah, I guess you're right. Most of the stuff was here when I was a kid. I never really thought about it." I pointed to an old table in the corner with a picture of my father and mother on their wedding day. "That may look like a 'retro' table, but it was new when my mother bought it, back in the seventies."

Cyndi laughed and it came out deep-throated, sexy. She'd finished her art inspection and came closer. "I think it's so nice of your father to make such generous donations to charity. Even though he was rich, he looked out for the little guy, huh?"

I nodded.

She took another step closer, faced me. With her heels, we were almost nose-to-nose. "I bet you had a great childhood, Josh."

"The usual, I guess," I said, as I waved off any further questions about my formative years. It was cold outside, but warming up nicely in here. "So, are you from around here?"

"We moved here when I was about nine," she said. "I love it here. Don't you?" She caught my eyes and held them. My breathing became shallower. And faster.

"Yeah, it's nice." I gathered myself. "Did, um, you and your boyfriend celebrate New Year's Eve in high style?" I asked, not sure whom I was channeling. Transparent questions like that weren't my thing.

Cyndi glanced at the floor, then back at me. Fluttered her lashes going for coy, but it came out closer to predatory. "Oh, I don't really have a boyfriend, Josh," she said. "But I'm working on it. Real hard." She reached out and grasped one of my hands in hers. "And I usually get what I want."

But was it what I wanted? For an instant, Rachel's face seemed superimposed upon Cyndi's body.

The doorbell rang.

Cyndi's hand jerked back. "Someone's here." Her eyes were wide, as if she'd been caught with her red talons in the money drawer at the bank.

"I'll get it. Just take a minute." I went to the door and threw it open.

It was Rachel.

TWENTY-FIVE

RACHEL PUSHED PAST ME into the foyer. "I need to talk with you, Josh. I thought about calling you today, but I thought we should have this discussion in person." She paused to catch her breath, but continued before I could break in. "I think that we—"

I followed her gaze over my shoulder into the doorway of the living room, where Cyndi stood. Her ever-present smile had taken on a different sheen, and she licked her lips as she studied Rachel.

Rachel's hand flew to her mouth. "Oh. I'm sorry," she said to me, then spoke to my guest. "I'm Rachel. And you are?"

Cyndi introduced herself, but didn't give any more information besides her name. I guess "Cyndi, the Very Friendly Neighborhood Banker Who Makes House Calls" would sound weird.

I had two drop-dead gorgeous women in my house, both expressing a definite interest in me. Why did I have the sour feeling this would end poorly? "Come on in. Visit for a while," I said to Rachel, while I consciously avoided looking at Cyndi.

Rachel bounced from me to Cyndi, then back to me. "No. I'm interrupting. I'd better go," she said, but she stood firmly in place.

Cyndi stayed silent, with one eyebrow arched. I guess it was up to me. "Um, well, why don't …" I paused, fifty feet up without a net.

Rachel's eyes narrowed at me, demanding some sort of face-saving comment. *Stay a while, you're not interrupting a thing.* Or *Please, don't go, Cyndi was just leaving.*

I graced her with more stammering. Out of the corner of my eye, I saw Cyndi. Beaming.

Rachel turned on her heels and bolted. I remained stuck in place, frozen with confusion, as the seconds ticked by. Cyndi said something from behind, but I wasn't listening. I unglued my feet from the floor and dashed after Rachel.

I raced out the door and down the steps, just in time to see her car peel away from the curb and zip up the street.

When I got back inside, Cyndi had her coat on, briefcase in hand. "Well, Josh. I'm glad we got our business taken care of. If there's anything else you need at Virginia Central Bank, please do not hesitate to ask." She flashed me one more goodbye smile and left. I watched in futility as her boot heels click-clacked down the walkway to her car. She started it up and drove off in the opposite direction from Rachel.

When you're hot, you're hot.

And when you're not, you're Josh Handleman, stud to dud in sixty seconds.

———

The next morning, Yakov Sapperstein hunched over the kitchen table, examining the diamonds spread out on a black cloth before him. He'd knocked on the door at precisely ten a.m. toting two bags, a large brown leather case and a smaller one that looked like an old-time doctor's bag. What did it say about society when doctors no longer made house calls but diamond merchants and bank managers did?

Yakov was a slight man, with thin dark hair and jug-handle ears. A bobby pin held a knitted blue *yarmulke* in place on his head. He set the diamond he was looking at in one of five piles he'd created, picked up a pencil, and jotted some numbers down on his pad.

For the past three hours, he'd been poring over the gems, making notes and sorting them into piles with the deftness of a concert pianist. He polished each one with a chamois and examined it under the microscope he'd brought. Most of the time he smiled, but sometimes he'd see something that set him frowning. There was a lot of head nodding.

"These are some fine-looking stones, Josh." Yakov put the loupe down next to the microscope and smiled. "Your father amassed a nice collection."

"Thanks."

He unscrewed the top off a bottle of water and gulped some of it. Wiped his mouth on his sleeve and glanced at his watch. "Let's take a break. I need to stretch." He pushed his chair out and stepped away from the table. Then he extended both arms to his sides and began slowly rotating them in widening circles. "I get stiff sitting in one place. And the ride down on the train last night didn't help."

I got up too, careful to avoid his windmilling arms, leaning back against the wall as a safety precaution. "What more can you tell me about my father's hobby?"

A short laugh burst forth from Yakov's mouth. "Hardly a hobby, Josh. I like to think of it as an investment. A very wise investment."

Up until now, Yakov had kept his salesman-shtick in check. Thankfully. "Okay, okay. I didn't mean any disrespect. Do you know where he got them from?"

"Your father and I talked on a few occasions. He was a warm man with a very genuine sense of humor. But he was somewhat evasive when I asked him about his collection. I gathered that he purchased his stones from a variety of places over the years." He shrugged. "I never sold him any."

"Then why did he call you to appraise them?"

"Some people like to keep the 'selling' separate from the 'appraising.' They're afraid of the process getting tainted. I do not blame them. It's like asking a car salesman how much your trade-in is worth." Yakov had stopped spinning his arms and was now working his neck back and forth. "You know, he did talk a lot about Israeli diamonds. So—if I had to guess—I'd say he got the majority of his gems from there."

Figures. "Are Israeli diamonds any better than other diamonds?"

Yakov laughed. "No. Just more kosher." He laughed again. I wondered how many times he'd dredged up that joke in the past.

"Do many people 'collect' diamonds like my father?"

Yakov braced himself with his arms against the wall and extended his right leg behind him. Stretched out his calf. "A lot of people collect precious gems, and I'd have to say that diamonds are indeed the most popular. But few collect so many, and very, very few are so secretive. Most have certificates and documentation." He stopped stretching and stared, trying to read me. "In fact, I was led to believe that these had such documentation."

I held my hands out. "They probably do. I just haven't found it yet."

Yakov searched my face some more. "In other circumstances, I might think these stones were hot."

"Believe me, they're not." After Detective Morris' identical comment, the thought had crossed my mind, but I'd dismissed it. I knew my father. Demanding, stubborn, unforgiving perhaps. But never a thief. He'd been the kind of guy to correct a grocery cashier for undercharging him a nickel on a tube of toothpaste.

"Well, most people have insurance on such valuable things. Did you try calling his insurance man?"

"Yeah. No luck." I'd called the guy who handled the homeowners and auto insurance, and he knew nothing about any diamonds. And I'd been through my dad's papers twice without success. "Do you think he might have gotten someone else to insure them? Someone who specializes in valuables like diamonds?"

Yakov smiled, patronizing. "I guess it's possible. Who knows? Like I said before, diamonds make some people act a little ... abnormal. The important thing is you got them back. Once I appraise them, you can go out and get your own insurance." His face became stern. "Which I highly recommend, by the way."

"Don't worry, I will." I pulled up a chair while Yakov did a few lunges. "How did my father get your name, if you don't mind me asking."

"My uncle's friend recommended me. That's how I get most of my business. Referrals. That's why treating my clients right—best service, best deal, best quality stones—is so important to me."

More salesman patter. Could he turn it off when he got home to his wife? "Who recommended you?"

Yakov straightened and picked his pad off the table. Flipped to the front and read the name. "Lady named Carol Wolfe. Know her?"

I swallowed. "Yes. I know her." On the surface, it smelled fishy, but who else would my father get advice from about diamonds, if not his girlfriend?

Yakov said, "My uncle met her through a friend of a friend. I think I sold her son an engagement ring a couple years back. Nice guy as I recall." He shook out his arms a final time and sat back in his chair. "Okay. Let's do it."

I put ideas of Carol's gold digging behind me and smiled at him.

He smiled back at me. "I'm ready," he said.

"Okay. Don't let me stop you. Do what you need to."

Yakov's brow furrowed. "I'm finished with these diamonds."

"Oh. Sure." I was new to the diamond game. I guess it was up to me to ask the value. "How much is the collection worth?" My heart sped up.

"I do not know yet."

"Oh." I relaxed. "Right. You need to do some calculations. So, what? You'll call me in a few days?"

"I think there must be a misunderstanding," Yakov said. His puzzled face set off warning bells in my head.

"Oh?"

"Over the phone, your father described his collection in vague terms, as I've mentioned. But he did give me some indication of the size. And … Is this all?" Yakov held up his hands, palms up.

I nodded, afraid of what was coming next.

"I was led to believe he had more than two hundred and fifty diamonds to be appraised." Yakov raised one eyebrow, hands still open. "Where are the rest of them?"

TWENTY-SIX

JEWS COME IN THREE flavors: Orthodox, Conservative, and Reform, or as my father liked to say, Jewish-Lite. I was raised Conservative, but I flushed all religious knowledge down the toilet the day after my Bar Mitzvah. I was still pissed at God for making me go to Hebrew School twice during the week and once on Sunday, which interfered with my Little League games. Because I was always late, I had to sub in at right field, the wasteland for losers. And although I still carried on some of the Jewish holiday traditions, considering them more of a cultural thing than a religious one, I really had no use for organized religion of any flavor.

So Aunt Shel was justifiably surprised when I told her I was taking her to Friday night services at B'nai Shalom, one of the two main synagogues in Reston and the only Conservative shul in the area. We got there early and stood outside the sanctuary in a reception area along with the other worshippers. The conversations ebbed and flowed, some hushed, others loud and boisterous. Aunt Shel and I waited in silence.

At the far end of the reception area, a couple of women prepared for the *kiddush* ceremony. A few white linen napkins covered the challahs, and one lady was pouring grape juice into little plastic cups lined up on the long table.

"Look, there's Lev and his family," Aunt Shel said, pointing through the window toward the parking lot. A minute later, Lev, Peter, Jenn and their two kids entered. They paused at the door and scanned the crowd. When they saw us, Lev headed our way and Peter leaned over and said something to Jenn. She gave us a half-hearted wave and herded the kids off down a hallway, no doubt in search of restrooms, while Peter caught up to his dad.

"Hello, Shel," Lev said. "How are you?"

She issued a protracted sigh. "Feeling better," she said, "now." She patted my arm and forced a smile. "Josh found what he'd been missing."

Lev squinted at me and Peter's eyes grew wide. "You found them," Lev said, not a question.

"Yes. And they're locked away in the vault." I'd taken the bag directly to Virginia Central after Yakov had left. I hadn't run into Cyndi, but Earl had given me a couple world-class sneers on my way out.

Peter said, "That's great. Now you can really get on with your life. Move forward and leave all this unpleasantness behind. I'm so happy for you." He winked at me. "And if you need help with any investing now that you'll have some extra cash..."

Yakov had given me a figure close to $200,000—which I guessed still had a little wiggle room built in. "Thanks. But I haven't decided what I'm going to do with them." I tried to be as ambiguous as possible, deciding not to tell anyone about the *additional* missing diamonds. Didn't want to wreck anyone's good mood.

Aunt Shel spoke up. "You're going to sell them. And invest wisely. Listen to Peter. He knows about money. Such a nice house he has." Then she reached up and poked me in the chest. "And you're going to get a job and make a living, too."

Jenn joined us and we chatted amiably about nothing. When I looked around our little circle, everybody seemed happy and relaxed. Everyone except stone-faced Lev, who stared at me until I looked away.

Lev wanted to be able to see better, so he and Peter and his family found an empty row close to the front of the sanctuary. Aunt Shel and I begged off, preferring to sit in the last row, on the aisle closest to the back door.

Up on the *bimah*, the Rabbi, a big bear of a man in a tight-fitting brown suit, began services with an upbeat hymn. Then, after a short greeting in English, he launched into a series of prayers in Hebrew, some spoken, some chanted. I recognized some of the words from twenty years ago, but the tunes and cadences seemed different to me now, not so dirge-like. Maybe Judaism had modernized when I wasn't looking.

The sanctuary itself was also more modern than the synagogues I remembered from my youth. The ark appeared to be made of some kind of brushed metal and the bimah had blond wood accents and lots of curved surfaces around the edges.

From my vantage in the back, I noticed a preponderance of gray heads. The synagogue was located only a few blocks from the Hebrew Home, so many of the more mobile residents attended. The average age of the congregants had to be over fifty-five, and that included the dozen or so kids I saw squirming in their seats. In front of me, a little girl, maybe three years old, peered over the seatback. She stuck her tongue out and I returned the favor. She giggled until her mother spun her around to face front. I got a nasty sideways glare from the mom, as if I had been the one to start things.

Most of the service was conducted in Hebrew. Next to me, Aunt Shel kept nodding off and I couldn't blame her. It was hard maintaining concentration when you didn't have any idea what was being said. My chin hit my chest a few times, too. An hour or so later, the Rabbi delivered a mini-sermon—thankfully, in English—and then led the congregation in *Aleinu*. After the prayer was over, he leaned in to the microphone, modulating his sonorous voice. "All mourners, please rise for the Mourner's Kaddish."

I helped Aunt Shel to her feet and held her arm as we stood together. About a dozen others also rose, most holding a *siddur*—prayer book—open in their hands. Aunt Shel and I would wing it without one. Lip-synching the prayers was the one thing I'd nailed back in Hebrew School. I felt the stares of all the "non-mourners" upon me as I prayed, judging me, Mr. Hypocrite, the man with no use for organized religion.

"*Yitgaddal v'yitqaddash …*"

———

I went straight home after dropping off Aunt Shel. Wanted nothing more than to watch some TV and get a good night's sleep. My stress level was through the roof and I had no real hope that it would lessen any time soon.

I managed to remove my coat and hang it up, but I only got as far as the stairs. I plopped down on the second stair and leaned back, resting my elbows on the step above. Stared at the spot where my father had died.

There hadn't been any blood and I hadn't seen it firsthand, but my imagination had taken over, generating photos every bit as vivid as the real ones in Morris' file must have been. Sometimes you hear that dead people looked like they were sleeping when they died. Not so in my version. There was no doubt my father was dead.

And what had he left me? A gigantic mess, that's what. His purported cousin, barely able to function on his own, was out wandering the streets. For all I knew, he was lying dead himself somewhere, in a morgue or an alley or a ditch in the woods, corpse being devoured by foxes. I figured he'd just run away, but maybe I should check out the area hospitals to see if he'd been admitted. Maybe I should call Carol to get her advice. She seemed like she would know better than I. But I didn't move. Kassian wasn't dead. He'd run off after I practically accused him of murdering my father. And, as sad as it sounded, I didn't have to worry about Kassian's survival. He could take care of himself on the streets better than most, given his extensive experience.

My father *had* left me a bag of diamonds and a boatload of questions. But—if Yakov Sapperstein can be believed—many more were still missing. Why would the thief return just *some* of the diamonds? Wasn't it an either/or proposition? Either you were a thief or you weren't. Was Kassian on his way to Atlantic City with the rest, looking to parlay his plunder into megamillions? Or was there someone else involved in the diamond theft? I thought about the facts. My father had taken the stones out of the bank on Thursday, in anticipation of Yakov's appraisal on Tuesday morning. He'd have to get them sometime before the holiday weekend because the bank wouldn't be open on Tuesday in time for his meeting. He could have gotten them on Friday sometime, but maybe he didn't want to go out if he was expecting Lev over to play chess. Besides, what's an extra day or two? I mean what are the odds you would get robbed of your diamonds on any particular day?

Who knew my father even had diamonds? Aunt Shel. Lev. Carol. Kassian, most probably, even though he claimed he didn't know. None of them seemed like prime suspects. Which brought me back to my original assumption. A stranger broke into the house, killed my father, took the diamonds.

But there had been no evidence of a break-in. Doors locked— dead bolts, too—and windows secure. Someone with a key? Kassian had a key. Carol had a key. I pictured Carol returning her key and hanging it on the hook next to the ... spare key. Only there hadn't been a spare key hanging there. Had the murderer coerced his way in and used the spare key to lock the door behind him?

I rubbed my face with my hands. My headache had returned, in spades. The more I thought about it, the more confused I got and the more I believed Kassian was the linchpin. He knew something he wasn't sharing with me, something important that would shed some light on my father's death and the diamond theft.

Mentally, I ticked off the supporting facts. He was living here when it happened. He knew my father's most recent activities. And he was playing woodsman watching Stephen Wentworth's house. I had a feeling if I found Kassian and got him to talk, the mysteries would start to unravel.

But where had he gone?

I went upstairs. Decided to skip TV and climb right into bed. Find a good book to take my mind off things. I emptied my pockets onto the top of my dresser and remembered I'd turned my phone off before we went into services. I turned it on, hoping there'd be a message from Rachel, but afraid there'd be a dozen messages from Dani. I wouldn't be surprised if she somehow had wheedled Heath to take her back and I was once again a smudge on the bottom of her shoe.

There were two messages and neither was from Rachel. One from Dani, the other from Erik. I listened to Dani's first.

Hello, Josh. Why won't you call me back? Sorry about the other night. I'm feeling better now, I can see that Heath was a big mistake. I'm really so sorry. We need to talk, Josh. I'd like to see if we can work things out, give ourselves another chance. We were good together, for a while. Next time, we'll have learned what we can…

I cut the message off while she was still rambling. *There won't be a next time, Dani,* I whispered to myself. *Fool me once…*

Erik's message simply said to call him, so I found his home number in my contacts list and clicked. He answered promptly, as usual. It didn't seem to matter whether it was his cell or home phone. "Hello."

"Hey, it's Josh."

"Yes, I know. It's this new thing, Caller ID. I hear they're working on something even better. A cordless phone." Erik paused. "Nice of you to return my call."

"You're welcome. What do you need?" I asked.

"Actually, it's what you need. I got you an appointment with your father's real estate guy. Terrible Teresywzki. And it wasn't too easy, let me tell you. That guy's calendar is jammed until Easter. But I got you in," Erik said. There was a moment of silence. "You still want to talk with him, don't you?"

"Yeah, sure. Thanks."

"There's only one catch," Erik said.

I sighed. Sounded like some hoop-jumping on the horizon. "What? I've got to ride with him in a cab to the airport or something?"

Erik laughed. "Worse. Six-thirty a.m. Monday morning. At Gerry's Gym. Wear workout clothes. He left your name at the front desk."

"Thanks."

"One more thing. Don't pull too many muscles." Erik was still laughing as I hung up.

TWENTY-SEVEN

With some assistance from the towel guy, I found Terry Teresywzki alone in the cardio room plugging away on a treadmill. His orange UVA T-shirt couldn't hide his barrel-chest, and his dark hair had probably been graying at the temples for years. Hawk eyes didn't miss a movement of mine as I approached, and when I got closer, I noticed he had the largest, most well-defined forearms I'd ever seen, with the possible exception of Popeye. He looked to be about sixty years old, but I'm sure he could take a man twenty-five years younger in a wrestling match. With one massive forearm tied behind his back.

I introduced myself and he nodded, unable—or unwilling—to interrupt his exercise to shake hands. "So you're Abe's boy? He was a good man. A real throwback. He will be missed." Teresywzki talked to me but kept his eyes forward, as if he were searching for a field mouse from two hundred feet up. "Hop on." He pointed to the machine next to him. "You look like you could use some exercise."

"Okay. Thanks." I peeled off my sweatpants and sweatshirt and climbed aboard the treadmill. After a minute of fumbling around with the controls, I got it going at a fairly slow pace. A pang of guilt hit me. After my New Year's Day run to kick off my get-in-shape regimen, I hadn't been out since.

Next to me, Teresywzki maintained his metronomic pace. "So what can I tell you about your father's real estate business?"

"Everything, I guess."

"I've been handling his deals for years. Smaller ones at first, then larger." Teresywzki punched a few buttons and increased his pace. I'd been going just barely faster than a walk for only a minute and was already feeling it. "These past few years, he'd gotten involved in some real money-makers." He glanced at me sideways, then focused straight ahead.

"Anything out of the ordinary?"

Teresywzki grunted. "No. Nothing complicated," he said. "Actually, that's not true. Many of his deals were quite complicated. I should have said there was nothing *unusual* about them. Office buildings, professional buildings, some light industrial locations. Mostly part-ownerships, but good, solid stuff. For an individual investor, he did quite well."

"That's good, I guess," I said.

"Yes it is. He did better than a lot of my institutional clients. They might have had more advisors and scads more money, but they didn't have more business acumen than Abe." Teresywzki spoke in a normal tone. No gasping for breath or pauses between words even though he was running seven-minute miles. Only the faintest sheen of sweat was visible on his forehead.

I'd compiled a list of questions in my head, but none seemed like the kind of question Mike Wallace would ask. Mine seemed so ... pedestrian. "Did you know anyone who might want to see my father fail?"

Teresywzki blew out some air. "Hmm. Not that I can think of. He was well-liked. Respected. Honorable. Don't recall him ever screwing anybody. Abe was a big proponent of the 'win-win' deal. He got his nickname honestly, if you'll pardon the pun. As I like to say, he was a good all-around shit."

I wasn't sure what I hoped to find out, but I guess knowing my father was a "good shit" made me feel more comfortable as I delved into his business dealings. "In the past few months, had he been talking about developing anything especially large, or controversial, or unpopular?"

Teresywzki thought about it. "Again, no, not that I can think of. He'd been talking about that Russian thing for the Hebrew Home, but that idea had been bouncing around for a while. Frankly, I think it would fill a need and knowing Abe, he'd give them a real sweetheart deal. In fact, the latest I heard was he was going to foot the whole bill."

"But nothing new lately?" I felt like I was grasping at straws.

"No, nothing new. And certainly nothing contentious." He swiveled his head and settled his carnivorous gaze directly on me, sending a ripple through my body. I could see how he earned his nickname. "Why are you asking these questions? Has something improper been discovered? Erik never mentioned anything to me."

I shook my head, getting a little winded. I cranked the speed down to a brisk walk and took a deep breath. "Just trying to get a better picture of my father, that's all. A few things don't really add up, but..."

"I assume you know about his other, um, investments?"

"His charities? Sure," I said, but the way Teresywzki phrased it made me think I was off base.

"Erik never mentioned his angel work?" Teresywzki asked.

"His what?"

"His angel work. Abe was a venture angel. He invested in people who had trouble securing traditional financing. People who had good ideas, or noble ideas, or people he just liked who might not have possessed the business experience or wherewithal to attract conventional money." Sweat had begun to form in earnest on Teresywzki's face. He grabbed a towel off the treadmill frame and wiped his face without breaking stride.

"All I know about is his stake in the video game company." And Erik hadn't mentioned it to me. That info came straight from Matt and Goose.

"There you go," Teresywzki said. "That's one of them."

"There were others?" For some reason, I pictured people in shiny, new meth labs—they probably had trouble securing traditional financing.

"Well, I don't really know many of the details. I handled his real estate, Erik handled his other investments. Abe told me about some of them in passing, but I'm a real estate guy. I know my area of expertise as well as anyone in the county, and I wouldn't want to hurt my rep getting involved in other arenas where I wasn't so...comfortable." Teresywzki glanced at his watch. "Still got forty minutes left," he said, as he toggled the speed on his machine a little faster.

Funny, Erik had no trouble keeping my father's angel investments secret while he blabbed to anyone with ears about my missing diamonds. What else was he keeping hidden? "Can you give me any more information?" I asked, anxious to have someone level with me for a change.

"Like I said, don't know too much about most of Abe's projects. There was one thing I remember him telling me about VidGamZZZ."

"Go ahead," I said, as I reduced the speed of my treadmill as far as it would go, disappointed there wasn't a button marked "saunter."

Teresywzki lowered his voice, although we had the cardio room to ourselves. "Abe said—this was about a month, six weeks ago—that a guy wanted to buy out his stake in the company. Abe told him he wasn't interested, but he persisted. I'm not sure what happened, I just know Abe was perturbed by the whole thing."

"Did he say who the guy was?"

"Yeah, that's why he brought it up, I guess. Abe figured I might know this guy, which I did. I'd met him at one of those silly Business Elite breakfast get-togethers. He's a real arsehole, pardon my English." Teresywzki swabbed his forehead with a towel before continuing. "Brandon Flannery's his name. I'm glad Abe didn't sell anything to that arrogant jerk."

Maybe Terrible Teresywzki wasn't so terrible after all.

TWENTY-EIGHT

I'D BEEN DRIVING HOME from the gym when I suddenly found myself parked in front of Erik's office. I had planned to cool down—emotionally—before confronting him, but I figured it would be a shame to lose my edge. I was hot and had a few things to say to my old friend.

It was barely seven-thirty and the receptionist hadn't arrived yet, so I made my way back to Erik's office unimpeded. He was chatting on speakerphone and he glanced at his watch as he motioned me in. I shut the door hard, the slam echoing in the office. Erik frowned, threw a "great talking to you" at the black box on his desk, and hung up quickly. He started speaking as he rose to greet me, but I hit him full blast before he could utter a full sentence.

"What the fuck is going on?"

Erik froze. "What's the matter?"

"Enough bullshit. How about coming clean for a change?"

Erik blinked rapidly. I'd blindsided him and he was mentally running through all the things that could be bothering me. He gestured toward the couch. "Let's have a seat."

"I don't feel like sitting."

Erik eyed me. "Suit yourself. What's the problem?"

"I just finished talking with Teresywzki. He mentioned my father's angel investments. Business you'd been handling." I hit the "you'd" hard and pointed at him. "How come you never mentioned it?"

Erik glanced across the office at something on the wall. When he refocused on me, his demeanor had changed. Colder. "I didn't think you'd want to hear about it."

"What? Why not? Is this more bullshit about your client's confidentiality? He was my father, for God's sake."

"When it came to the confidentiality pertaining to your father's will, I had no discretion. He specifically asked me not to divulge anything, and as my client, his wishes were sacrosanct. This other stuff . . . Well, I guess that was my decision to keep quiet."

"Why don't you tell me about it now?" The words squeezed out through clenched teeth. It had been a long time since I'd been this mad at somebody I cared about. Even with Dani, my anger had seemed muted much of the time.

He sighed. "Sure, Josh. But let's take a seat. Please. We'll be more comfortable."

We took our seats on the couch, facing each other across the empty middle cushion.

Erik stared at me as if probing my depths for something. "Your father helped a lot of people. He was a very good man, despite how you felt about him."

"I know about Matt and Goose. Who else?"

"Dylan Wernicke. Suzanne Miller. Tony Stokes. Truck Taylor." He paused and fixed his attention across the room again.

I shifted on the couch. They were all friends I had growing up. "There were others, too. Weren't there?"

Erik nodded without looking at me. "Yeah. Lots. Abe didn't wait for people to come to him. He sought them out. And I—"

"Helped. You helped, didn't you?" These just weren't *my* friends. Growing up, Erik and I had many of the same friends. We hung in the same circle.

He nodded again. "Yes, I did. Your father came to me with his idea. Explained it in such glowing terms. He'd help these people with their business ventures. He liked the idea of being an angel on everybody's shoulders. But he wanted to make sure he was only helping good people."

"So you steered him to all of our friends?"

A rueful smile grew on Erik's face. "Make no mistake, Josh. These were all *your* friends. If they were good enough for you, they were good enough for him." Erik's voice had diminished to a whisper. "Abe wanted to help *your* friends. Because you wouldn't let him help *you*."

I rose and walked to the window, the faint tick-tock of a desk clock the only noise in the office. I thought back to the arguments my father and I had when I'd dropped out of college with ideas of starting my own business. He'd wanted me to continue my studies, but when I wasn't dissuaded, he'd insisted on funding the start-up. I'd refused, wanting to succeed on my own, and *not* wanting to be under his thumb. I returned to my spot on the couch. Erik hadn't moved a muscle.

"Why didn't you tell me?"

"Considering your relationship with your dad, I thought if you knew he was loaning them money…" Erik laughed. "Loaning. Hell, he was practically giving away loads of cash with very little chance of ever seeing it again. I pointed that out on many occasions, but he just smiled and said it didn't really matter." He shook his head. "Anyway, I thought if you knew about it, your relationship with him would become even more strained. And I didn't believe either of you wanted that."

I swallowed. I was pissed now, hearing about it, but was I torqued at knowing the details, or because people had been keeping me in the dark? "So, all of my old friends got money from my father over the years? And no one mentioned anything to me?"

Erik licked his lips. "Abe didn't *want* his angel activities to be secret—his goal was for people in need to come to him. But he didn't want the specifics of his involvement known, so he made confidentiality part of the agreement. The recipients were prohibited from mentioning the source of the money." He held his hand out. "I didn't see any upside to telling you about all this. I'm sorry, Josh."

"Got anything else you're keeping from me?"

He shook his head slowly. "No. Nothing else."

"What about Brandon Flannery? Are you telling me you didn't know about his desire to buy my father's stake in Matt and Goose's company?"

Erik's brow furrowed. "I don't know anything about that. Brandon's simply a workout buddy of mine. I referred him to your father, but we don't really talk much business."

"Come on. All you Business Elite guys seem to know everything about everyone's business." I'd become tired of all the bullshit raining down on me.

Erik laughed. "The Business Elite? That's a joke. A sham. Nothing but a bunch of fat and happy yuppies having a good chuckle at their own expense. And parties, lots of parties."

I squinted at him. "What are you talking about?"

Erik sprang from the couch and circled his desk. Pulled something out of the top drawer and returned. Flung it into my lap. "You're a member of the Northern Virginia Business Elite. Congratu-fucking-lations."

I picked up the scrap of paper he'd thrown at me. A membership card to the Elite, my name engraved in a fancy gold script. "What's this?"

"You're in. You are officially one of the most highly regarded and most influential businessmen in Northern Virginia." He laughed again, a joyless sound. "I was trying to figure out a good practical joke to pull on you using your new membership." He surrounded the word membership with air quotes.

"I don't even live here. How can I be a member?"

"Thirty-five bucks gets you in. That's the only requirement. We network, we throw parties, we give speeches. We have a newsletter mostly made up of pictures of us giving speeches at parties. It's a phony-boloney boys' and girls' club in suits. Shit, I even signed my dog up. Scout Nolan is a member of the Elite, too. Arf, arf."

———

My talk with Erik hadn't left me in a very good mood. My best friend had kept important things from me, and my father felt he needed to give money to my friends as a proxy for giving money to his son. How much of what had happened was my fault? The older I got, the larger my portion of the blame seemed to grow.

I drove home with the radio loud, trying to blast away my sour thoughts about the last few days, but the volume level only went so high. I'd spent most of the weekend engaged in two pursuits: cruising around town looking for Kassian and trying to connect on the phone with Rachel. I'd laid goose eggs on both accounts and the failure grated on me.

When I got home the phone was ringing as loud as my ears were. "Hello?"

"Hello, Josh. This is Carol."

I rubbed my face with my hand. "Yes?"

"Can you come over? I need to ... talk to you." Tense.

"Now?" I was looking forward to a hot shower. And maybe a nap.

"Please, Josh. It's important."

I sighed. "Where do you live?"

She gave me directions and I grabbed a banana on my way out.

Carol lived fifteen minutes away in Chantilly, in a subdivision not too far from the hustle and bustle along Route 50. After I turned off the busy commercial strip, I passed a school and a library, and there were sidewalks and playgrounds and baseball fields. Suburban living at its finest.

I turned down her street and rolled along, searching the house numbers on the mailboxes for the address she'd given me. I found the right one and turned into the driveway. Carol sat on the porch in a white glider built for two, bundled up in a black ski jacket. When I got to the porch, she rose and clapped her gloved hands together. Stressed or not, she radiated kindness, and I knew my father had been happy the last couple years.

"Thanks for coming, Josh." A smile accentuated her gratitude.

"Sure. What's going on?"

"Please," she said, and gestured for me to go inside. "We can talk where it's warmer."

She took my coat and removed hers, hanging both up in the closet while I waited patiently. It was a large house in a neighborhood of large houses. Not mansion-large like Peter's or Erik's, but big enough for a full family. I wondered what happened to hers.

"Can I get you something to drink?" she asked over her shoulder as she led me down the entrance hallway.

"No thanks. I'm good," I said, following her. "Nice house."

She nodded thanks from behind, but didn't comment, just kept walking. We entered the kitchen and she stepped to the left and stopped. Off to the right was a small table with four chairs. Sitting in one of them was Kassian.

"Kassian! Are you okay?" I wanted to rush over and hug him, but refrained. Relief flowed through me. I spun around to Carol. "How long has he...?" I spun back to Kassian. "How long have you been here?"

He pursed his lips, not sure how to react to my show of emotion. I suspected he didn't realize I'd been worried about him since he'd disappeared. "I came here after we argued. You told me to leave, yes?"

"No, not…" I glanced at Carol, anticipating a disapproving look, but she wasn't showing her hand. Kassian stared at me. I cleared my throat and started again. "I'm sorry for what I did and said that night. I'd been drinking and I was upset. Why don't you come back? That's what my father would have wanted. Please—" I held my arms out, not sure what else I could say to get Kassian to see how bad I felt about the whole thing.

Carol stepped up and touched me on my arm. "I'm sorry I didn't call sooner." She tipped her head at Kassian. "But he told me you knew he was here. I'm sure you must have been worried."

I took a deep breath and exhaled. "Yeah. Actually, I was. Very worried."

Kassian hung his head.

Carol said, "Kassian feels like you're mad at him. Like maybe you believe Abe's death was his fault somehow." Steely eyes met mine. "He's afraid he might not feel welcome there."

"No. I mean…" I looked back at Kassian, then at her. "That's not what I meant. It's just that some things weren't adding up. My father had left me something, and I couldn't find it, and I maybe jumped to the wrong—"

Carol came closer and touched my arm. "Josh. Relax. We're all on the same side here. I know about the missing diamonds."

I glanced at Kassian and his face drooped. "Can I talk with you? Privately?" I asked Carol.

She nodded and smiled at Kassian. "We'll be right back, dear." She led me through the dining room into the living room, stopping near a shiny black baby grand piano, the top covered with framed photographs. She whispered, "He says you believe he might have something to do with the missing diamonds, too."

I exhaled. I didn't really believe Kassian had taken the diamonds and then returned them—it didn't make any sense. But nothing made much sense regarding those stones, and I didn't know whom to trust. So I was distrustful of everyone, including myself. Especially myself. I wasn't sure I could handle anything properly, considering the emotional roller-coaster I'd been riding. "What do you know about them?"

"Abe told me about the diamonds. How he'd been collecting them for years. He wanted them to be his special gift to you. Eventually." She glanced over her shoulder to make sure Kassian hadn't snuck up on us. "He asked me if I knew someone who could give him an appraisal and I gave him a name. I never even saw any diamonds, except for the earrings and ring he gave me."

Her gaze drifted to a family portrait hanging on the wall. In it, three brown-haired kids and a gap-toothed husband surrounded a much younger Carol. "I know about family dynamics. And about leaving keepsakes and strained relationships. Believe me, Josh. Your father loved you and he wanted you to have his collection."

He hadn't told me about the diamonds. He hadn't told me about his upcoming marriage. He hadn't told me about his "cousin" staying in his basement. What had my father been waiting for? Now, of course, it was too late. My throat tightened and I forced myself to take a breath. "Do you believe Kassian?"

"About what?" Carol asked, as she stiffened.

"About everything. About anything. Did my father tell you Kassian claims he's related to us?"

A half smile appeared on Carol's otherwise staid face. "Yes. Abe mentioned it."

"What did he say? Is Kassian his cousin?"

The smile faded. "I don't know. But it didn't matter to Abe. Cousin or not, Abe would have taken him in. That was one of the things I loved most about your father. His compassion."

"What about Kassian and the diamonds?" I asked, more for confirmation than for anything else.

Carol shook her head. "Kassian did not take them. He isn't like that." She said it firmly and absolutely, in a way that invited no argument.

"Then who did?"

"That I don't know. I hope they will be recovered."

"They have been," I said. *At least some of them.*

Carol brightened. "You found them? Oh, that's terrific. Why didn't you … Never mind. Kassian will be relieved. And I'm sure you are, too." She started to leave the room but stopped short. "He came to me because he had nowhere else to go, and he trusted me because Abe did. But all he does here is mope around like a wounded puppy. I'll be leaving town to attend a conference for a few days, so … I assume you will take him back? He's comfortable there."

I didn't answer, ran through my options in my head. Nothing jumped out at me.

"He trusts you, Josh. You are Abe's son. To him, you're family."

I found myself nodding. "Sure. He can come back."

Carol smiled, then her expression hardened. "Of course, you must not berate him again. He deserves your respect." Her admonition made me feel even worse.

I nodded. "I won't. I just lost it. Won't happen again."

"And for his part, Kassian must abide by Abe's condition," she said, smiling once again. I was reminded of my father's stories about Henry Kissinger brokering peace in the Mideast.

I cocked my head. "Condition?"

"No drinking," she said.

Sounded like a good rule. For him and for me. Carol touched my arm. "Come on, let's go tell Kassian he's going home."

Home?

TWENTY-NINE

I TOOK KASSIAN STRAIGHT home and made sure he got settled in. We hadn't talked much in the car. Actually, I'd talked in my most soothing voice, but he'd just grunted a few answers, still plenty upset at me for what I'd done. Either that, or he was offended by both Carol and me for treating him like an unwanted child, passing him back and forth, custody going to the biggest loser. After apologizing again and swearing I'd never touch him in anger, I left him in his room, in his chair reading his magazine. Nice to get back to routine.

It was a little after three o'clock, and I needed to get going if I was going to meet Rachel at her school. She didn't know it, of course, but I thought she might appreciate the surprise gesture. A sign of caring. On the other hand, she might accuse me of stalking her. At this point, what did I have to lose?

Twenty minutes later, I pulled into a spot reserved for the Principal's Secretary, according to the white letters stenciled on the asphalt. There were about a dozen cars left in the lot, one of which was Rachel's Prius. I hopped out and took a position near the back door to wait for her. I leaned against the side of the building, one foot on the ground, the other flat against the red brick. All I needed was a cigarette dangling from the corner of my mouth and a surly sneer to make my juvenile delinquent pose authentic.

A couple teachers passed, eyed me with disdain, and hustled to their cars. Hopefully, Rachel would come out before one of them called the cops. I waited against the wall for about ten minutes, watching the vapor from my breath rise before my eyes in wispy streams. Then the door swung open and Rachel came striding out, carrying a tote bag overflowing with papers. She ducked her head against a gust of wind and when she raised it, she saw me and stopped walking. After a couple seconds, she came my way.

"Hey, good looking," I said in a tough-guy accent. "Wanna go to the malt shop and get a shake?" The idea that I watched too much *Happy Days* on TV Land crossed my mind.

A smile flirted with her lips. "Hello, Josh Handleman. How are you?"

I slicked the hair back behind my ears with my hands. "I'm cool," I said. "Real cool." I dropped the accent. "Actually, I'm freezing. Can we go somewhere and talk?"

She nodded and her smile grew.

We drove to a nearby Starbucks and parked our cars next to each other. I wanted to hold her hand as we went into the store, but I kept my hands jammed in my pockets. So did she.

We sat in the back while we sipped our coffees.

"I tried calling you over the weekend," I said.

Rachel stared down at her drink, and spoke without looking at me. "I know. I'm sorry. I was …"

231

"Listen, about the other night—"

She held up her hand. "I'm sorry, Josh. I shouldn't have come over like that without calling. That was rude." She reached out and touched my hand. "Please forgive me."

I wasn't expecting this. I'd been the one who'd been a jerk. "No, it wasn't—"

"Josh. Please. I need to say a few things." She stopped and waited for me to nod before continuing. "After we went out on New Year's Eve, I thought I'd finally met someone..." She choked up a bit and took a sip of coffee to clear her throat. "I thought I'd met someone who I could really get to know. Develop a relationship with. I know we'd only gone out a couple of times, but... well, it was really great. And I thought you—"

"I felt the same way, Rachel. Really. I wanted—"

She didn't let me complete my sentence. "Please, let me finish. This is hard for me." Another sip of coffee. "I thought you felt the same way. And I think you might *think* you do, but..."

I nodded. I'd heard a lot of this Dr. Phil talk from Dani, but I never really understood most of it. I didn't know what to say, so I simply nodded again.

"Josh, when you got that call from your ex-wife, I was jealous. How ridiculous. I mean, we'd just started dating. I hated myself for feeling that way."

My father's well-worn adage, *Save Your Hate for Hitler*, sprang to mind. As a teen, every time he said it, I peppered all my conversations with the word *hate*. "Don't be silly. There's nothing going on with me and Dani. Nothing." I put as much reassurance behind my statement as I could.

She shook her head. "That's not the point. I don't want to be so wrapped up in a guy that little stuff sets me off. I'm ashamed of how I've behaved since then. Not returning your calls, barging in."

"Come on. I'd really like to get to know you better, too. Think about New Year's Eve."

Instead of the smile I thought the memory would elicit, her eyes flashed. "What about Cyndi? You seemed like you wanted to get to know her the other night."

"Believe it or not, she came on to me."

Rachel gave me a *come on, get serious* look.

I held my hands out. "Really," I said. "Nothing going on there either. Not my type."

Her look intensified and she all but *harrumphed.* "So you don't like gorgeous women?"

"Just one, at the moment." I grinned, hoping to break her barriers down.

Her lopsided smile made a brief appearance. "I'm not sure it's wise for me to get involved. We're both on the rebound, and…"

"Why don't we start from scratch? Start all over. And this time we'll go real slow." I closed my eyes and brought both hands up in front of my face like a screen. Then I parted the screen and opened my eyes. "Why, hello there. I'm Josh Handleman."

She glanced at me, then stared at the ceiling, lips moving wordlessly, as if she were working out some calculus problem. After thirty seconds, she threw her hands up. "What the hell? Why not? Nana likes you, and she's got pretty good taste." She extended her hand. "I'm Rachel Rosen. Nice to meet you, Josh Handleman."

I asked Rachel to dinner, but she declined, saying she had some exercise plans with her iron-woman-in-training friend. I wondered if her plans included running on a treadmill next to a fitness maniac named Terrible. But we settled on going out tomorrow. It would be difficult, but I could wait another day.

On the way home, I stopped at the store and picked up a rotisserie chicken, some already-steamed broccoli, and a baguette for a "welcome back" dinner with Kassian. If I was going to live with the guy, I might as well try to make it as pleasant as possible. I didn't want to admit it, but I felt sorry for him.

When I pulled up, Lev's RX300 was parked in the driveway. I left the Taurus on the street, grabbed my grocery bag, and jogged to the door, girding myself for some kind of altercation.

Good thing.

I heard Lev yelling as I turned the key in the lock. I threw the door open and found them in the kitchen, Kassian sitting in a chair in the corner, Lev looming above him with his back to me, still in his coat, bellowing in Russian. Kassian's eyes were wide with fright, but to his credit, he hadn't run off. My arrival hadn't done anything to suppress Lev's rage.

Maybe they hadn't heard me above the din. "Hey. Cut it out," I shouted at them. Lev whipped around, and when he saw me, he took a small step away from Kassian. The fury drained from his face and his breathing slowed. Two seconds later the stone-faced scowl returned to its customary place.

"Hello, Joshua," Lev said, voice calm. He acted like I'd just dropped in from Jupiter without witnessing any of the tirade.

"What the hell is going on?"

"We were having a small discussion, Kassian and I," Lev said, as if it were the most logical, most reasonable thing in the world. Never mind he was shouting and had Kassian pinned in the corner, cowering. I thought of how I'd bullied Kassian and felt like a jerk. Again.

"A discussion? Sounded more like you were about to tear his head off. Tell me what's going on."

"Yes, a discussion," Lev said, shrugging. *No big deal.*

I addressed Kassian. "What's the problem? Lev was screaming at you."

Kassian eyed Lev, but was met with studied impassiveness. I wouldn't want to face Lev in a poker showdown. Kassian didn't answer me, but his eyes kept pinballing between Lev and me. I knew Kassian feared Lev. Up until now, I hadn't known why. Of course, I still didn't really know why, but with what I'd just seen, I figured Kassian had reason to be worried.

I set my groceries on the kitchen table and moved closer to Kassian. Lev drifted away and I planted myself between the two combatants. "Kassian, why did you let him in?"

Another timid glance at Lev. "I didn't—"

Lev said, "It was a misunderstanding."

I glared at Lev. "I'm trying to talk to Kassian. Please let me." I turned back to Kassian. "Why did you let him in? I told you not to answer the door."

Kassian mumbled something under his breath.

"What? Speak up."

Kassian cleared his throat and spoke to me, although his eyes didn't leave Lev. "He threatened to burn down your house if I did not let him in." Kassian's lower lip trembled.

"It was a misunderstanding. I meant no harm," Lev said. He bowed his head slightly to Kassian and spoke through clenched jaw. "Please forgive me. I need to be going now. Perhaps we can continue our conversation in the near future. In the meantime, you should think about what we have discussed. Remember, you are a Russian Jew. It is never too late to begin acting like one." With a curt nod, Lev started toward the door.

I held up my hand like a traffic cop. "Hold on. No one's leaving until I know what's going on."

Lev stopped moving and faced me. There was something behind his stoic face that I'd never seen or felt before. Something I couldn't quite make out, something I wasn't sure I wanted to. He didn't speak, but turned and left the kitchen. I glanced at Kassian, who still looked like a critter in the headlights, and followed Lev.

I caught up to him just as he was opening the front door. I grabbed his coat sleeve. "Lev, hold up. We need to talk."

Lev didn't move his body, simply swiveled his head. "Joshua. Please unhand me." His voice was low and steady, but I could tell he was fuming inside. I let go and he faced me full on. "I have given you many chances to serve justice for your father. And you have not chosen to do so. Instead, you harbor the man—the animal— responsible for his death. I do not know what runs through your mind as you are doing this. But I am sure that Abe did not raise you to behave in this fashion. He would not even recognize you." As Lev talked, his words came out more rapidly, with more force.

"Kassian did not kill my father." I was sick of saying it, just as I was sure Lev was sick of hearing it. But the truth was like that sometimes.

Lev straightened. "There are many things you do not know about Kassian. And about your father. Things you would not understand even if you did know." His eyes had focused elsewhere, and now they came back to me. "But you have failed, so I shall take

236

care of things in my own way. Goodbye, Joshua." He opened the door and stepped out onto the porch.

"Wait, Lev," I called out.

He drew up and turned, the light spilling out of the front door illuminating his face, like a body-less ghoul at the haunted house. "I have already waited too long, Joshua. Now it is time for action." A small, sinister smile formed on his ghostly face as he disappeared into the pitch-black night.

THIRTY

I TRIED TO COAX Kassian into telling me what he and Lev had been arguing about. I asked pointed questions; Kassian remained mute. I shifted tactics and asked about his forest hideaway and got the same results. He kept shaking his head, refusing to speak. For some reason, I'd left Wentworth's name out of it, but I don't think it would have mattered had I invoked the name of Joseph Stalin. Kassian wasn't talking. And the more questions I fired at him, the more agitated he became. If his anxiety was simply an act meant to put me off, he'd missed his calling on the silver screen.

When I finished my fruitless interrogation, Kassian paced around the house, wringing his hands and mumbling to himself in at least two languages. Every time he sat, he'd bounce back up within ten seconds. I tried to calm him down with little success. Talking in a soothing voice didn't work. Getting him to eat was futile. I thought about offering him a drink but didn't want to go down that path. Finally, after showing him I'd locked every door and window in the house, I managed to get him into his bed. I turned the TV on to keep him company and said goodnight, promising to keep the light on in his bathroom all night. I guess these were some of the joys I missed by not having kids.

I went upstairs and booted my laptop. Navigated my way to Google. Called up my previous searches and hit Wentworth again, and dozens of listings materialized. Probably the same pages as before, except now I was determined—and resigned—to read them carefully. There had to be something I missed the first time.

Forty-five minutes reading various websites and insider blogs and news releases gave me a pretty clear picture of Stephen Robert Wentworth, Digitelex V.P. Unfortunately for me and my conspiracy theories, he seemed like your basic, run-of-the-mill corporate citizen. A stand-up guy. Not a whiff of scandal or controversy. Of course, maybe that made him *unlike* your run-of-the-mill corporate executive.

I'd come across a handful of photos, most showing a smiling, handsome guy, about thirty-five or so, shaking hands or slapping backs or standing shoulder-to-shoulder with other young executives, also handsome and smiling. Cookie-cutter execs. Ho-hum.

I kept mousing and clicking, determined to find some connection between Kassian and Wentworth. But what could an old Russian Jew and a young, up-and-coming WASPy telecom executive have in common? A love of vodka?

I'd plowed through twenty-four pages of Google effluent, when I hit upon a Business Elite newsletter, a couple years old. In it, there was a small spotlight article on Wentworth, and in addition to the usual fluff about his company and its fiscal goals, there were a few paragraphs on his personal life, including a photo of him and his wife. Both were dressed for fun in the sun, walking hand-in-hand at some kind of fair or carnival. Of course, Wentworth looked corporate, even in casual clothes, but it was the picture of his wife that captured my attention. The brunette in white shorts looked familiar.

I scrolled down to the caption: *Stephen Wentworth and wife, Suzanne Miller, cavort at the Elite Spring Festival.* I'd gone to high school with Suzanne. In fact, she ran with Tammy's group of friends, and I'd hung out with her on more than one occasion. More importantly, I'd heard the name recently. Erik said she was a recipient of one of my father's angel loans.

Small world.

———

I'd finally arranged to have my mail forwarded and was catching up on the bundle that had arrived today when the doorbell rang. Instinctively, I glanced at my watch: 10:45. It had been a long day and I was dragging, but my spirits perked up. Could it be Rachel, coming by for a nightcap, or for something even more intoxicating? I chided myself for thinking such thoughts as I rushed to the door and peeked through the peephole. My hopes were dashed. The visitor was Brandon Flannery, wearing a black leather duster, a backward baseball cap, and a sneer.

"Yes?" I asked, cracking the door open.

"I need to talk to you," he said, as he put his palm flat against the door and pushed.

I resisted briefly, for show, then allowed the door to swing open. "Please, come in."

Brandon entered and I could tell he was pissed. About what, I didn't know, but I had the feeling I was going to find out.

"What the fuck do you think you're doing asking around about me?" Before I could answer, he stepped forward and poked his finger in my chest. Just like the pissed-off guys did in the movies before they kicked the shit out of someone. "Huh? Answer me, you little prick."

"What are you talking about? And calm down, will you?" I smiled and feigned ignorance, trying to defuse things. Backing up, I led him into the kitchen. Motioned to a chair. He followed, but didn't sit, preferring to intimidate me from a standing position.

"You were asking about my interest in VidGamZZZ?" A bit of slobber leaked from his mouth. I wondered who had blabbed about my questions. Terrible Teresywzki or my best friend who had trouble knowing when to keep his mouth shut and when to divulge information. At the moment, it didn't matter. I was more concerned with my physical well-being than about placing blame.

"Oh, that. My father was involved with them. Just trying to see what he was up to. Your name came up." I shuffled to my right, putting a chair between Brandon and me. "Nothing special."

"Your questions can screw things up for me. People find out I'm interested, they're going to jack up the price. Could cost me some serious coin." He jabbed a finger at me, but it didn't find any mark—my chest was out of range. "Besides, it's none of your fucking business."

"But is it true? Are you interested in buying my father's share?"

He cocked his head at me. "You don't even own it. Fuck you." The words were tough, but his tone had reduced to a simmer. "You got any say about what happens to his piece?" A glimmer of something shined through Brandon's mask of hostility.

I smiled, like I knew something he didn't. "Nope. 'Fraid not." I kept the smile propped up as I watched his face sag. "Anything else you'd like to ask me? You know, while we're here, just shooting the breeze?"

Like a switch had been flipped, Belligerent Brandon returned. "Stay the fuck out of my business. I wouldn't want you to get hurt or anything. Wouldn't want another accident to befall the Handleman family. That would be truly tragic." His head whipped to one side.

Kassian stood in the kitchen doorway, wide-eyed.

"The fuck you looking at?" Brandon said.

Kassian retreated a few steps, then turned and fled into the living room.

Brandon's cold eyes settled on mine. "Keep away from me, Handleman. And keep your little friend away from me too. No telling what might happen if you don't," he growled.

The door slammed on his way out.

When the coast was clear, Kassian emerged from his hiding spot. "He is an angry man."

I sighed. "Yeah. More bark than bite, I think." At least I hoped so.

"I have seen him before. He was angry then, too," Kassian said, eyes on mine.

"What do you mean?"

"He visited Abe here. They argued. About what, I do not know," Kassian said, anticipating my questions. "I do not think Abe liked him very much."

"Anything else you can remember about their argument?"

Kassian shook his head. "Sorry. I closed my door that day and turned the TV on. I could hear their loud voices, but not their words. When he left, Abe was quite upset. Used some bad language." He seemed apologetic for having to tell me that.

"Okay, Kassian. Thanks. Time to get some sleep, huh?" I said, but Kassian looked more frightened than tired. Twenty minutes later—after some placating discussion about the weather—I managed to persuade Kassian to return to his room and go to sleep.

Then I went to the kitchen and guzzled two beers standing at the sink, barely pausing to breathe. Finished with my mini-binge, I rinsed out the cans and tossed them into the recycling bin. I went upstairs, brushed my teeth, and hopped into bed, struggling to quell the adrenaline rush and quiet the cacophony of voices in my head. Finally, the beer took effect and the voices trailed off as I tumbled down the rabbit hole into a deep dark slumber.

A hand on my arm. A voice calling my name. Darkness all around, but the pressure on my arm remained and I heard my name again. And again. "Joshua. Wake up."

I broke through my sleepy fog. Kassian sat on the bed, shaking me. My room was dark except for a very faint glow from a light somewhere down the hall. "What's wrong?"

"I must talk with you," he said.

I glanced at the clock. "At 3:14? Can't it wait?"

"No. It cannot." Kassian's hand still rested on my arm, but he'd stopped the shaking.

"Is the house on fire?" I asked, then felt bad, considering how Lev had threatened Kassian earlier. "Sorry. Bad choice of words.

Hang on." I pushed the covers down a bit and Kassian's hand slid off with them. "Let me turn the lamp on."

"No!" Kassian said, then softer, "Please do not. For what I have to say, I would prefer the dark."

I knew there were many things best said under cover of darkness, things that might seem unbearable in the light. What was Kassian about to lay on me? I braced myself for bad news. Three-in-the-morning news. "Okay. What's so important?"

"I have done many terrible things in my life. From when I was small, until this day. Sometimes the things I have done were out of necessity. Sometimes not." He paused, and I felt him shift on the bed next to me. It was too dark to make out even the most shadowy of shadows. "Most of these things I have regretted. Not always at the time, but later. Often, I have sought forgiveness. Even when it has not been given, I have felt better. I wasted a lot of my life, Joshua, and I have only just begun to care that I do not have much of that life left."

I pushed myself higher against the headboard, propping myself into a sitting position. As I moved, so did Kassian. He was practically sitting in my lap. "Look, Kassian. We all make mistakes. We're human. Don't be too hard on yourself."

He didn't answer me and a sour feeling took root in my stomach. Was he about to confess that he killed my father? My stomach clenched tighter. Had Lev been right? "Is there something you're trying to get off your chest?"

Kassian's warm breath hit me as he exhaled. He'd inched closer. Darkness also broke down the barriers of personal space. "Joshua. I lied to your father and I lied to you. I am sorry."

"Lied about what?"

"About my relationship to him. I told him I was his cousin, but I am not. I am not related to him—or to you—in any way." His hand found my arm again. "Please forgive me."

Kassian's revelation wasn't news to me, but I was glad he'd decided to tell the truth about it, for his sake. "Don't worry about it. Obviously, my father cared for you as a person, not just as some distant twig of the family tree. I'm glad you told me. Thanks, Kassian."

"I do not deserve your thanks. Maybe you should not call me Kassian. I was not born with that name. It was the only way I could escape and get to this country."

I didn't know what to say to that so I kept quiet. Sniffling filled the void, halting at first, sounding more like whimpering as the seconds ticked by.

"Hey," I said. "You might not have been born with the name, but that's how I know you. Would it be okay if I kept calling you Kassian?" I said it like I was talking to a child who'd just dropped his ice cream cone.

I guess it worked because he stopped crying. "I have been known as Kassian for so long, I would . . . Yes, please call me Kassian. That would be nice."

I patted his arm. "Good, good. Now why don't you go back to sleep? We can talk more in the morning, if you want. And really, I'm sure my father wouldn't have cared so much about the little white lie." Which might or might not have been true. At this point, it surely didn't matter one whit. It did feel a little weird, though, speaking for my father.

Kassian didn't respond, but he hadn't left. I could still feel his weight on the side of the bed and hear his raspy breathing. Close, like he was about ten inches away. "Kassian?"

A small voice answered. "Yes. I am here."

"Is there something else?"

"I am afraid," he said, voice tremulous.

"Go to sleep, Kassian. The house is locked. No one will bother us."

"I have not told you the complete truth," he said. "About the day your father died."

I reached over to the lamp on my nightstand and flicked the switch. Kassian and I both shielded our eyes. "What are you talking about?" I asked, squinting through my fingers.

Kassian kept his hand over his eyes while he spoke. "The day your father died, I saw someone come in the morning before I left."

"Who?"

He shook his head, eyes still covered, head down. I thought he was going to clam up, reconsider his admission. But he raised up and exposed his face, jaw set with determination. "I heard the knock on the door, so I peeked out the window. His car was in the driveway."

"Whose car?"

Kassian's face tightened. "Lev's. He came over that morning."

THIRTY-ONE

"Lev was here? That morning?" I opened my eyes wider as they adjusted to the light. "Are you sure?"

"Yes. As soon as I saw him, I left. Quickly. You have seen how he treats me."

"Yeah, I've seen." I shook my head. "But you must be confused."

"I know what I saw."

"Then why did you wait until now to tell me?" I knew exactly why—now he was angry at Lev and wanted to get him into hot water. This was Kassian's attempt at revenge. Maybe Lev was right, maybe Kassian was nothing more than an unscrupulous liar.

"I was afraid," Kassian said, not meeting my eyes.

"Afraid of what?"

"Lev. He has friends. In the Russian mafia." Kassian turned his head away and stared at the window. Never mind that that the curtains were drawn.

"Come on. Lev? Russian mafia? Gimme a break," I laughed, then stopped when I realized Kassian wasn't laughing along. "You're serious? Lev isn't any more connected than I am. And trust me, I'm not."

"I am telling you the truth. I know what I saw. If Lev lied to me about his friends…" He shrugged and paused, thinking. "But I believe him. It does not surprise me that he would know such people."

"Kassian, what you're telling me doesn't make much sense." I was always taught it was bad form to call someone a flat-out liar. Too many nuances in life to be sure.

He exhaled. "I do not blame you for not believing me. I am like the boy who cried wolf. I have told many stories. But this is true, I swear it."

"Okay. Listen. Why don't we talk more about this in the morning? Things may seem different in the light of day."

Kassian slowly got up off the bed, hangdog look plastered on his face. He trudged out the door, not glancing back. I called out to him, "Goodnight. Sleep well," and felt like a fool doing so. He wasn't going to sleep any more than I was.

———

I'm sure I must have gotten fifteen or twenty good minutes of sleep the rest of the night, and when I awoke, I stayed in bed for a couple of minutes while my thoughts coalesced. A few questions tugged at me. Why was Kassian so afraid of Lev? Was that what the yelling was all about? Could Kassian be right about seeing Lev earlier that morning? It seemed doubtful, but there was an easy way to find out.

I got up to go to the bathroom and almost tripped over Kassian. He'd dragged a folding chair into the hallway and was sitting watch right outside my room.

"What are you doing?" I asked, trying to repress my snarl. I wasn't a morning person.

"I am afraid."

I tried hard not to roll my eyes. "I told you, you're safe here. Nothing's going to happen," I said. "As long as you don't open the damn door," I added, practically barking at him. He shrunk in his chair, looking tiny and alone. Shit. I was so much more pleasant after a cup of coffee.

I took a deep breath and kneeled. Spoke gently. "How about this? How about I take you out to breakfast and we can talk things over some more?"

"That would be good, Joshua." He bit his lower lip. "Thank you."

"Give me about fifteen minutes. I need to get dressed and I've got a call to make, okay?"

Kassian shuffled off, and I waited until he was out of earshot before I called Lev. Peter answered and after we exchanged pleasantries, I asked to speak to his father. I needed to get this cleared up ASAP.

"Sorry, just missed him. Said he was going to run a few errands before he set out for Pikesville," Peter said. Chewing noises accompanied his answer.

Pikesville was on the north side of Baltimore. An hour and a half drive, more with traffic. "What's in Pikesville?"

"Some kind of Jewish Aging Conference. Ever since he got involved with the home, it's been one boondoggle after another," Peter said, a touch of amusement in his voice.

Carol mentioned something about a conference, too. "Know when he'll be back?" Probably an all-day affair at the least.

I heard the sound of paper rustling. "Let's see. It's marked on the calendar as being a two-day thing, but sometimes he only goes for part of the time. You never know with him." Peter swallowed something. "Why? What's up?"

I lowered my voice in case Kassian was wandering around. "Kassian's got some wild story about seeing Lev at the house the morning my father died. *Hours* before he said he came over. I was just going to ask Lev about it. I'll try his cell."

Peter snorted. "Good luck."

"Thanks."

"If he checks in, I'll tell him you called. Will you be at home?"

"Kassian and I are going out to breakfast now. I guess I'll be in and out. You've got my cell, right?"

"Sure. Have a good one," Peter said, and hung up.

Kassian and I settled on IHOP, and we took a booth in the rear. He insisted on sitting with his back to the wall, so he could see who entered the restaurant, as if he were a notorious gunslinger in the Wild Wild West. Kassian the Kid rides again.

Over pecan pancakes, I attempted to assuage his fear. Tried a host of different arguments—logical, emotional, spiritual—all in vain. He was terrified of Lev and of Lev's supposed mafia friends, who in Kassian's mind were anxious to get some much-needed torturing practice. No matter what I said, he countered with his version of the truth—he saw Lev that morning and Lev was going to hurt him. Finally, I'd had enough. Time to put the ol' Handleman foot down.

"I've known Lev a long time. Since I was a child. And I know he's gruff and rough and rude at times, but he is a man of his word and he would never actually hurt anyone. Not on purpose. You have nothing to worry about."

Kassian stared at me. "I saw him that morning. Perhaps he had something to do with Abe's death."

"Here's what I think." I pushed my coffee cup to the side and leaned forward, ready to put my proverbial cards on the table. "I think Lev accused you of having something to do with my father's death." I paused and examined Kassian's face. His eyes darted around and I knew I'd nailed it. "And I think you made up that story about Lev being there to get back at him. Striking back is a natural human reaction. But you can't go around accusing people of stuff you know they didn't do. It isn't right." It seemed I was saying that a lot lately. Maybe things were different in Russia. Maybe in Russia, accusing innocent people was a parlor game.

Kassian shook his head. "I did not make it up."

"Then why didn't you tell me sooner?" My patience had evaporated. Sometimes you had to treat children like children. I slid out of the booth. "Enough stories. Let's go."

"I told you, I was—"

"Enough. I've heard enough." I reached into my wallet, threw a five on the table for a tip and stalked off to pay the cashier, leaving Kassian talking to himself.

On the drive home, I cranked the volume on the radio high enough to make conversation impossible. Not that Kassian wanted to talk. He stared out the passenger window the entire time, as if it were the first time he'd seen the Northern Virginia landscape. When we got home, he let me get out of the car first, and he trudged around to his separate entrance in the back, the first time he'd ever done that when we'd arrived together. Maybe he'd finally gotten the message.

I was hanging up my coat in the closet when I heard Kassian's strangled scream. I dashed downstairs and into his bedroom. One of the ancient windows facing the backyard was wide open, glass sliders broken on the floor, as if someone had kicked them in. Kassian huddled in his chair with his knees up, hands clasped around them. Panic had seized him and he stared at me with wild eyes.

"What the hell?" I asked, but I knew Kassian didn't have a clue what had happened. He didn't answer, but pointed to his bed. There, on top of the covers, was his busted picture frame. The glass in the frame had been smashed, a few shards still clung to the wood. Carefully, I picked it up and examined the photo, heart skipping a few beats. Someone had scratched out the eyes of a much younger Kassian.

THIRTY-TWO

I TOLD KASSIAN TO stay where he was as I went through the house to make sure everything was okay. Room-by-room, I searched for any sign of an intruder. Nothing else seemed touched, let alone missing. Whoever had done this had broken in through the window, left their message, and departed. How many times would my house be broken into? As soon as I had a free minute, my first call would be to a security outfit to get an alarm system installed.

My shoes crunched on the broken glass as I boarded up the window. Kassian rocked in his chair and watched. It didn't take a genius to come up with a list of suspects—and it was a mighty short list. After the tongue-lashing Lev gave Kassian last night—not to mention the not-so-veiled threat—his name was number one with a bullet. Peter had said Lev was planning to run errands before he headed to his conference. Go to the bank, drop off some dry cleaning, break in and terrorize an old man. Just crossing a few items off the to-do list.

I pulled out my phone and called Lev's cell phone. After a few rings, it rolled into voice mail. I left a message asking Lev to call me as soon as he could, but I knew if he'd been the one to do this, he wouldn't bother.

I put the phone down and mumbled something about reporting the break-in to the cops, and Kassian erupted. He pleaded with me not to involve them. Of course, calling them was the right thing to do, but I knew nothing would come of it, just like my plea to Detective Morris had fallen on jaded ears. The police spent their resources on serious crimes. I'm sure they would have been interested in the breaking and entering, but photograph defacing wasn't high on their list. Whatever was going on was connected to Kassian. And with Kassian so spooked, he wouldn't hold up well under police questioning, even if I could persuade him to cooperate. Maybe when he calmed down, we'd report it. For now, it would have to wait.

I'd planned on talking with Goose about Flannery's desire to buy into his company, and I'd planned on talking to him alone. But in light of what had transpired, I decided to take Kassian with me. When I suggested it to Kassian, he hadn't needed any convincing.

We arrived at VidGamZZZ, and I was about to ask Kassian to stay in the car, but one look at his face told me that wouldn't fly. Today was going to be a long day, just me and my Russian shadow. We entered the warehouse and a gangly guy who couldn't have been older than fifteen asked if he could help us. We told him we were there to see Goose, and he announced it over the intercom, then went back to his computer screen, not giving another thought to me or Kassian. Live bodies with physical constraints paled next to untethered pixels.

At least we were entertained while we waited. Instead of basketball, this time two guys faced off in some kind of duel involving slingshots, Velcro-covered ping-pong balls, and fuzzy sweaters. Kassian seemed enthralled by their American ingenuity and creative spirit.

Finally, Goose called to us from down the hall and we made our way back, slowly. I had to stop every couple steps to nudge Kassian along as he paused to peer at all the crazy games being developed on the monitors we passed.

"So, this must be Kassian," Goose said, as we took seats around a small Formica-topped table. The sign on the door read *Conference Room*, but there was only room for about five people. Maybe six, if they were all as skinny as Goose and the gangly fifteen-year-old. "Heard a lot about you. You can call me Goose."

"Hello, Mr. Goose," Kassian said. He folded his hands together and placed them on the table.

Goose smiled and looked at me. Probably wasn't used to Russian manners. "I need to talk to you about something, and Kassian here is just along for the ride. I'm sure we won't even know he's here," I said.

"Okie dokie, gents. What's on your mind, Josh?"

"Brandon Flannery, that's what."

As soon as I said the name, Goose leaned back in his chair and slapped himself on the forehead. "This about your dust-up at the poker game? He's a dipshit, all right, but sometimes we need him to have enough for a game. Don't mind taking his money, though."

"It's not about that. This is serious. I—"

"You seemed pretty serious at the game, pardner. I haven't seen you that mad for a long time." Goose gave Kassian a sidelong glance then looked back at me.

I glared at him. "Would you please listen? What's the deal with him trying to buy into your company?"

Goose blew out some air. "Fat fucking chance." He glanced again at Kassian, whose eyelids had started to droop. He seemed to be entering another zone. "Brandon came to us a few months ago, wanting a piece of the pie. Said he had some ideas that would really help us. Can you believe that? We hardly even know this guy, just through Erik and even then, we've just played poker with him a handful of times. Why he thinks we want him in our business is beyond me."

"What did you tell him?"

Goose looked at me as if I believed video games were for geeks. "Told him to fuck off. Whaddya think? Course we phrased it a little nicer. Didn't want to lose a poker player."

"So he tried to buy my father's stake?"

"He tried. Two seconds after Brandon asked your father about it, Abe called us. Let us know what the jerk was trying to do. And he told us we could relax, he wasn't planning to sell it to him. I guess your father didn't like him either." Goose pulled out a chair next to him, turned sideways, and rested his foot on it. "Maybe Flannery hatred is on the Handleman gene."

"Or maybe nobody likes him because he's an ass," I said. Next to me, Kassian's eyes had closed. Guess that's what happens when you don't sleep at night. A nap sounded good to me, too. "Why does he want to get in so badly?"

Goose was taken aback. "Because we're a great company with a tremendous upside, that's why. Your father knew a good investment when he saw one."

"No offense." I held up my hands. "How did Flannery even know my father invested in you?"

"Yeah, Matt and I wondered that. Coulda been through Erik, although Matt thinks we might have said something about it during one of our poker games. Can't remember for sure. Doesn't matter. He's not getting a part of me. No way, no how." Goose nodded toward Kassian and whispered to me, "What's with the side-kick?"

"Long story. Where's *yours*?"

"Carla? At work, I think. Why?" Goose seemed alarmed.

"I meant Matt."

Goose exhaled. "Oh, right. He's around someplace. Probably kicking someone's ass. He's the bad cop around here and I'm the good one. At least this month. We switch it up every so often or people will get wise." Another glance at Kassian. "Want me to get a pillow for your friend?"

Kassian's head tipped back slightly and his lips parted, but he stayed asleep. I nodded toward the door and got up. Goose followed me into the hallway.

I kept my voice low, just in case Kassian woke up and was listening at the door. "You remember Suzanne Miller?"

"Sure. Why?"

"Know anything about her recent activities?"

"Her 'recent activities'? You've been watching too many detective movies." Goose smiled, but I didn't return it. He wiped it off his face. "I saw her a couple of years ago, I think, at a party or something. Talked to her for a couple of minutes. Can't say I remember a whole lot." He stopped and looked at me. "Why?"

"Anything else?"

Goose, tapped his head with a pen he'd taken out of his pocket. "Let's see. She was married. Kids." Then he jabbed his pen into the air. "I remember. I saw her at an Elite party. Her husband is a telecom guy. Successful, too."

"You're in the Elite." A statement.

"Yeah. So what?" More tapping, this time his chin.

"Nothing," I said, shaking it off. Of course he was in the Elite. Everyone in Northern Virginia was, myself included. I felt somehow remiss in not signing up Kassian, although I guess it wouldn't surprise me if he were already a member too. "Did you know if my father had any business dealings with her?"

Goose's eyebrows came together. "Hmm. Don't know, but it would make sense. She's in the county's planning office. You know, parks and trails and things. Abe might have worked with her on some of his development projects."

"Did you know she was one of his 'angels,' too?"

He shook his head. "No. We didn't have any club meetings. Besides, Abe's interest in our company was more of a straight investment, not so much an 'angel' thing."

"Why do you think that was?"

Goose twirled the pen in his hand. "I told you. Because we're a great company with a tremendous upside. Why else?"

I rolled my eyes. "Know anything else about Suzanne?"

"Nope. Why don't you look up Tammy and ask her about Suzanne? They were pretty tight, weren't they?" he said, then he snapped his fingers. "Hey, did you know Tammy was—"

I held up my hand. "Yes. I know."

Goose shook his head. "And you didn't have a clue back then, did you?" He tried to hold back a snicker but didn't have much success. "Tammy was always a great practical joker." His snicker transformed into a full-blown belly-buster.

"Yeah, well, I got the last laugh. I'm dating her sister Rachel." I grinned. "In fact, I'm going out with her tonight."

His mouth opened. "No shit? Wasn't she a little scrawny?"

"Not anymore, my friend. Not anymore."

THIRTY-THREE

I USUALLY DON'T AGREE with restaurant reviews I read in the papers, but I took Rachel to a new seafood place in Great Falls that had just opened to accolades. White linens on the table, waiters in black suits, terrific wine list. Lobster to die for. There I was, gazing over an intimate candlelit table at a beautiful girl, everything perfect. Everything except the old Russian sitting next to us.

Rachel was being a good sport about having Kassian along. In fact, when I'd suggested it, she thought it was a terrific idea and agreed without hesitation. I'm not sure what that said about my dinner companionship, but I admired her flexibility. She'd been perky on the drive up, telling stories about her students and about some of the other teachers at her school. All through the first course, she'd turned on the charm, trying to engage Kassian in conversation. And she'd been successful. Slowly, she'd chipped away at his hard shell and he'd responded, becoming more animated. The change was remarkable. I got the feeling I could have uttered the exact words, and Kassian wouldn't have said "boo!" to me. For the most part, I'd picked up on that and kept quiet, letting Rachel steer the conversation. Play to your strengths, my father always told me.

"So, Kassian. Tell me about your family," she said, giving him her full attention. If I wasn't finding Kassian's transformation so fascinating, I might have been miffed about her barely looking in my direction all evening.

Kassian glanced at me, then smiled and turned to Rachel. "I was married once. A long time ago." He stopped talking, but didn't take his eyes off Rachel.

She leaned in. "What happened?"

"I walked away one night and never returned. I wasn't a good husband." He cast his eyes downward. "Or a good father."

I remembered Kassian's photograph on the dresser. Husband, wife, baby, all smiling. Then an image of the destroyed photo, smile almost literally wiped off their faces. I could feel Kassian's sorrow.

Rachel looked my way, then asked him in a soft voice. "That must have been very difficult, leaving your wife and child."

Kassian nodded, still looking away.

"Was your child a boy or a girl?"

Kassian mouthed the word girl, then repeated it, barely audible. "Girl. We called her Mischa, after my grandmother. Ah, that was many years ago. Many hard and unpleasant years."

Rachel leaned closer to him, touched his arm. "But you're turning things around now, right? That's what counts. We can only move forward, and from what I can tell, you're doing a fine job."

Kassian nodded. "You are very kind, Miss Rachel. Very kind."

She glanced at me and smiled, obviously pleased with herself. I'd told Rachel a little of Kassian's recent history. She'd asked me a few questions about him, and I hadn't had any answers, causing her to look at me funny—and to take him on as a challenge. For some reason, I'd never really asked him about what happened before he showed up at my father's doorstep. Seemed irrelevant, but maybe I was insensitive. Dani always used to wonder about my lack of curiosity about stuff like that, too. Must be a girl-guy thing.

Our main courses arrived. Rachel and I both got lobster—tail for me, ravioli for her. Kassian ordered a lamb chop. We'd tried steering him toward some fish or shrimp dish, but he had his heart set on lamb. After two bites, he declared he wasn't really hungry. Rachel and I had no problem finishing our meals.

We ordered coffee and once our dinner plates were cleared away, Rachel resumed her soft-pedal probe. "What was it like growing up in Russia?" she asked, eyes twinkling at Kassian as if he were the only other one in the room.

He blinked rapidly. "Hard. My parents left me when I was eleven."

Rachel gasped. "Oh my God. That's terrible. They just left?"

Kassian nodded. I thought I detected a tear. "Left or died. One day they did not come home. My aunt sent me to live in an orphanage with many others. They did not treat us well. Not well at all. They locked us in at night. To keep us safe." Something painful flashed across his face, then disappeared.

"I'm so sorry. That must have been very difficult for you." Rachel reached out again for Kassian's arm, but he slipped it under the table.

"Yes. Terrible." Kassian turned to me. "Joshua. I am very tired. Perhaps we could go now?"

I looked from him to Rachel, both seemed spent. Emotions will do that to you, I guess. "Sure. No problem." I motioned to the waiter, told him we decided to skip our coffee, and paid the bill.

When we got to Rachel's condo, I walked her to the door and we necked like horny teenagers for a couple minutes. She disengaged first. "I've got to get up for school in the morning. And you've got your roomie to think about," she said. Then she wrapped me up in another hug and whispered in my ear. "You're a good person, Josh Handleman. Take care of Kassian, okay?"

I drove home in silence, savoring the taste and smell and feel of Rachel, while Kassian remained mum in the back seat.

Two hours later, I was reading in my bed when Kassian knocked on my door. "What's up?" I asked. *Another midnight confession?*

"I have a favor to ask, Joshua." Standing in the doorway in his pajamas, Kassian looked like a frightened boy. And it wasn't just his size. He said, "Can I sleep in your room with you?"

I sighed, got up, dragged an air mattress from a closet in the study, and set it up on the floor. Found him a blanket and got him tucked in.

"Good night, Kassian. Sleep well."

"Thank you, Joshua. Good night."

———

The next morning at breakfast, I told Kassian I had more people to see. An hour later when I went to the car, I found him in the backseat already buckled in.

"What are you doing?"

"I am afraid to be alone today. I will be quiet. You will not notice me."

I'd had enough of the me-and-my-shadow routine yesterday. And I did notice him—or at least what he was wearing. His gray cardigan sweater and no coat. "You're going to be cold today. Frigid." The weather guy on the news said today would be the coldest day of the winter so far, wind chills flirting with the zero mark and nasty weather on the way. For once, it seemed like he knew what he was talking about. The morning sky was flat and gray and close, and I could already feel the impending snow on the back of my neck.

Kassian stared at me.

"Why don't you get a coat? I'll wait."

He cocked his head at me, as if I were going to burn rubber as soon as he stepped from the car. "Go ahead. I promise I'll wait for you."

Kassian eyed me again, then got out and walked—quickly—up the walk and into the house.

I'd hoped he'd be calm enough to be on his own today, but I can't say that I really blamed him. Someone bashing into my room and scratching the eyes out of a photo would have me spooked too, if I was the one in the portrait.

I felt bad for what I was about to do—the old bait and switch—but I didn't want him around when I spoke to the people on my list today. Hopefully, he'd go along without a fuss.

He darted out of the house, then slowed when he saw I had, in fact, waited for him. He wore a blue, puffy ski jacket, two sizes too big. It looked ridiculous, but when the wind whipped through him, he wouldn't care what other people thought.

Ten minutes later, Kassian and I signed in at the front desk of the Hebrew Home and I asked the attendant there to page DeRon. A short while later, he showed up, looking fresh and crisp in his white uniform. He smiled broadly at Kassian. "Hello, Mr. Kassian. How are you?"

Kassian nodded tentatively and his eyes darted around the lobby. I had to cajole him big time to get him out of the car, making wild-ass promises that Lev wouldn't be around today, although I had no idea where Lev was. Not yet, anyway. My first task was tracking him down.

DeRon spoke to me. "And how are you, Mr. Handleman?"

I shook his hand, and whatever had rubbed him wrong the other day seemed to have been forgotten. "Fine. Please call me Josh, okay?" I kept my own smile bright, making sure I was on my best behavior. Didn't want to say something to set him off, especially since I needed his help.

"Where have you been? Haven't seen much of you lately. Miss our little chats," DeRon said to Kassian, who was practically floating with the attention.

"I've been around. Just around," Kassian said.

"You going to spend the day with us?" DeRon asked, looking back and forth from Kassian to me.

"Yes, that would be terrific. Kassian's been saying how much he likes it here. What's on tap today, activity-wise?" I said.

DeRon eyed me strangely, but answered. "We've got card games starting in a few minutes, followed by a book discussion later. You always like those, don't you, Mr. Kassian?"

Kassian nodded and scoped out the lobby again. As long as Lev didn't show up, things would go smoothly. "Sounds fun," I said, winking at DeRon. "I'll pick you up here later. Sometime this afternoon. Okay?" Kassian's attention had drifted to two little girls playing with dolls on the floor, next to an older lady in a wheelchair. One of them combed her doll's long blond hair, while the other made her doll walk in little halting steps. I touched Kassian on the shoulder to get his attention. "I'll pick you up later, okay?"

He nodded at me, then refocused on the little girls. I steered DeRon over to the side. "He's a bit nervous. A little under the weather. If you can keep an eye on him today, I would be very, very appreciative."

DeRon studied me, trying to gauge my sincerity, I guess. I didn't know what I'd do long-term with Kassian if I didn't figure out what was going on, but I'd worry about that later. I needed him to be taken care of today. DeRon slowly nodded. "I'll watch him. It's not exactly my job here, you know, but I'll see what I can do. I like Mr. Kassian." He broke away from me and returned to Kassian. Said a few words and pointed him in the direction of the card room. At least that's where I hoped he was pointing him. Kassian shuffled off without a backward glance. Why was I always pissing him off? Rachel's words echoed in my ears as a counterpoint, "You're a good person, Josh Handleman." Then why did I feel like a selfish one?

I took a moment to clear my head outside the Hebrew Home. The first flakes of snow had begun to fall, big, heavy flakes, fast and thick. If I didn't know what a mess it would make on the roads later, I'd say it looked kind of pretty.

The snow didn't matter to me. I was determined to uncover the truth, no matter how deep the obstacles. My first order of business was to talk to Lev. I was hoping he'd returned from the conference so I could confront him about the photo, as well as hear what he had to say about Kassian's assertion that he'd seen Lev's car that morning. I wasn't looking forward to going up against him. Too stubborn, too ornery, and it reminded me too much of dealing with my father. But sometimes you just gotta forge ahead regardless of the consequences.

I called Lev at home. No answer. I tried him on his cell, but there was no answer there either, it just rolled into voice mail like it had yesterday. I didn't leave a message this time. I tried Peter's cell, to see if he knew where his father was. Again, no answer. I decided to swing by his house—maybe Lev was there and had come to the conclusion that he was being an ass, and that he was too embarrassed to talk to me. Yeah, and maybe I'd be marrying the Pope's daughter.

When I got to his house, Jenn was pulling up in her car. She came up beside me in the circular drive and rolled down the passenger window. "Meet me in the garage," she said, then drove around a hedge and off to the side of the house where the garage was located. I cut the engine and followed on foot. The snow had begun to stick and I left a footprint trail. When I got around to the garage, she'd already opened the trunk, revealing about a dozen grocery bags squished together.

"Here, let me give you a hand," I said. She smiled and handed me a couple of the heavier bags.

"Thanks. The worst part of shopping is putting away all the stuff," she said over her shoulder, as she led me into the house. She set her bags on the floor of the mudroom and finger-combed her hair. I leaned over and kissed her hello. "I'm sure you didn't come to see me, but Peter's at work," she said. "Someone has to pay for all the stuff I buy."

Jenn was a stay-at-home mom, but I knew from my friends that it was harder than many office jobs, and a lot more tedious. "Actually, I was looking for Lev. Know where he might have gone?"

She tilted her head. "Well, he's here somewhere. Come on."

I followed her into the kitchen, wondering why Lev hadn't picked up the phone. Probably knew it was me from the caller ID and wanted to avoid a confrontation.

Jenn punched the intercom button and called for Lev. After a moment, he answered.

"I'm back from the store. And you have a visitor. Where are you?"

Lev's voice, distorted by the intercom, said simply, "Sunroom."

Jenn turned to me. "He's probably listening to his music. In the sunroom. To the back, make a right." She pointed through the kitchen and through the dining room. "You know, Josh, he hasn't really been himself lately. Surlier than usual. Your father's death really shook him up. He's so angry, it's almost unbearable."

I nodded. "Need some help with the rest of the groceries?"

"No thanks. I need the exercise. Besides, I'm sure Lev is anxious to talk to you." She started back out to the garage, then stopped. "Maybe you can cheer him up."

I nodded again to be polite, but I was pretty sure Lev wouldn't be feeling much cheerier after I finished talking to him. Or me, either.

As I made my way back to the sunroom, the music became clearer. Some kind of upbeat jazz, heavy on the horns. Good jazz seemed so improvisational and I always wondered if the musicians could play their songs the same way twice.

I'd never been in the sunroom before, and it was, to borrow Jenn's word, cheery. Lots of large windows, lots of plants. Probably got lots of sun, too, when it wasn't snowing. Lev eyed me from his wicker chair. He was dressed more casually than I ever recalled seeing him—Virginia Tech sweatshirt and gray sweatpants. Socks on his feet. Just a retired guy chilling out to some jazz. Of course, I knew better. Lev never chilled out.

"I figured you more for Rimsky-Korsakov or Tchaikovsky," I said, naming the only two Russian composers I could think of.

He picked up a remote control and pressed a button. The volume of the music decreased, although it was still audible. "Your narrow view of me is appalling, Joshua. I am a big fan of your country. Big Macs, *American Idol*, jazz. Free speech. Free enterprise. All good things. I especially like American justice." He hissed out the last part of the word, as if he were some anthropomorphic snake in a child's cartoon.

"Mind if I sit?" I asked, pointing to a chair on the other side of a small glass-topped table on Lev's right.

He dipped his head. "Please."

I moved the floral-patterned cushion to the side of the chair and leaned against it so I could see Lev better. "What were you arguing with Kassian about?"

Lev waved his hand. "It is no concern of yours. I was simply reminding him what it was like to be raised a Russian Jew. Honor, integrity, honesty. He seems to be lacking in those important qualities."

"And this required backing him into a corner and screaming at him?"

Lev half-shrugged. "I wanted to make sure he understood my point."

"Uh huh." I shifted the cushion in the chair, trying to get comfortable. "Kassian thinks you do not like Russian Jews."

"Why would he think that?" Lev asked, inflection flat.

"Because you did not want my father to build a Russian Unit at the Home. He says you two argued about it."

Lev sighed. "First of all, we did not argue. I explained my position and Abe explained his. Do you understand?"

"Tell me again."

Lev sighed again, louder, as if I were a slow child unable to grasp his meaning. "It is true that I do not want that unit to be built. It is not true that I do not like Russian Jews. There is only one Russian Jew I do not like." He glared at me.

"Why don't you want the unit built? Seems like it would be a good thing."

Lev frowned. "Would you say the same if it was a unit built for Italians? Or Catholics? Or Iranians?" He paused and waited for a reaction.

"I'm not sure what you're getting at."

"Why should it be limited to a certain group of people? I have been campaigning for years for the Home to be more open, more inclusive. Expand the services for everyone in the community. Not restrict things. I wanted everyone to benefit from your father's generosity, not only a few," Lev said. "Besides…" Lev's mouth tightened. He picked up the remote and turned it slowly in his hands.

"What?"

Lev shook his head as if he were done speaking, then he slapped the remote down on the table between us. "Russians should take care of their own. As Peter has done with me. That is the respectful way. It is not right to send your elders away to die by themselves. A good Russian is raised to look out for his own."

"That's what my father wanted to do. Provide a good home for Russians. In case there is no family to look out for an 'elder.' Like in Kassian's case," I said, not quite seeing Lev's side of things.

He glared at me again. "Maybe it is a semantic issue. By calling it a Russian Unit, we would be singling them out, saying an entire culture cannot take care of their own. That is not right." Lev softened. "I am sure that given time, we would have arrived at a compromise."

I let it go and admired the greenery. Plants in a variety of pots and containers lined the floors, their vines and runners and tendrils intermingling in an indoor jungle. Broad, glossy green leaves—round, oval, heart-shaped—formed a living carpet along the floor. The thick foliage reminded me of Kassian's hideaway in the holly trees, and I wondered if that was somehow connected to Lev's anger toward the little man.

Time to get to the issue at hand. "Kassian says he saw you on the morning my father died. At around nine-thirty." I stopped for a response, but Lev stared straight ahead. I prodded him for an answer. "That true?"

Lev jerked his head toward me, as if he'd been released from a trance. "No. It is not. As I have said, he is a liar."

"You're sure you didn't make a mistake about the time? Or maybe you came by first, had a talk with him, then left. Came back later to find—"

"Do not insult me, Joshua. I am sure about this. I was at the dentist that morning. That is why I had to delay our game of chess until the afternoon."

"Kassian says he saw your car, plain as day, in our driveway, before he went to the Hebrew Home that morning."

"He is mistaken," Lev said. "If you do not believe me, you may call my dentist. Dr. William Brock. I will even give you his number." His stare challenged me. "Or would you prefer to see the crown he worked on?" Lev began to open his mouth, taunting me.

I didn't take the bait. "Kassian swears he saw you. Why do you think he would lie about that?" I was pretty sure I knew the answer, but I wanted to get Lev's thoughts.

"It is obvious, no? He is angry with me so he tries to destroy me. I should have expected such desperation from him," Lev said. "A coward does cowardly things."

"Speaking of cowardly things, someone broke into my house—Kassian's room, to be exact—and vandalized his belongings. Know anything about that?"

Lev opened his mouth, then closed it. Shook his head slowly. "No, I do not," he said softly. It was a strange reaction from someone who had been so adamant in his other denials. And it wasn't what I'd expect from someone who was guilty. But if Lev didn't threaten Kassian, who did?

"Any idea who might have done that?"

Lev stared out the window into the distance. "No." He didn't look at me when he answered, just kept his gaze out the window, as if he were searching for answers in the swirling snow.

"Did Kassian have any enemies?"

Lev shook his head.

Nothing was adding up. I wasn't any closer to unraveling the knotted mess, except now I was even more pissed at Lev. He knew something and due to some kind of warped Russian pride, he wasn't telling. I tried one more time. "If you have any information to give me—about my father's death, his diamonds, Kassian, or anything else I might give a shit about—now's the time to level with me."

His mouth remained closed, lips pressed together as if something inside was trying to escape.

I got up, frustration churning inside. "Well, would you at least talk to Kassian? Nicely, this time, with me present? Tell him you won't hurt him. Tell him you're not part of the Russian mob. He had nothing to do with my father's death. You need to stop harassing him."

No answer.

I stood before him, bending over to get in his face. "Goddamn it, Lev. Answer me, you old bastard!" My hands balled up into fists, but I kept them at my sides. I might as well have been talking to the plants.

He simply stared out the window, a stubborn old man aboard a wicker chair floating in a sea of greenery. A snake in the garden.

I let myself out.

THIRTY-FOUR

I THOUGHT ABOUT CALLING Suzanne Miller before I dropped by, but I wanted to see her face when I spoke to her. There were too many times when I was convinced I lost out by not being able to gauge a person's nonverbal cues. And now was one time when I needed all the information I could get.

Before I left the house this morning, I'd gone to the Fairfax County Government's website and spent a few minutes surfing around. Found the home page for the County's Parks and Recreation Services Division, and drilled down until I found Suzanne's name on the contact page: Assistant Director of Recreational Facilities Development and Acquisition. A mouthful, but there wasn't any additional information about what she actually did. I guess I'd have to ask her.

I drove from Lev's place to the Fairfax County Government Center, a multi-building complex that housed most of the county's administrative offices. When the first building had been erected, it had only been partially filled, and the local press had stirred up a ruckus about wasted tax dollars. Now, fifteen years later, several other buildings had been built to handle the load generated by the county's population explosion, with more in the offing. Not that I was complaining. That explosion had fueled much of my father's success.

I entered through the revolving front doors of the imposing horseshoe-shaped main building and shook the snow from the hood of my parka, the one I'd "borrowed" from my father. I passed by the watchful eye of the security guard and found the building directory where I looked up Suzanne's department. Took the stairs to her office on the second floor. A young dark-haired man dressed entirely in black sat behind a counter, poring over a series of blue-lined architectural drawings. When he saw me, he smiled. "How can I help you today?" he asked in a cheerful voice, as if he were about to break into song.

"Hello. I'm looking for Suzanne Miller. Is she in?" A strong chemical smell wafted up from the drawings.

"Oh, sure. Suzanne is in. Who shall I say is visiting?" He was far too upbeat for a government drone. Maybe he was a temp, or maybe the chemical fumes had gotten to him.

"My name's Josh Handleman."

"Okay, Mr. Handleman. It'll just be a second!" He picked up the phone and punched in four numbers. Announced me like I was a visiting ambassador at an official State Dinner. Then he hung up and flashed his pearly whites. "Follow me. I shall take you to her office!" he trilled. Whatever was emanating from those drawings, I wanted some.

I followed him through the ubiquitous cubicle maze, worker bees tapping away at their computers or chatting on the phone.

One guy was tilted all the way back in his chair, eyes closed. Inspiration arrives in different ways.

When we reached the far corner, my guide stopped and let me pass, pointing out Suzanne's office. It was nice to know she'd risen high enough in the ranks to earn her own workspace with walls and an actual door. When she saw me, she came around her desk and hugged me. I hugged her back, feeling awkward. Back when I knew her better, I don't think we ever touched. "Wow, this is a surprise."

I shrugged. "I was in the neighborhood so I thought I'd drop in."

"Glad you did," she said, as she offered me a chair and returned to her own. "I'm so sorry about your father. He was a charming man. Tough losing a parent."

I nodded.

Her sad smile gave way to a more engaging one. "You're living in San Francisco, right?"

"I was. I'm going to stick around here. For a while at least."

"Moving the family? That's a pretty big deal," she said.

I shook my head. "Getting a divorce. No kids. I think I could use a change of scenery."

"And you came back here?" she said with a little laugh. "Have you spoken to Tammy yet?"

"Yeah. Ran into her."

"Then you know. She came out of the closet a few years ago. Best thing she did. She was so unhappy trying to keep it a secret. I knew, of course, but not too many others did. It was weird. When she made it public, no one really cared. I think it might have hurt her feelings a little."

"Knowing Tammy, I'm sure she got over it quickly," I said, pointing at a picture of two little girls on her worktable. "Those your girls?"

She beamed as she followed my glance. "Yes they are. Haley and Madison. Two little imps." She sighed. "When we were back in high school, we didn't have a clue, did we? How life really was?" She sighed again. "So what brings you here? I'm guessing you didn't stop by just to hear the latest gossip."

On the ride over, I'd gone back and forth about how to broach the subject. Unfortunately, nothing came to me then, just as nothing clever came to me now. Might as well fly direct. "Do you know an old guy named Kassian?"

"A small man with an accent? Very polite? Did something happen to him?" She looked concerned.

"No, he's okay." I eyed her. "How do you know him?"

"He's your father's friend, right? Or cousin. Something like that." Her face had relaxed. "Abe was in the building one day—about three or four months ago—and stopped by to see me. Had Kassian with him and we chatted for a few minutes. A couple of weeks after that, he brought him by again. Why do you ask, anyway?"

How to answer? *He's been spying on you* didn't seem like the prudent response. "Uh, I was explaining some of my father's investments and your name came up. He thought he might have met you, but he wasn't sure, so…" I held my hands out, palms up. *Ergo.*

Suzanne seemed a little puzzled by my explanation, but didn't ask for clarification.

I took the initiative. "I'm a little fuzzy. What did my father invest in with you?"

She stared at me for a beat, then smiled. "He really came through for us." She swiveled in her chair and opened a file drawer in the cabinet next to her. Paged through it and extracted a thick brown accordion file. Plopped it on her desk. "Determination Playground at Cool Falls."

Now it was my turn to be puzzled. "I'm not sure I follow." Cool Falls was a landmark in the western part of the county, near where the W&OD Trail cuts into Loudoun County.

"He never mentioned it?" Suzanne said. She seemed disappointed, as if my father had neglected to tell me he'd won the Nobel Prize.

"No. Sorry."

"Well, he provided the lion's share of the private investment in the project." She opened the file and removed a small stack of pictures. Handed them across the desk to me. "Determination Playground is an all-accessible playground catering to physically challenged kids. Specially designed and constructed to accommodate their needs. It really is spectacular. It had always been a dream of mine—I have a challenged niece whom I adore—so my boss gave me the green light."

I sifted through the pictures as she talked. Red and yellow plastic structures abounded. Slides and ramps, swings and bridges. In the pictures everything seemed new and shiny and clean. I glanced up at Suzanne. Her face lit up as she saw me studying the pictures. Her baby.

She continued, features tightened a little. "Only there was a catch. My boss wanted it to be an example of a public-private partnership. Which meant I had to go out and hustle up some money. For weeks I asked anyone—and everyone—I could think of. They all thought it was a great idea, but no one wanted to pony up. Finally, I heard from a friend of a friend of a friend that your father might be interested in this type of project."

"And I guess he was," I said. I'd come back to the first photo, so I squared the stack and placed it on her desk.

"Oh, he was more than just interested. With his backing, we were able to double the scope of the project *and* package the concept for other donors who want to duplicate our results." Suzanne stopped and waited a moment to make sure she had my attention. "In the four years since, we've been able to put up two other playgrounds and we have two more in the pipeline, all thanks to your father's help."

She looked like she was about to shed some tears of joy. "I do feel bad about one thing, though. Not very many people know of his involvement in this. He insisted—adamantly, as I'm sure you can imagine—that his contributions remain anonymous." She plucked a tissue from a box on her desk and blew her nose.

Glad I asked.

THIRTY-FIVE

FIVE MORE MINUTES OF chatting with Suzanne didn't yield any more useful information, and after a promise that we'd try to get together to talk over old times—along with Tammy and a few others—I left. The happy guy at the front counter gave me a big smile and a wiggly finger wave as I pushed through the glass doors.

I walked through the main hall of Government Center and pulled out my cell phone. Called information and got the listing for Dr. Brock, Lev's dentist. Punched in his number. I felt like a worm for checking up on him, but I needed to be sure.

"Hello, Dr. Brock's office. Can you hold?" An officious voice switched me over to Muzak without even waiting for my reply. I reached the center of the building, a five-story atrium, and leaned over a railing overlooking a small amphitheater. Tall windows rose beyond the stage, and the grassy field behind the building was white. The snow was still falling, just as heavily as it had been earlier.

"Dr. Brock's office. How may I help you?"

"Uh, yeah. Hi. This is Daniel Yurishenko, Lev's son. He was in a few weeks ago, and I was double-checking what day that was. I think it was December 22. In the morning. Am I remembering it correctly?"

"Please hold." No questions. Too busy for questions.

A group of workers, ID badges dangling from their necks, passed by, talking about the weather. As I remembered from when I was a boy, there was always an extra buzz in the air whenever a big snow was predicted. Brought back memories. We didn't get much snow in the Bay Area.

The receptionist returned to the line. "Yes, Mr. Yurishenko. Your father was here that morning. Is there a problem?"

"Oh no. No problem. Thanks so much." I clicked off, trying to assimilate the information. It seemed obvious that Kassian lied about seeing Lev that morning. A mini-movie of Kassian kicking in the window and wrecking his own photo played in my mind. I saw him cowering in his chair, acting like he'd seen the devil. Was that all it was, acting? Could he have gone to such great lengths to try to frame Lev? Seemed improbable to me, and it begged the question, why? What would he have to gain?

My stomach soured. If Lev was right and Kassian had killed my father, then Kassian would have plenty to gain by framing Lev. It didn't seem to matter which road I headed down, Kassian was at the end of every one of them. Maybe I should have listened to Lev from the beginning instead of relying on my gut.

I needed to talk to Kassian.

Traffic was heavier than normal because of the snow—both inches of it. Drivers crawled along, some putting their flashers on as if they were hauling toxic waste. If we were in Buffalo or Sioux Falls, no one would think twice about the weather. But this was Washington, where people went into a tizzy over the slightest dusting, descending on the grocery stores for milk and toilet paper the second a weather forecaster uttered the words "possible accumulation."

The fifteen-minute drive had stretched into forty, but when I got to the Hebrew Home at least I didn't have any trouble parking. The lot had emptied, friends and relatives deciding to cut short their visits and get home before the roads worsened.

I logged in at the front desk and the hairy guy from last week asked for my ID. I glared at him and handed it over, and he inspected it for ten full seconds. "Okay," he said, "you may enter."

"Thanks. Is there a listing of today's activities?"

"Sure," he said, staring at me.

Games, games, games, everybody plays them. "Where is it?" I asked, trying to keep my frustration at bay.

"Over there. On the board." He jerked his thumb at a bulletin board on the wall.

"Thanks." I started for it.

"Won't do you any good, though. We've cancelled all non-essential activities."

I stopped and faced him.

"The weather, you know. It's snowing." He winked at me and returned to some paperwork.

I checked the activity schedule anyway and headed back to the library where a book talk had been listed for 3:00. It was about 3:20 now, so I figured it still should be going on, unless they were discussing a picture book. When I opened the heavy wood doors, the library was empty. I guess book discussions weren't essential, after all.

After the library, I checked the card room, the cafeteria, the TV lounge, and the exercise room, although I was pretty sure I wouldn't find Kassian there. He wasn't in the gift shop or the vending area or in the non-denominational chapel, decorated equitably with a Star of David *and* a cross. I wondered if Muslims felt left out.

I returned to the front desk. The hairy guy didn't look up, even though I was sure he knew I was there. More games. "Excuse me. Could you page DeRon Woodson please?"

He lifted his head, gave me a "surprised to see you" look, and said, "Sure." He picked up his phone and called for DeRon. Then he handed the phone to me.

"Hello?" I said.

The hairy guy said, "He's not on yet. Give him a few minutes, sheesh." He shook his head as he busied himself again shuffling papers.

I waited for a few minutes and no one picked up. "Excuse me. Are you sure you paged him? He hasn't answered yet."

The hairy guy didn't get up from his chair. "What? You think he's just sitting around waiting for your call? I'm sure he's busy. Give him a break. He'll get to you."

Two minutes later, DeRon picked up. "This is DeRon."

"Hey DeRon. This is Josh Handleman. Do you know where Kassian is? I've looked everywhere."

There was silence on the other end of the phone. "Did you try the TV room?"

"Yes. He wasn't there."

"Well, that's where I saw him last. About an hour, hour and a half ago. Gave him a box of Junior Mints and set up a movie for him to watch with about five other folks. Then I got called to help with a patient, then another patient vomited all over the hallway, and ... well, I've been pretty busy." He paused. "I'll be down in a minute, help you look. Don't worry, we'll find him."

I handed the phone back to the hairy guy and grabbed a seat in the lobby. DeRon arrived a few minutes later. "Come on, let's take a look around," he said.

DeRon and I retraced my earlier rounds with no luck. No sign of Kassian, and the few people DeRon questioned hadn't seen him either. "Any secret hiding places around here?" I asked, hoping DeRon had been holding out on me.

He shook his head. "Nope. Mr. Kassian isn't here. He must have left." DeRon gazed out the front window. "Not a good time to be out wandering around. Hope he went straight home."

"Hope so." I pictured Kassian trudging through the snow, barely able to stay upright in the wind. At least I'd persuaded him to wear his winter coat. "I better go after him."

DeRon caught me by my arm. "Good luck, Josh. If I spot him here, I'll let you know."

"Thanks." I hustled out the front door, not even bothering to sign out on the visitor's log. Take that, hairy guy.

When I got outside, I huddled against the wall for a moment, mentally outlining my course of action. Kassian's most likely destination had to be the house. I figured it was about a three-mile hike; in normal conditions it might take him an hour or less. In a blizzard, who knew?

If I'd just missed him, he'd still be on the path and I could track him down and catch him, before he froze to death or got blown into a ditch or just got disoriented and lost. He'd had plenty of experience surviving the elements when he lived on the streets, but I don't think he grew up in Siberia.

Of course, if he'd left an hour and a half ago, he might already be at the house. I pulled out my phone and called home, but I knew it would be fruitless as I hit the last digit—Kassian never picked up the phone. It rang and rang before the call rolled into my father's voicemail. "Hello. I'm sorry I missed your call. Please leave me a message and I'll get back to you as soon as I can. And have a great, great day." My father's voice, speaking to me from beyond the grave. Telling me to have a great, great day. I felt my knees start to wobble and I braced myself against the brick wall. Why hadn't I listened all those times he'd told me in person to have a great day? Why had I been so preoccupied with myself, with being independent, that I couldn't take what he'd been offering? Why had I been such a know-it-all?

I pushed away from the wall. My father took Kassian in, looked after him. Now it fell to me. I decided to leave my car in the lot and take off after him on foot.

Thankfully, I was wearing my father's parka. I cinched up the fur-lined hood and secured my gloves. Set off around the side of the building where I would connect with a side street leading to the trail access point. I walked as quickly as I could without losing my footing. The wind whipped the falling snow into a frenzy, nipping at the exposed part of my face. I trundled along, keeping my head down, looking up every twenty seconds or so trying to spot Kassian.

I seemed to be the only pedestrian out for a stroll today.

Across the street, at the edge of the woods, a sign marked the trailhead. I looked back at the Hebrew Home and was dismayed by how little ground I'd covered. I could have sworn I'd gone half a mile already, when in fact I'd only gone a couple hundred yards. On the main road on the other side of the home, I saw a few vehicles making their way on the snow-dusted streets, which gave me hope that conditions might not be too bad.

I entered the woods on the path, and the windbreak provided by the trees tempered the wind from gale force to something more bearable. But it still roared in my ears, like a leaf blower gone berserk—even through my thick hood. I realized I wouldn't be able to hear my cell phone in my pocket if DeRon called, so I stopped for a minute and dug it out of my inside coat pocket. I removed a glove and quickly turned up the ringer volume to the max and set it to vibrate as well. Then I slipped the phone into the front pocket of my jeans. Didn't want to take any chances of missing the call. I allowed myself a small smile as I put my glove back on. *Is that your crotch ringing, or are you just happy to see me?*

I set off again, trying to keep my head up as best I could so I could follow the abrupt twists and turns of the trail—and avoid bashing into any tree trunks—but I had to maintain a constant squint against the blowing snow. The canopy of trees provided some cover, but most of the taller ones were bare and the snow eventually filtered its way down to the ground.

Along the way, I searched for size six footprints. The blowing and drifting snow made it impossible for me to make out much of anything. As soon as I left a footprint, the wind whisked it away. I plowed on in search of Kassian.

I figured I was about halfway home when I felt a buzzing on my thigh. I grabbed off a glove and yanked out my phone. Flipped it open and tucked it inside my hood, pressed onto my ear. "Hello?" I shouted.

"Hello? Josh?"

It was a woman's voice, but I could barely hear it. "Who is this? Rachel?"

"Yes." She shouted back, and I shifted positions until I could hear her better. "Where are you? I saw your car in the parking lot."

"What do you mean? Where are you?" I asked.

"At the Hebrew Home. Visiting Nana."

"In this weather? Are you crazy?" I slipped the glove back on my exposed hand.

The wind abated for a moment, and I could hear her laugh, as if I were standing right next to her. "I went to Cornell. This is nothing."

"You drove in your Prius?" I moved closer to a large tree trunk and leaned my head against it.

"I'm not that stupid. It was Tammy's night to visit Nana, so I traded with her. And I took her Land Rover. Actually, the roads aren't too bad yet. The more chicken drivers that stay home, the easier it is for the rest of us." She laughed again. "Where are you?"

"I'm traipsing through the woods looking for Kassian."

"*What?*"

"He's missing, and I think he might have headed home. On the paths."

"Oh no, Josh. What can I do to help? I'm pretty good in the woods, too."

"Thanks, but I can handle it. Listen, if you see him there, you know, wandering the halls, give me a call, okay?" I didn't want to drag her into my *michigas*. "Be very careful driving, okay?"

"I plan to. And you be careful out in the woods. Let me know when you find him. Good luck."

"Thanks." I hung up and put the phone back in my pants pocket. Continued down the path, hands jammed into my parka for warmth.

Twenty minutes later, I approached the house. Ran the last forty yards and let myself in through Kassian's door, gasping for breath. "Kassian? You here?"

Silence was the answer I dreaded.

Silence was the answer I got.

THIRTY-SIX

I SAT AT THE kitchen table, cradling a mug of steaming coffee in my hands, trying to put myself in Kassian's shoes and not having much luck. Still in my coat, my body temperature was slowly rising and feeling was returning to my cheeks. I gripped the mug tighter, relishing its warmth, tempted to pour its contents over my head. What I really wanted to do was crawl into bed, pull up the covers, and awaken a month from now, all the lies and half-truths and deceptions exposed, arguments settled. But this wasn't about my wishes. I couldn't run and hide. Kassian, if no one else, was counting on me.

As soon as I'd arrived, I'd called Carol on the off chance that she'd taken him in again. There'd been no answer—she was probably still at her conference—so I left a message for her to call me as soon as she could. I didn't really think he'd be able to get to her house without a ride, but I needed to cover all my bases.

I took a long slurp of coffee, not even tasting it, just gulping it to feel the warmth as the liquid rushed down my gullet. I put the mug against my cheek. Where would an old guy like Kassian go in the middle of a snowstorm? Did something happen at the Home that spooked him? Did his "stalker" track him down and threaten him in person? Or worse?

I didn't let the logical side of my brain catch up to my emotional side. I picked up the phone and called Lev. Jenn answered. "Hey, cold enough for you? Hold on, I'm putting you on speaker." I heard a bunch of clattering, dishes and silverware being unloaded from the dishwasher. "It's Josh."

Peter's voice came from the background, sounding as if he were in a long tunnel. "What's up, Josh?"

"Is Lev around?" I tried to tamp down my anxiety.

"Funny you should ask. We were just wondering where he was," Peter said. "I've tried his cell, but—surprise—no answer. I should give him another talking to about that."

The background clattering subsided and Jenn said, "Is anything wrong? He stormed out of here about an hour after you left, grumbling about something. With this weather, I'd feel a lot better if he were home."

"Yeah, it's getting nastier out there, but I'm sure he's okay," I said. An image of Lev ambushing Kassian along the wooded trail popped into my head and I had trouble shaking it.

"I hope so, too." Peter said. "Why did you want to speak to him?"

"I don't know where Kassian is. I thought maybe Lev would know where he was." I heard Jenn say something to Peter and Peter answer, but I couldn't make out the words.

A moment later, Peter's voice came over the phone, louder. He'd taken me off speaker. "He's missing? Where did you last see him?"

I explained that I'd left him at the Hebrew Home, under the not-watchful-enough eye of one of the workers there. I condensed my fruitless hour walk in the frigid wilderness into a single sentence.

"So he's not at your house, and he's not at the Hebrew Home where you left him," Peter said. "He have any friends?"

"None that I know of." Now that Abe was gone, that is.

"What's your best guess? Where do you think he might be? He can't just be meandering through the woods. It's cold out there," Peter said.

"If I had to guess, I'd say that's exactly what he's doing. Or what he started to do. He might have started out on a walk, not realizing how cold it was. Maybe he ducked into a store or a restaurant. Hell, for all I know, he could be sitting in some stranger's living room right now, sipping tea. I don't know." The more I talked, the crazier I sounded. And the more worried I became. Kassian wasn't the type to venture into an unknown store or restaurant. Certainly not some stranger's home. "He's an old, depressed guy. The cold could kill him." I'd read about mountain climbers who got too tired to continue, lay down, and never got up again.

"Hang on," Peter said, and then I heard his muffled voice talking to Jenn. A minute later, he was back with me. "Okay. How about this? I'm going to drive over to the Home and look around. Maybe he returned there. If I can't find him, I'll drive around the area, looking for him. You search around your house. Maybe he lost his key and went to a neighbor's house. Sound like a plan?"

I thought a moment. No sense trying to save my pride any more. I'd "lost" Kassian and needed all the help I could get. "Thanks so much, Peter. You don't have to do this, you know."

"Hey, you'd do the same if it were Lev who'd wandered off, right?"

"Sure," I said. "Sure."

———

I took Peter's suggestion and went out to canvass the neighbors. No one at the first two houses remembered seeing Kassian, but an elderly lady at the third house recalled something.

"The older fella? Kinda short?" she said, squinching her eyes together. "Yeah, I think I saw him."

"Today?"

"Yeah. Today," she said. "Or…" Her head tilted, and she squeezed her eyes until they closed completely. Visualizing.

"Yes?"

"Or maybe it was a few days ago?" The eyes opened. "And I think I'm getting him confused with another guy. The MacKenzies' plumber, across the way. He was short and old too. Although he was kinda fat and had a bushy moustache." She shrugged. "Sorry."

I tried three other houses on the street and came up empty. Given that Kassian used his side door and got around town via the trail system in the woods out back, the neighbors probably wouldn't have seen him no matter how many times he'd come and gone.

I returned home, but didn't go in. Stood outside Kassian's door and watched the snowflakes flutter. The blizzard had eased, but the wind still gusted, and with night approaching, it had gotten even colder. I pulled out my cell and checked for messages. None. He was still missing.

I flipped open my phone and called Erik. His buddy Brandon had been pretty hot the other night. What if he was trying to follow through on his threat? Could he have broken in and wrecked Kassian's photo? Terrorize me by terrorizing Kassian? Could he have snatched him from the Hebrew Home?

Erik answered after the first ring. "Hello?"

"Hey, this is Josh. Can you do me a favor?"

"Sure. Name it," Erik said.

"Can you call Brandon and find out what he's doing right now?"

There was a pause. "Why?"

I didn't feel like explaining, especially if I was way off base. "Can you just do it? Please?"

There was another pause. "Okay."

"Great. Call me back, will you?" I hung up. Took a deep breath. It was a long shot, but I wanted to be thorough.

I took another deep breath, knowing what had to be done.

There was one place I hadn't looked yet and I'd been putting it off, not exactly sure why. I guess I didn't want to believe that Kassian would choose that place over coming home, that my house—with me in it—was so terrible. But it would be dark soon and I couldn't leave Kassian there, if that's where he was. It was time to check his hidey-hole in the woods.

I'd left my car at the Hebrew Home, so I had no choice but to hoof it. Which was good, really. I wouldn't want to miss him coming back, if I was on the road and he was walking on the path. I ran back inside to go to the bathroom and get a flashlight, then I decided to change into my hiking boots. No telling how much snow I'd have to wade through. I took the cell phone out of my pocket and wedged it into the back of my glove so I'd be sure to feel it vibrate. It looked like some kind of grotesque, rectangular-shaped tumor. I slipped the other glove on, tied my hood up tight, and closed the door behind me, making sure it was unlocked. Just in case Kassian found his own way home and had somehow lost his key.

I stomped through the backyard and out to the trail behind the house. I'd come this way only about forty-five minutes ago, but the blowing snow had already wiped away my footprints leaving no sign that I'd been there. Ahead, the pristine path beckoned. With a quick glance back at the house, I set off to find Kassian.

It felt surreal in the woods, all alone, bringing back childhood daydreams of being stranded under twenty-foot snowfalls where the only way to get around was to tunnel through the snow. The snow seemed to dampen the sounds of the woods, turning my footfalls into muffled steps, more pressure than noise. The only thing I heard was the pulse pounding in my ears. I didn't know whether it was an acoustical property of the snow itself, or whether all the animals had simply gone to ground, but everything was muted. And it wasn't only the sound; the colors also seemed strangely bleached, as if I were the last human on earth walking in a frigid dreamscape. Funny how the cold could play tricks on the mind.

It was darker in the woods than out in the open due to the tree canopy, and it pained me to think of Kassian sitting on the ledge, tucked into the small cave, shivering. All alone in the world. I picked up the pace, breaking into a slow jog. When I got to the fork in the trail, I stopped, flicking my flashlight on to examine the path heading toward the Hebrew Home. The snow appeared un-disturbed. I thought about going to get my car, but it would take too long. Quicker—if colder—on foot. I took a big breath and jogged off down the path toward the golf course.

I ran along, arms pumping and breath churning from my mouth like a steam locomotive. I settled into a rhythm and soon realized running in hiking boots was a lot more strenuous than flying along in running shoes. I was sure I'd have blisters tomorrow. Despite my exertion, I was damned cold. Poor Kassian.

I emerged from the woods and the golf clubhouse rose into view, covered in white frosting like a fairy tale gingerbread house. I half-expected to bump into Hansel and Gretel walking along, hand-in-hand. Too bad Kassian hadn't thought to leave a trail of bread crumbs for me to follow. A couple of spotlights highlighted a sign that read "Reston Hills Golf Course," but there were no vehicles in the parking lot, just a couple abandoned golf carts parked by the side entrance.

I stopped for a minute to get my bearings, ignoring the protests from my aching feet.

On the other side of the putting green was the tenth tee, although I could barely make it out, the darkness outside of the woods catching up. I loped off again, down the right side of the tenth fairway. For a while I found decent footing on the cart path, which curved along with the treeline, but then I lost contact with it, running on the grass of the golf course itself. My way was more direct and faster, if a little bumpier. I switched on the flashlight and left it on, every so often shining it down at my feet to make sure I didn't stray into a bunker or water hazard.

When I reached the tenth green, I veered right, back onto the wooded path, toward my goal. I picked up the pace and kept my head raised, hoping—praying—I'd see Kassian walking toward me. But I was the only fool out in this weather. Even the animals had more sense than I did.

I slowed as I approached Kassian's cave. Although it had to be only fifteen or twenty yards away, it was hard to tell exactly where things were in the snow. Everything seemed whitewashed, making it difficult to get any real depth perception.

"Kassian," I called out. His name sounded strange in the dark woods. Alien. There was no answer as I drew closer. I swept my light across the path. Small depressions—footprint sized—seemed evident, but it could have been my imagination. I wanted so badly to find Kassian it was possible I was seeing things where none existed. I examined the hill leading up to his ledge. Again, it looked like something had disturbed the snow. The wind? Perhaps. A squirrel, a fox? Hard to guess.

"Kassian," I called out again. The wind whistled through the trees in response.

I scanned the area and broke a small branch off a tree. Clambered up the hill, grabbing on to whatever I could to pull myself up. A tree trunk, a rock, a bush. I slipped and scrabbled, but I made it. I stopped just short of the ledge and held the stick—pointy side out—in one hand, flashlight in the other. I didn't want to corner a rabid fox in the cave completely unarmed. I counted to three and hoisted my body up the last few feet onto the ledge, stick poised for action.

The cave was empty, save for a single piece of trash.

An empty Junior Mints box.

THIRTY-SEVEN

So Kassian had been here recently. Very recently.

I brushed aside some snow from the ledge and eased my aching body down. Tried to think this through. It had been about two hours since I'd left the Hebrew Home. And Kassian could have left there anywhere from an hour to an hour and a half earlier. After that, he'd come here and stayed for … Who knows? I could have just missed him. Or he could have been here two hours ago. This is what I knew: I didn't pass him on my way here. He wasn't home. He wasn't at the Hebrew Home. He couldn't have just disappeared.

I pulled off my glove—the one with the phone tucked into it—and called Peter. "Hey. Kassian's been here. In the woods. He's—"

"What are you talking about?" he asked.

"He's been here. I'm not sure when, though. I didn't actually see him." My mouth was half-frozen and I was having trouble forming the words properly. "I don't suppose you've found him yet."

"No. Of course not. He wasn't at the Hebrew Home and I'm still cruising the streets. Shall I come there and help you look?"

"Hang on." I tried to think like an old Russian. Where would he go? If it were me, I'd head home. Could I have missed him in the woods? Maybe he knew another way back. "Okay. Why don't you head over to my house? See if he went there. I guess that's the most logical place."

"Okay. I'm on it," Peter said. "Bye."

I hung up and jammed my glove on. Stuffed the phone back inside. I made my way down from Kassian's ledge, slip-sliding the last ten feet, catching myself on a sapling before I skidded completely out of control. I thought about heading farther along the path and then cutting across the golf course, but it was almost totally dark now, and I didn't want to stumble into a creek or step in a hole and sprain my ankle. Besides, I could wander around all night in the woods and not find Kassian. I had no clue where he might be.

I decided to head back toward home. Maybe he'd gotten confused and taken a side path. Circled around a few times until he found his way. I walked along, shining my flashlight ahead of me. Walked going back—I guessed there was as much chance running into him walking as there was running. And my feet hurt.

I passed the clubhouse and my hand zizzed. Stopping, I pulled off my glove and answered the phone. It was Rachel. "He's here."

My heart skipped a beat. Or three. "What?" I asked, although I'd heard her clearly.

"Kassian's here. In the snackbar."

Thank God. My heart resumed its normal cadence and relief pulsed through me. "You sure?" I said, stupidly. Rachel wouldn't be yanking my chain, not about this. I just wanted to hear it again.

"Yes, I'm sure. He's here. Talking to his friend."

"His friend? You mean DeRon?" I asked.

"No. The old grizzled guy. With the accent. Lev."

My heart stuttered again. What was Lev doing with Kassian? Something wasn't right. "Lev's there? What are they doing?"

"Nothing. Just talking," Rachel said. "Why? Is something wrong?"

I hoped to hell nothing was wrong. But I had my doubts. "Okay. I'm coming over. Where are you now?"

"Josh, what's wrong? You don't sound happy to have found Kassian."

"Where are you? Are you in the snackbar with them?"

Rachel paused. "No. I was walking with Nana and we saw them. Drinking coffee. Kassian seemed fine to me."

"Hey, can you do me a favor? Can you keep an eye on him? Just until I get there?" I didn't want to lose him again, and I didn't want Lev to bully him either. He'd be less likely to try something with Rachel nearby.

"Be happy to. Let me get Nana back to her room and I'll do that," she said.

"You're a peach. Thanks. I owe you."

"Relax, okay? You sound awfully tense."

I'll relax when I'm standing next to Kassian and Lev's out of the picture. "Okay. I'll be there soon." I clicked off.

I was about to return the phone to my glove when I remembered Peter. I could use his help with Lev, although I hoped it wouldn't come to that. I hit the send button and his name came up, hit it again and the phone dialed his number. He picked up on the first ring. "Hello."

"We've located Kassian. He's at the Hebrew Home. I—"

"Thank God," Peter said. "And he's okay?"

"Yeah. Listen. Your father's with him and they've been arguing a lot lately. Maybe you could swing over there and make sure things don't get out of hand."

"Arguing? About what?" he asked.

"I don't have time to get into it now. I'll explain later."

"Sure. I'll head over there and get Pops. Nice to know he's okay, too. Don't worry, Josh. I've got everything under control."

"Okay. I'll be there shortly." I hung up and stuffed the phone away. Picked up my pace. *Don't worry, don't worry.* Why was everyone telling me that? Was I that much of a worrywart? I knew the answer. I guess I got the worry genes from Mom's side of the family.

The beam of light from the flashlight bobbed as I walked along, creating bizarre shadows. It was too dark to run, so I walked as fast as I could, careful to dodge the branches and limbs protruding from the trees closest to the path. Something tugged at my brain as I lumbered along; my intuition sensed that something was off. What was Lev doing with Kassian right now? I remembered the expression on Lev's face in the sunroom, after I told him Kassian saw him at my father's house that morning. At the time, I thought it reflected Lev's stubbornness. Anger, perhaps. Now I knew it for what it was. Resignation. But what had he decided to do? Apologize?

A coldness spiked through me, building from my core, and it wasn't from the arctic wind. I'd believed—all along—that Lev was angry because he thought Kassian murdered my father. But what if that wasn't the case? What if Kassian had told Lev he'd seen him at the house that morning? What if Lev had been threatening him to keep quiet about what he'd seen? The arguing and yelling. The bullying. Kassian had been petrified, of Lev and his fictional mob ties. The breaking in and smashing of his picture was a little warning of what might happen if Kassian ratted Lev out.

Lev had strung me along, and I'd fallen for it. His insistence that Kassian was the guilty party, when in fact it was Lev. The coldness spiked through me again. Now that I'd revealed to Lev what Kassian had told me, maybe Lev felt compelled to shut him up before he could tell his story to the police. Shut him up for good.

I broke into a jog, slipping and sliding. The path had mostly disappeared under the blanket of snow, identifiable only by the lack of trees, but I ran anyway, feeling the terrain rise and fall, stumbling over tree roots and into gullies, branches clawing at my face as if I were an escaped convict and they were trying to recapture me.

My anger for Lev rose. All along I'd thought Kassian was making up the fact he saw Lev that morning. Telling stories to get back at Lev. But he'd been telling the truth—I just hadn't believed him because, deep down, I thought he was nothing more than a homeless, unreliable drunk. I felt like a complete shit. And worse, I was terrified my telling Lev what Kassian had told me in confidence would lead to harm. His harm. I stopped in a small clearing, gasping for air, lungs racked from the cold. I hunched over, hands on my knees, trying to get my breathing under control. I whipped out my phone and called Rachel. "Where are you now?"

"Josh? What's wrong? You sound awful," Rachel said.

I drew in air rapidly like a panting dog. "Where are you now?"

"In Nana's room. Getting her settled. Changing the routines because of the snow has set her off a bit."

"Rachel, please, it's important. Can you go find Kassian? Now? I think Lev might try to hurt him."

"What? Lev hurt Kassian? Why?" Rachel's questions, all logical, only fueled my desperation.

I shouted into the phone. "Rachel, please. Find Kassian. And call me when you do." I clicked off, took a single deep breath, and started running. Fast.

As I ran, Lev's motives jelled in my head. Those arguments about the Russian unit. What if they had snowballed into something larger, more serious? One likely scenario: My father—stubborn man that he was—refused to change his mind. Lev—also no slouch in the stubbornness department—lost his cool and pushed my father down the stairs. Then Lev found the diamonds lying around. Hell, my father might even have told Lev about the appraisal he was getting. So Lev stole them to frame Kassian for the murder. And busted my balls about it every chance he could. Trying to manipulate me to go to the cops and implicate Kassian.

When he saw that wasn't going to work, he gave the diamonds back to me, claiming Kassian must have had a change of heart. Bullshit!

The trees grew closer together and the underbrush seemed thicker. I must have lost the path. Up ahead, a fallen tree blocked my way. I shortened my steps to time my jump and leapt over it. I'd almost cleared it when my back foot caught on something. I spun backward and instead of making a clean landing, I tumbled onto the ground, banging my right side against a stump. The pain throbbed in my side as I scrambled to my feet. I was too young to have broken my hip, but it hurt like the devil. You'd think it would be cold enough to dull the pain. But I wasn't so lucky.

I didn't have time to waste. I wasn't too far from the Home, maybe another four or five minutes. I checked to make sure I hadn't dropped my cell phone. Still there. I took off again, pain shooting down my right leg with every step.

Thoughts went back to Lev. He had an alibi—the dentist. But it wasn't airtight. He could have kept his appointment after murdering my father. You'd have to be a stone-cold bastard to be able to pull that one off, but if anyone could do it, Lev could. I didn't know anyone colder than Lev Yurishenko.

But was I being fair? Was I getting too wrapped up in the emotions of the situation? I considered my conclusions about Lev. Could it have happened that way? Or was it all too fantastic? Like some storyteller around the campfire making things up as he went along, weaving together scraps of truth to fashion a blanket of lies.

I tried to shake it off as fiction, but the facts seemed to fit. That was why Lev couldn't go to the police. Because *he was guilty*, not because he was some senile Russkie whom the cops would never believe. And he had the perfect patsy in Kassian. But give Kassian credit, he'd finally done what was right. He'd finally trusted me. My father had seen something in the old guy, and—I've come to realize—my father's judgment was usually spot-on.

Lev had almost played it brilliantly, but he'd overestimated his ability to keep Kassian quiet with his threats about his connections to the Russian mob. He'd underestimated Kassian, just as I had.

My lungs burned from the cold and the exertion. My right side screamed with every breath, with every step. But all the pain—as intense as it was—paled next to how I felt about that old man who had claimed to be my father's best friend.

The vibrating cell phone brought me out of my fury. I flipped it open. "Hello?"

"It's Rachel. Kassian's gone."

THIRTY-EIGHT

"WHAT DO YOU MEAN he's gone?" I shouted to be heard above the wind, shouted because the cold had numbed my mouth. Mostly, I shouted because I couldn't believe what was happening. "How can he be gone?"

"Josh, I'm sorry. They're not in the snackbar. I don't know where they are."

"Well, goddamnit, find them!" I hung up and dashed ahead, feeling things spiral out of control. I could apologize to Rachel when we found Kassian.

I came to the end of the trail and broke through the trees. Off to my right, the lights of the Hebrew Home shone brightly. The snow had tapered to flurries, although the wind still howled.

Despite the pain in my hip, I sprinted the last hundred yards to the Home and circled around to the front entrance. In the first row of the parking lot, in the handicapped spaces, I noticed Lev's SUV, covered with about a half inch of snow. Next to it was Peter's identical black vehicle, barely dusted. STOX1 and STOX3, side-by-side. Thank God Peter was here to help. I wondered what he would think when he found out what his father had done. All we had to do was find them before it was too late.

The bottom dropped out of my stomach as a sudden, sick realization hit. Maybe Kassian *hadn't* seen Lev's car that morning. Maybe he'd seen Peter's. They were the same model SUV, same color. Kassian wouldn't know the difference. I remembered the expression on Lev's face when I'd told him what Kassian had seen. Had he realized it, too?

I didn't have a clue why Peter would want my father dead, but my feeling of dread grew. Peter hadn't seemed his usual self lately. More uptight. I'd interpreted it as concern for his father, but it could have been guilt. Or the fear of being caught. Whatever Peter's motives, I'm sure they had something to do with my father's wealth. Peter always was a money guy, always angling for more.

My stomach tumbled again. I'd called Peter to help hunt for Kassian, leading the wolf to the sheep. What would he do if he found him? Silence his only witness for good? I needed to find Kassian, and fast.

I barged through the front doors and tore past the reception desk, ignoring the calls to stop and sign in. There was no sign of anybody: Kassian, Peter, Lev, or Rachel. Just a few residents, their cozy, snowy evening in the lobby interrupted by a crazed madman bursting in from a hike in the frozen woods. My head whipped around, scanning the lobby, in case I'd missed something.

I ran to the snackbar to double-check Rachel. Maybe Kassian and Lev had simply taken a break and gone to the men's room. Six vending machines, no people. I hustled to the game room. Four old guys and a much younger lady sat around a card table playing poker. No Kassian.

I barreled back into the hallway, still breathing hard from my streak through the woods. Pausing to catch my breath, I removed my gloves and stuffed them into my coat pocket. Put my phone in my jeans pocket. Where was Kassian? Maybe in the TV lounge. As I started across the lobby, I saw Lev go into the men's room.

I raced after him, caught him washing his hands at the sink. When he spotted me in the mirror, his eyes went wide and he spun around. "Joshua!"

"Where is he? Where's Kassian?" I moved closer. We were the only ones in the small room. "Come on, I know he's here somewhere."

Lev said, "Yes. He's in the library. The *Handleman* Library." Wary, as if he knew he was about to be busted. "Is something wrong?"

"Don't give me that shit. Where's Peter? He was the one, wasn't he? I figured it out. Peter murdered my father."

Lev stared at me, eyes flat and dead. He didn't speak. He didn't have to.

"How long have you known?" Spittle flew from my lips.

A small downward glance, then his trademarked stone expression reappeared. I felt like slapping it off his smug face. Instead, I grabbed his arm. "Come on, you old fool." He protested for a moment, then stopped struggling when he realized I meant business. I led him out of the men's room, gripping his bicep as if he were an eel. We needed to get to Kassian before Peter did. I didn't know where Peter was, but he couldn't be far. I perp-walked Lev across the lobby toward the library as fast as we could manage. The pain in my side had waned—I had more important things to concentrate on.

"Josh!" Rachel called out, as she hurried down the hall from the direction of the cafeteria. "You found Lev."

"We need to get Kassian. I'll explain when we find him." I squeezed Lev's arm and jerked him forward. It must have hurt, but he didn't utter a sound. "Come on, he's in the library." The two of us escorted Lev, one on each side. I could see the questions in Rachel's eyes, but I didn't fill her in yet, just pressed on. I wanted Kassian to hear every word about Peter killing my father. I wanted him to know I was sorry for not believing him, for not trusting him.

We were ten feet from the library doors when we heard a giant crash and the sound of breaking glass. I leapt forward, swung open the heavy wood doors, and darted into the library, followed closely by Rachel and Lev. The back windows were shattered, broken glass everywhere, a chair upended. Incongruously, a copper birdbath sat on its side in the middle of the library floor. Above, the two stained-glass panels had been spared, but were hanging slightly off-kilter.

In the midst of the debris, Peter dragged Kassian toward the opening where the window had been, an arm crooked around his captive's neck. When he saw us, he stopped and straightened, but didn't let go of Kassian. His face appeared calm, only the blaze in his eyes betrayed his true emotional state. He opened his mouth to speak, but closed it before anything came out. What could he say? Get out of here and pretend you never saw this? On my left, Rachel drew quick shallow breaths, one hand covering her mouth, face ashen.

Lev stepped forward. "Peter. Stop this. We know what has happened. It is time for you to be a man and face this."

"You don't know what really happened, Pops," Peter said. The words squeezed out in a strange monotone, as if he were possessed by aliens. He scuttled to a shelf, took his arm away from Kassian's throat, snatched a book, then threw it at Rachel. It caromed off her thigh and fell to the floor. "Do me a favor, will you? Cram it into the door handles," Peter said, nodding at the doors to the library. He grabbed Kassian around the throat again.

Rachel stared at the book at her feet.

"Do it. Now," Peter said, and he slowly pulled his other hand from behind Kassian's back to reveal a gun, just to show us he was serious. This wasn't the Peter I knew. This was some kind of crazed-maniac Peter.

Rachel bent over and picked up the book. With trembling hands, she stuffed it between the door handles, effectively locking people out. The cold air rushed into the room through the wide-open holes where the windows had been—Peter's escape route. Would he kill us all so we wouldn't talk? Or was he planning to flee to South America and live in hiding like a Nazi?

Lev tried again. "Peter. We know you killed Abe. Kassian saw your car there that morning."

"It was an accident. An accident. I didn't mean to kill him. We were talking and he tripped." Peter pleaded with us to understand his version. I didn't know what the truth was, but he'd gone to an awful lot of trouble to cover up an accident.

Lev stepped closer to his son. "I know Abe turned you down for a loan. But that was at my insistence. He wanted to give you the money you asked for." He paused and set his jaw. "I told him not to."

Peter studied his father, eyes wavering in and out of focus. "You? You told him not to? I needed that money. *We* needed that money. You think that big house you live in is free, old man? And that car you drive?" Tears formed at the edges of Peter's eyes.

"Do not lie to me, son. I have overheard many discussions about your sure-fire investments that lose money. The angry people whose money you lost. I knew you were going down the wrong path. I tried to warn you. *Do not take risks with your money. Do not take risks with other people's money.* But you did not listen. Instead, you gambled. And you lost." Lev remained stone-faced. He clasped his hands behind his back, like a professor delivering a lecture to his class. "You brought shame to all of us."

Rachel reached out and took my hand. Squeezed it. I squeezed back, then pulled it away. It was because of me that Kassian was in this position. I wasn't going to let him die, not if I could help it. I inched forward. Peter still had an arm around Kassian's neck with the gun in his back. But Peter's eyes were glued to Lev.

Lev shifted slightly to his right, away from me, as he spoke. "I wanted you to live up to your own responsibilities and obligations. No one named Yurishenko takes charity. We work honestly for what we have. And we take care of things in our own house." He slowly shook his head. "Ironic, isn't it? That my beliefs cost the life of my best friend."

Peter brought the gun up to Kassian's head. Waved it around. "It was an accident," he said, voice hoarse.

Lev held out his hand and stepped forward. "Give me the gun, Peter. Let him go. It is time to be a man. Be brave and accept what you deserve."

Peter stared at his father. I wasn't sure if what Lev said sunk in, or whether Peter was too far gone for anything to make sense. Either way, he didn't give up the gun or release Kassian. He dragged Kassian back a couple of steps toward the hole in the wall, feet crunching on broken glass. "Charity? You didn't seem to have any problem sponging off of me."

"You are my son. That is what sons do. Perhaps I did not raise you right." Lev pointed at Peter. "Because I have raised a cowardly murderer."

Peter aimed his gun at Lev and stepped back, but slipped on the glass. He let go of Kassian as he thrust his arms out to regain his balance. I lunged forward and drove my shoulder into Peter's chest, propelling all three of us into the window frame. The impact knocked the stained glass panels loose and they crashed to the floor in an explosion of brightly colored glass pieces.

We fell as one into a heap on the floor. Kassian rolled off the pile and I felt Lev dive into the fray next to me and I lay atop Peter, clawing and scratching after the gun in his hand, finally getting both hands on his wrist where I twisted and squeezed and pried, bending back his fingers, their snapping noises spurring me on. Lev pummeled Peter's face with a series of punches. Rachel's screams provided the soundtrack for our struggle, until a loud roar echoed in the room. Peter's gun discharged, the bullet flying through the window opening into the black night.

I had to get the gun.

I redoubled my effort, kneeing Peter in the groin, putting all of my weight behind it. Then I elbowed him in the face. Twice. He lost his grip on the gun and it went sliding away on the tiled floor. My hand reached for it but touched something else on the floor, and my fingers closed around it, a razor-sharp shard of dazzling blue glass. I held it tightly in my raised hand, summoning the strength to ram it into Peter's chest when I heard Rachel scream, "Stop. Stop. He's got the gun. Everybody stop."

I held my hand steady and glanced to my side. There was Kassian, good ol' Kassian, holding Peter's gun with two shaking hands. Inside the library, everything went quiet. Outside, in the lobby, there was banging and yelling and more banging on the library doors. Kassian pointed the gun vaguely in Peter's direction.

I scrambled to my feet, still holding the triangular glass dagger, a thin trail of red in my palm. I stared at the blood, thankful for Kassian's intervention. I'd been about to kill another human being. I felt Lev, next to me, remove the glass from my hand, but I stared down at Peter, who lay motionless on the ground. His eyes were shut, but I could see his chest rise and fall. Battered and bruised, he was still alive.

Kassian inched closer to us, fingers gripping the gun so tightly his knuckles were white. It danced in his hands.

"Kassian. Put the gun down. Please." He turned toward me, and the barrel of the gun followed his eyes. Both pointed in my direction. "Hey, watch it. Put it down."

He looked at his hands and his eyes grew wide for a second, as if he'd just noticed what he was holding. Then he brought the gun up slowly and aimed it at Lev. The barrel wobbled, but he kept it focused on Lev's chest.

Lev remained still. No evasive maneuvers, no expression of fear—or of anything else. He glanced from Kassian to Peter, then back to Kassian.

I eased between Kassian and Lev. Reached my hand out. Shut out everything in the room, everything in my world. The screaming and the banging and the timpani of my pounding heart. Concentrated on one thing: the gun.

Kassian's finger trembled against the trigger guard.

I held my breath and extended my arm, placing my hand on top of the gun, bracing for the explosion. Slowly I pushed the barrel down so that it aimed at the floor. Exhaled.

Motion on my right caught my eye. In a flurry of waving arms, Lev toppled over onto Peter. Peter gasped, then twitched, finally going limp beneath Lev.

"Oh, shit," I said, as I hauled Lev up. "Shit, shit, shit." Peter lay there, the shard of dazzling blue glass embedded in his neck. Blood streamed from the gash, pooling on the floor beside him. Lev knelt next to his son and grasped his hand, chanting something in Russian.

Rachel ran for the doors, yanked the book from the handles, and flung the doors open. "Call 911. See if there are any doctors around. And call some nurses. We've got a man hurt in here. Hurry." I could hear her in the hall, answering questions and taking charge.

I stood there, transfixed. Kassian huddled in a corner, hands over his head. He hadn't seen a thing, no doubt. Lev prayed over his dying son. Had he tripped, or had it been intentional? I replayed what I saw several times and honestly didn't know. It all happened too fast.

Finished barking orders for now, Rachel joined me in the library and we locked eyes. I could see the unanswered question deep within her, and in that instant, I realized she didn't know what really happened either. We'd both been standing right there, but we didn't know the truth. We didn't know the truth about many things.

Maybe it was better that way.

THIRTY-NINE

Two weeks later, I visited Erik at work. There was a different receptionist out front, just as protective as the previous one. But she was no match for my persuasive argument that all I needed was five minutes. She led me back to his office, glaring at me the whole way.

Today's suit was a glen plaid, with a cream-colored shirt and abstract multi-hued tie. He hugged me, like always, and we sat on the couch. I hadn't seen much of him since the incident at the Hebrew Home. "So," he said. "Things settled down yet?"

I nodded. "Getting there. It'll take some time."

"I'll bet. You started with Goose and Matt?" Erik glanced at me, then stared off into space.

"Yeah. Couple of days ago. It's not my life's work, but it'll do until I figure out what I want to be when I grow up."

Erik let out a small laugh. "Good luck with that," he said. "How're things with Rachel?"

"Good. Real good." We'd gone out four or five times and things were moving along nicely. At a comfortable pace, for both of us. "We should all go out sometime."

"Yeah. Katy would like that. I don't think she liked Dani too much."

I nodded, as if it were news to me, although I'd known Katy's feelings almost since the day she met Dani. "Then I guess she'll be happy. Yesterday, I filed the divorce papers."

A grin spread across Erik's face. "That's good. I never really liked Dani much either."

"What?" I said, acting pissed off, then breaking into my own smile. We sat for a moment in silence, before Erik cleared his throat.

"You had no idea Peter was in financial trouble?" he asked.

"No. How would I? He lived in a big house, had a small fleet of cars, vacationed all over the world," I said. "He'd been diverting funds from his clients' accounts for years, chasing wilder and wilder investment returns. When one thing tanked, he took from someone else. Some kind of twisted Ponzi scheme, except he was the ultimate victim."

Erik shook his head. "Man."

"Peter leveraged everything he owned and it finally caught up with him," I said. "I guess desperation makes people do desperate things."

"And he came to your father for help?" Erik asked. "Your father was an angel, but he'd never go for that."

"Well, he almost did. He would have given Peter the money he asked for—I'm sure Peter made up some story to cover up his illegal activities—except that Lev begged him not to. Wanted Peter to earn his dough, not get a hand-out."

"So when your father refused, Peter just killed him?"

I shrugged. "Who really knows? Best guess: They were in my father's office upstairs discussing Peter's request. When my father turned him down, they argued and Peter pushed him down the stairs—Lev says Peter had quite a temper when crossed. I suppose it could have been an accident. We'll never know. But it's obvious that Peter was there, and that he covered it up."

"Peter just went off the deep end?" Erik asked. "Unbelievable."

"Yeah." It really was hard to fathom. How did he think he could possibly get away with killing Kassian? I'd thought about it a lot over the past couple weeks. I guess if you believed you could get away with stealing money from your clients, you believed you could get away with murder, too. Tough to suss out a psycho.

"He must've been quite pleased his father was trying to pin it on Kassian."

I nodded. "Sure. Took the heat off him. Almost worked, too."

Erik shook his head. "What about the diamonds?"

"Well, they would have been just a band-aid for Peter's financial problems. He was in debt to the tune of about three million dollars." I paused, wondering how things could have gotten so out of hand. "They turned up in one of Peter's safe deposit boxes. Close to 300 stones."

Erik let out a low whistle. "Not bad. Those are yours, my friend."

I nodded. Ironically, Peter kept them in the same bank—Virginia Central—that my father had. In his box we'd found two more full velvet bags along with a sheaf of documentation. Each diamond was safely tucked into its own tiny numbered poly bag; the numbers corresponded to the data on GIA certificates, insurance papers, and old appraisal records that he'd taken from my father's filing cabinets.

Turned out the insurance company—one that specialized in precious gems—wanted to update the policy and had asked my father for a more complete appraisal. That's what got the whole thing rolling.

Erik shook his head. "But why give some back?" A damn good question.

"He must have wanted me to stop poking around. When he realized I didn't know how many diamonds there were, he figured fifty would get me off his scent. He also figured I'd think it was Kassian who took them, then changed his mind and returned them." I paused. Erik was still shaking his head. "Peter purposely jumbled the diamonds all together—without numbers or any identifying characteristics—hoping their lack of paperwork would make it more difficult for me to determine what had happened." He'd been right about that.

Erik snorted. "Man," he said, giving his head one last shake.

The diamonds were nice to have, but now that they were in my possession, it all seemed a bit anticlimactic. A lot of anxiety and anguish for a bunch of sparkling stones.

Erik cleared his throat and looked at me, a question on the tip of his tongue. But he kept staring.

"What?"

"What really happened between Lev and Peter? At the end? Did he kill him on purpose?" Erik asked.

The details reported in the paper were sketchy, and in the end, it had been declared a tragic accident. Like my father's death had been. I said nothing to challenge that version of reality. "It was an accident. Lev slipped and Peter got impaled. Freaky, but that's what happened."

Erik eyed me, brow furrowed, trying to determine if I were telling the truth or not. I maintained a poker face. When he realized I wasn't going to say anything else, he rose and glanced at his watch. Busy man. I got up, too. "Hey, what's the deal with Brandon?" I asked. I'd heard a vague rumor about some trouble he'd gotten into.

A worried look clouded Erik's face. He took a deep breath. "Terrible Teresywzki got his teeth into him and wouldn't let go. Called on his buddies to investigate some of Brandon's activities."

The thought of Terrible T on my ass gave me shivers. So much for members of the Elite sticking up for one another. "What's he guilty of?" Being an asshole wasn't a crime.

"The rumor mill has it that Brandon will be indicted within the next few weeks on some kind of insider trading scandal. Friend of a friend kind of thing," Erik said, looking as if he'd eaten some bad sushi.

"What?"

Erik shook his head, kept his lips pressed together.

"What's wrong?"

He closed his eyes for a second, then opened them. Cocked his head to one side, contrite. "I'm clean in this, Josh. But sometimes investigators—in their zeal—paint things with a broad brush, start pointing fingers at everyone around the guilty party. I've made a few investments based on Brandon's advice, but nothing illegal." His eyes pleaded with me. "You've got to believe me."

I told him I did. And left, shaking my head.

What money does to good people never ceases to amaze—and infuriate—me.

———

Four weeks later, Lev died.

A massive coronary, in his sleep, took him quickly. Jenn and the kids held up well, considering what they'd already been through. At the funeral, she told me she would be moving back to New York to be closer to her relatives, once she sold the house. She had trouble looking me in the eye, and I felt her pain.

No one sat shiva for Lev.

———

Eight weeks later, I piled Kassian, Aunt Shel, and Rachel into my new Beamer and we drove to the Hebrew Home. I dropped the ladies off at the Judaica shop—Aunt Shel had a hankering to haggle over half-price menorahs—while Kassian and I met with Carol in her office. She'd called, wanting to tell me something in person.

"Good to see you again, Josh," she said. "And you too, Kassian." She winked at him. I knew they saw each other frequently. "I'm glad you could come in today."

"Sure," I said.

"Last night at a board meeting, we voted to go ahead with the Russian Unit development." She beamed at me. "Thanks to your father's funding—and his vision—that unit will become a reality. Congratulations, Josh."

I didn't know what to say. I'd been too busy getting my life back on track over the past two months to pay much attention to the goings-on at the Hebrew Home.

Carol's smile brightened even more. "I know Abe would be happy. It was the one thing he talked about most," she said, then something twinkled in her eyes. "Besides you, of course."

She got up from behind her desk. "I'll be sure to invite you to the dedication. Both of you. I think we might call it The Handleman Home for Russian Jews. What do you think?"

I told her I thought it was nice. Very nice.

Kassian and I left Carol in her office. Side by side, we walked down the hall toward the gift shop to meet Rachel and Aunt Shel. There'd been something I'd been meaning to ask him, but it never seemed like the right place or the right time. I was tired of waiting. "Kassian?"

"Yes?"

"What's the story with you and Stephen Wentworth?"

Kassian stopped short. "Nothing."

Not, "*Who's Stephen Wentworth?*" I tried to make my voice as casual as possible. "Then you know him?"

No answer.

"How about Suzanne Miller? Know her?"

Kassian's features sharpened. "I believe so."

"How?"

"How?" he asked.

"Yes. How do you know her?"

He studied my face, searching for something. Something that would tell him if his secret would be safe with me. All at once he relaxed, and I saw a side of Kassian I hadn't yet seen. "She is my daughter."

I'm sure my surprise was evident, although I tried to be cool. "Your daughter?" Inside, I was screaming.

"Yes. When I left my wife, my daughter was only a baby. I lost contact with them. I lived on the streets and was drinking and even if I could have found them, I would not have wanted them to see me like I was. Then, many years later, with the help of some very kind people, I got better. My life had been wasted, but I wanted to find my daughter. I spent many months searching in vain. I was very sad. So sad. Thought about killing…" His voice caught and he swallowed to clear his throat. "It was then I wrote to Abe. He sent me money to come down here. He promised he would help me."

A couple passed us in the hall, and Kassian waited for them to move out of earshot before he continued. "Abe talked with me. Consoled me. Told me he would help find my daughter. Once he started, he found her in a matter of weeks. Said she'd changed her name, but she was my Mischa." A proud look spread on Kassian's face.

I knew Suzanne Miller wasn't really Kassian's daughter. And my father knew it, too. The white lie was simply my father's attempt to bring peace to an old man who'd led a hard life. Another act of kindness from "Honest" Abe. "So my father introduced her to you?"

"Yes, at her office. But he warned me not to mention a word of it to anyone. Not a word, even to her. He said that she would not believe I was her father, and that she would think I was some kind of stalker or molester. A bad man. I promised him I would never tell. Anyone." Kassian eyed me. "And now..."

I patted his shoulder. "It's okay. I am his son, after all. He wouldn't care if you told me. He'd probably be happy about it. But he is right. You must never tell anyone else, including Suzanne."

Kassian nodded solemnly.

"And that's why you were in the woods?"

His face turned crimson. "I only wanted to see her. And my grandchildren. You have seen them?" He smiled, rotten teeth and all. His eyes misted. "They are beautiful grandchildren, yes?"

"Yes they are, Kassian," I said. "Yes they are."

———

We caught up with Rachel and Aunt Shel outside the gift shop. Aunt Shel had a couple plastic bags in her hands, stuffed with menorahs and other Jewish tchotchkes. I'd probably see a few of them as gifts somewhere along the line.

I pulled Rachel aside. "Why don't you take Kassian up to visit Nana now?" I'd been joking that she should try to fix her grandmother up with Kassian. She hadn't thought it was too funny.

"Where are you going? You're not ditching him with me, are you?" She asked, smiling as she said it.

"No. I want to show Aunt Shel something. We'll be up in a few minutes."

I watched Rachel and Kassian walk over to the elevator, realizing—not for the first time—how lucky I felt being with Rachel. We were getting along, as Aunt Shel would say, famously. Rachel had even invited me to a spring picnic for the faculty at her school—a sure sign that something special was happening. If only my father were around to meet her. I don't believe he liked Dani much either.

Dani. I'd called her about a week ago to tell her I was filing for divorce and to see how she was doing. The conversation had been pleasantly devoid of any rancor. No caustic words. None of Dani's neediness or bossiness or self-focused rants. Hearing her laugh reminded me of the good times we had. In fact, I *almost* remembered why I'd been attracted to her in the first place. Though drama still ruled her life—she'd gone back to Heath, then broke it off again— this time she seemed more resilient. More hopeful. More *mature.* Even talking about the finality of our divorce hadn't spun her out. The idea of remaining friendly with her now didn't seem out of the realm of possibility—as long as she stayed on the West Coast.

Across the lobby, the elevator arrived and Rachel gave me a little wave as she and Kassian boarded. After the elevator doors whooshed shut, I took Aunt Shel by the arm and guided her to the library. Stopped outside the entrance. "Look," I said, pointing at the brass plaque.

She stared at it, tears welling up. "Your father would be so proud. Of this. Of you. He'd be *kvelling,* all right. In fact, I'm sure he's doing that right now." Her eyes rolled upward a fraction, then she winked at me.

I nodded and blinked back my own tears. Pulling the doors open, I held them while Aunt Shel shuffled in. "I want to show you something."

There were a couple residents at one of the tables, a book open between them. The younger woman read something in Hebrew to the man, who leaned back with a faraway look in his eye and a faint smile on his lips. She kept on reading, strange words to me, comforting words to them.

"Over here."

I led her to the windows. Pointed up. The stained-glass panels had been restored. I sold some of the diamonds and had to pay extra for the rush job, but it was worth it. The Star of David sparkled in the sunlight. Red, blue, white, pieced together like an iridescent jigsaw puzzle. Aunt Shel's mouth parted slightly as she admired the beauty.

"This is what Dad commissioned. To make the library special. He wanted a little bit of himself to be preserved here. Through the art he adored." I took one of Aunt Shel's hands. "Pretty neat, huh?"

She nodded, unable to speak, tears running down her cheeks.

It was the best $84,000 I ever spent, not that I really had any choice.

After all, it *was* the *Handleman* Library.

ACKNOWLEDGMENTS

I don't know if it takes an entire village to publish a book, but it sure took a lot of very talented, very generous people to get this one published and on the shelves. My sincere gratitude goes to:

My critique group partners, Dan Phythyon and Ayesha Court. It's no exaggeration to say this book wouldn't have come to fruition without their considerable input.

Megan Plyler and Dorothy Patton, for their invaluable critiques and eagle-eyed line edits. Mark Skehan and Doug Bell for their very helpful comments. My Dallas posse: John Stevenson (oldest friend and still a trusted voice), Jill Balboni, Kim Stevenson, and Samantha Stevenson. It's nice to have a Texas fan club.

My cadre of readers for their insightful feedback and first-rate opinions: Myra Angel, Katherine Clay, Sam Feigeles, Christopher J. Ferguson, Ruth Field, Dana Forrest, Pat Humphlett, Marion May, Steve Orr, Sue Ousterhout, Mike White, and Chris Wilsher.

Technical experts: John Schulien, for his stained glass knowledge. Manny Gordon for the lesson on diamonds. Officer Dexter Morgan and the rest of the Herndon PD, including those involved with the eye-opening Citizen's Police Academy, for their crime-fighting expertise. Special Agent Rick McMahan for, well, I can't tell you.

The P. J. Parrish sisters (Kris Montee and Kelly Nichols) for their kind words—and excellent writing pointers. Elaine Raco Chase and Ann McLaughlin for getting me started in the right direction. Tim Bent for his "book biz" recommendations. P. J. Nunn for her promotional experience and wisdom.

Superb storyteller John Gilstrap, infinitely generous with his time and career advice.

The indomitable Noreen Wald for her inspiration, encouragement, and support—along with a kick in the pants. And a tip of the hat to her workshop participants for all their suggestions (they had plenty!).

My terrific agent Kathy Green for her unwavering confidence in my work (and in me).

The fabulous Midnight Ink team—they know how to do it right: Bill Krause, Brian Farrey, Terri Bischoff, Connie Hill, Donna Burch, Steven Pomije, Courtney Kish, and Ellen Dahl. GO TEAM!

My mother-in-law Ruth for her unbelievable belief in me. Karen, Jamie, and Emma; David and Wendy; Susan, Becca, and Phillip; and Lisa for their unbridled enthusiasm. Family rules!

My mom, Bev, for everything. My late father, Leonard, for everything, too.

My children, Mark and Stuart, and my wife, Janet. I can't say enough—your love is what keeps me going.

Thanks!

© Lifetouch Portrait Studios Inc.

ABOUT THE AUTHOR

Before Alan stepped off the corporate merry-go-round, he held a variety of positions at a number of prominent companies, including General Electric, *The Washington Post*, and Arbitron Ratings. In the nineties, he founded Environmental Newsletters, Inc. to help organizations reduce their negative impact on the environment.

Alan earned a B.S. degree in Mechanical Engineering from the University of Maryland and an M.B.A. from MIT/Sloan. He belongs to Mystery Writers of America, International Thriller Writers, and The Writer's Center in Bethesda, MD.

Residing in Northern Virginia with his diamond-loving wife and two sons, he's currently hard at work on his next novel.